MADLY

By

Winston J. Knowlton

Copyright

Masq

Copyright © 2013, Winston J. Knowlton

2nd edition

February 2014

Published in the United States of America, 2013

www.wynsyn.com

Special editing thanks to: Mellissa Duclos and Gerald (Jerry) Madsen

Interior illustration by: Mark Childers

For Nichole, my memory...

"We understand how dangerous a mask can be. We all become what we pretend to be.

-Patrick Rothfuss, The Name of the Wind

One

The clouds moved slowly across the dismal sky. As I stared up at them on yet another dreary day, it was hard to imagine the darkness would ever end. Rain seemed cocked and ready to fall at any moment, as if the sky were an angry man holding a loaded weapon. Funny, I thought looking up into the pale sky, and reaching down to feel the smooth pistol strapped to my shoulder. Funny how similar I felt to the coming storm. This was, I realized, the first time I could touch the weapon without shaking and seeing visions of all that blood. I didn't know how to feel.

I could go farther back, I suppose, but the rest of my past isn't important. For me, this is where the story began.

I let go of the pistol and walked over to the sofa, leaving alone the cloudy landscape that stretched out from my window. I had been off the scene long enough that I didn't even know what was going on in the world anymore, never mind who any of the major players were. I took a long look at the brown sofa before crashing down on top of it, realizing as I did how well I knew the simple piece of furniture, from each and every stain down to that tiny tear on the left side, the one I hid so well. I shook from my mind the strange sensation that I wasn't really in the room. It was a familiar feeling, one that made me feel like some kind of zombie. I needed a distraction. The remote was close enough that I didn't even have to move to push the red power button, activating my flat screen TV. Instantly voices began to chirp before I even saw the image of two news reporters sitting above the name, Channel 12 News.

"In today's top story, an all-out war has broken out between politicians over whether or not America is ready to lift the masq policy. As politicians prepare for the upcoming vote, polls show that the majority of people favor keeping the masq policy for at least another six year term." The man sounded warm and friendly, and I pictured a tan face underneath the smiling mask he wore. The female newscaster hadn't spoken yet, but looking at her I could almost tell she was aging fast and that she supported the masq policies. I watched as she nodded her head, the green and blue feathers on her mask waving back and forth.

"The politicians are not yet in full agreement, but no word has been given on which representatives are standing up against the policies," she said as the camera panned backward, taking in the studio before zooming in again on the woman as she launched into her next segment.

"In other news, the unmask group known as face again caused panic as they ran through the streets without their masks on. According to our report, they were trying to enlist others at the local New York mall to take off their masks and join the movement. Police were on the scene and were able to apprehend several of the individuals but many others got away." The TV screen flipped to a blurred out image of the group, showing the rough outlines of the people involved in the movement but obscuring their faces. I noticed the female running at the head of the group; she wore a tattered army jacket and had short blonde hair. The image disappeared and the news reporters started making comments about the situation that I didn't care to hear, so I simply stopped listening. Instead I focused on the tapping sound that had started slowly but then picked up speed. I'd always loved the rain and for a split second I thought I loved it again.

"Tune in next week for the ultimate thrill ride, the greatest thing to happen in action and romance history." I turned back to the TV to see a commercial starring the all two famous actors everyone had been buzzing about.

"Starring Eli Phaunt and P Feather—don't miss the amazing story." The commercial droned on but I stopped listening, looking instead at the famous actors on the screen. The man was all muscles and wore a peculiar mask with a long trunk, much like an elephant's. The toned woman beside him danced gracefully under what looked like a mass of peacock feathers and dazzling diamonds. I couldn't figure out what struck me about her, until the news returned and I realized that the female reporter was wearing a knock off version of P Feather's mask. I couldn't help but shake my head at what the world had become.

"Crime is still at an all-time low, and records continue to crash as the world moves further and further to a time of all out peace."

I wondered at that moment at what cost were we getting all this peace, and whether it was really worth it.

"We now go live to the political conference in D.C. For those of you just joining us, remember how important this meeting is. After this conference the fate of America will be decided for the next six years. Although the votes won't actually be cast for two months, the decisions made today by these representatives will likely indicate the outcome of the vote." I leaned forward on the couch finally taking some extra interest in what was going on in the country today.

A noise, exploding from the kitchen startled me and I jumped out my seat, reaching within inches of my weapon. When I realized what it was, I quickly shut off the TV and walked over to pick up the phone.

"Hello?" I asked questioningly into the receiver. I hadn't been expecting a call today, at least not yet anyway.

"Detective Wink, its Mac. I've got orders." For a moment I just stood there. It had been a while since I heard that voice, and the first time I had heard that name.

"Captain, I hadn't expected your call so soon. I was only reinstated today, was told not to even come in." I knew it was the Captain despite his new name. Again I couldn't help but wonder about the price of this time of peace.

"Yeah, well I need someone I can trust, and you're the only one left who isn't a part of this mask movement. You're the only one I know face to face." Because I hadn't been back to the office since all this started, the captain still knew the real me. I wondered how it felt to command a group of men and women who he couldn't even see. I was a little honored the captain thought of me in this way but I still felt a little awkward talking to the gruff old man.

"What is it you need me to do, Captain?" I tried not to sound intimidated, even though I was more than that on my first day back.

"It's nothing difficult: all I need you to do is attend a certain party and keep your eyes open for anything suspicious. Only if you're up to it of course. I don't want you waltzing out if you're not ready after what—" His voice froze for a long moment and I knew exactly what the captain was thinking about.

"I'm sorry, Wink, I wasn't thinking clearly, I was just—"

I cut him off there, not wanting this awkward moment to go on any longer, for either of us. "Look its fine Captain, I'm over it. At least I'm over that part of it anyway so you don't have to worry." I almost said you don't have to worry about my missing eye, but I caught myself, realizing how strange it would be to utter those words out loud. While I was speaking I subconsciously rubbed the wrinkled scar where my eye had once been. Against my fingers the rough feeling of the skin reminded me of all the pain I had gone through, inside and out.

"Anyway, Captain, what party? And why is it so important?" I tried to picture my Captain beside the phone giving out orders and kept getting stuck. I could see the old bulky body, the large ape-like fists gripping at the phone clumsily; I could even see the balding head. However anytime I tried to picture his face my mind could only conjure a mysterious mask. I paused, suddenly frightened at the prospect; as I thought more about it I realized I couldn't picture anyone's real face—not my friends, coworkers, even my parents seemed fuzzy. Only one person's face came to my mind clear as day, but the image only made my heart sink even more.

"Well le t's just say I had a tip come down the wire about something big going down tonight, something at that party." The Captain's voice broke me away from my dreary thoughts and those old images faded away, much like a pillar of drifting cigarette smoke.

"This tip of yours must have been important, I mean if you're actually thinking about keeping watch and all." Something didn't feel right about this, and I wondered when the Captain started taking tips so seriously. I forced myself to stop thinking about it, though, and decided it was just another thing I had to get used to, after being gone for so long.

"Well, I don't even know for sure who sent the tip down but as quiet as things have been, I guess I'm just waiting for something big to happen." His voice broke off for a split second before he recovered, just one more thing to send my teeth on edge. I could tell he was holding something back but for the time being it didn't really matter. I dropped it and moved on.

"I guess it can't hurt to start out with something small like a party and an unknown tip. I think I'm ready to get back to work, and if you think this tip might mean something, I have no problem checking it out." I swallowed hard. It all sounded good, but then a new fear began creeping up my back and breathing down my neck. For whatever reason I didn't feel right about this. Maybe it was simply that I just wasn't ready to get back out there, especially somewhere like a party. Whatever the feeling was, I shook it off, knowing full well there was no going back without humiliation on my part, now that I had agreed to go.

"Great to hear you're back and ready for orders, Wink. I knew I could count on you. Now listen, everything that goes on needs to be reported directly to me and no one else. The last thing I want is journalists or activists from Face getting a hold of anything they can use against the department." I was listening but absently, my mind was in a million places at once, the phone cord holding most of my attention as I twirled it around my hands.

"Yeah, I understand, Captain: low key is the name of the game." At this point I was growing very tired of the conversation. What only moments ago had felt like hearing from an old friend very quickly became work.

"Good, now let me know of anything suspicious as soon as it happens."

I heard the inflection in his voice and knew he was about to end the call, even before I had all the details. "Captain, you still haven't told me what party this even is?"

He paused, and then coughed awkwardly before he spoke again, gruffly. "For some reason I thought you already knew. The masquerade party is being thrown by Funny Bunny."

Instantly my mind surged with images and news reports—everything I knew about the rich man and his crazy parties. "Funny Bunny? Are you serious?" I asked only to buy myself some time to think. Funny Bunny was perhaps the most famous person alive right now. I remembered hearing all about the billionaire who'd celebrated the masq policy with a series of masquerade parties. Each party had a different theme and various styles of entertainment. Even I understood that Funny Bunny and his parties epitomized the time in which we were all living.

"You heard me right. I would give you directions but I assume you already know where the party is being held."

I nodded, not even speaking anymore. My mind was swimming with questions about this tip and why a reinstated detective would be sent to such a high profile place. It took me a few moments before I was able to regain my composure and continue the conversation.

"What time does this masquerade start?" I asked while rubbing my hands together and feeling the cold sweat that lingered at the base of my palms.

"The word is this thing starts at about ten and goes on till morning." I blinked my one remaining eye over and over, trying to at least clear the world in front of me. I knew that no active police had ever been allowed in one of those masquerade parties, and that the sight of an officer there tonight would likely cause a panic; the revelers would not know what to do.

"Captain, are you sure this is what you want? I mean, I don't know how a detective is going to go over at this kind of thing." I was picturing the mansion in my mind, though I had only seen it from the back and could only imagine what the rest of it looked like. Funny Bunny was protective of his estate. There were high trees and massive stretches of lawn, all gated off and surrounded by stone slabs.

"That's another reason I chose you for this job, Detective Wink. You have been out of the game long enough that no one will know who you are—just another partier is all anyone will think. Besides, you're the only one in the department whose badge and badge number haven't been painted onto your mask yet. Once that happens, this would be impossible." I'd heard about this new practice: federal and state laws required officers to affix the badges to their masks. Since I'd just been reinstated, I still had one month to get mine taken care of.

I finally understood why I was chosen for this job, and I felt a little disappointed but at the same time a sense of invincibility compared with the other cops.

"Right now," the Captain continued, "you can go to the party, keep a look out and no one will know you're police. That's why you're the perfect man for the job; in fact you're the only man for the job that I've got."

"Alright I got it, Captain. I'll report in as soon as I know anything," I said and then slammed the phone down on the receiver without giving the man another moment to speak. I felt new excitement flood into me: for the first time in what seemed like forever, I felt like a real detective again.

Looking back on that conversation, I wince; I was supposed to be a detective and still I missed every little sign. If only I had known then what I was walking straight into.

*****

The rain poured down, and I could barely see out of my windshield, even with the wipers moving back and forth in rapid, animal-like movements, as fast and they could go. I drove slowly in a clog of traffic, doing my best to avoid the masked men and woman who walked across the streets. At one point I almost hit a car that stopped suddenly in front of me for a red light.

"Shit." I hit the brakes hard, racking my body against the seatbelt that seemed in that moment to be a coiled snake. I looked back and watched the cars behind me each do the same thing, all of them coming within inches of hitting the car in front of them. After a few moments at the red light, I turned my head to look out the passenger window, and my eye locked on a little kid standing next to his mother, both of them waiting for the bus. Heavy sheets of rain fell down around them, though they were protected by the bus stop canopy. The child wore a strange white mask with big round eyes, and shades of blue and pink polka dots from top to bottom. In place of the child's mouth was a crude drawing of a giant smile, inside of which were rows of sharp pointed teeth. The teeth were crowding one another in a tangled mass that reminded me of a shark.

A series of harsh honks broke the silence and I looked up to see I was the only car in front of the light. I was holding up the line and the drivers were angry. As I sped off quickly just making the light, I looked back at all the cars that were unable to go thanks to me and felt a grip of fear and awkwardness right in the center of my chest. Already today I had frozen up more than once; this wasn't a good sign for a detective who needed to be alert and focused.

It was going to be dark soon but I still had around three hours before the party actually started, so I figured I would get something to eat. I didn't have any food at the house since I hadn't been there much lately, so I had no choice but to go out. The place I had in mind came into view, a popular diner that wasn't too expensive but was still nice. Once I got there, though, I felt that same pang in my chest and couldn't stop thinking about how alone I had become. Instead of finishing the thought I drove on right past the little diner and headed for the nearest fast food joint. I parked behind the building and ran in as quickly as I could to avoid the downpour of rain.

"Hi, what can I get you for today?" I looked over the counter at the serving girl and studied her all pink mask that had hair clips that hooked into her pigtails. This strange mask made her head look larger than it should have, which I assumed was the new fashion for her age group. I couldn't help but lose my appetite staring at those bodies running back and forth taking money, and cooking and handing out food, and all in those ugly masks. Still I had to eat, so I ordered my food, which amounted to a flat burger and stale fries.

Later I watched the rain from the seat of my Jeep and wondered how such a large party could happen with this much water pouring down. Naturally you would think it would be canceled or moved to another day. I wondered how a party could be so important to people, but I knew I would have to wait until later to get the answers I wanted so badly, so I let my thoughts drift.

*****

"How are you feeling today, Mr. Wink?" I had looked up from the hospital bed not all that long ago into the strange eyes of the nurse who stood over me. Her mask was split down the middle, with one side blue and the other purple. The Red Cross was attached to the top middle of the mask, signifying that she was a nurse.

"Get away from me. I want a real nurse not you and that god damned mask." I gritted the words out from in-between my teeth. I could not handle how much things had changed in the world since I had first been hospitalized.

"I'm sorry, Mr. Wink, but you know that I cannot do that. It is now hospital policy, as well as the law, for everyone to wear a mask once in the public eye. I know it's hard for you to understand but if you just read over the sheet I gave you, everything will start to make more sense."

I picked up the sheet while the nurse fluffed my pillow and then walked toward the door.

"If there's anything you need, Mr. Wink, don't hesitate to ask," she said from the doorway before she slipped out of the room. I held the sheet in my hand for a long moment; at this point I wasn't ready to accept what was all around me. Finally I looked down at the piece of paper, ignoring the way it felt to read something with only one eye.

According to the new masq policy all of America is now required to follow these simple guidelines. As long as you—the public—follow these simple rules, this transition will be fun and exciting for all of us in this great nation.

1.   Everyone is expected to have a mask on at all times while in the public eye.

2.   When you remove your mask in the privacy of your own home, keep it close by in case someone comes to your home.

3.   Masks must be worn by government officials and state professionals at all times of business. This includes police officers, health care officials such as doctors and nurses, and judges and political officials.

4.   Masks must be personal enough to differentiate. Individuality is still important even in these trying times, and we encourage everyone to put creativity into their masks.

5.   All individual names must also be changed. Birth certificates and other official documentation will retain legal birth names.

6.   Last of all, remember that this policy is being enforced for the public's safety. We reserve the right to dissolve or change certain policies and rules at any time during this process.

It was all too insane to comprehend; it seemed like some strange joke that the office cooked up as my reward for finally leaving that place. When I finally got out of the hospital, though, there wasn't really any choice for me but to put the mask on, the one I had made just to play along. I looked at it before wearing it for the first time: it was slightly twisted but that was how I felt on the inside. The mask was gray and covered most of my face, with just a small section open leaving a portion of my mouth visible. One of the eyes was closed appearing to be winking. It would, of course, never open again. A long tear starting at the eye and trailing all the way down the face to the chin was colored blood red.

*****

The rain was starting to let up. I looked the car up and down through my mask, out of the one eye that I had left. With its rubber steering wheel, the dirt that had gathered on the floor, even the smudges that stained the dash, it was the only thing that still felt real. I touched the leather with my hand caressing the passenger seat; I couldn't help but wish I weren't alone. I wished she was sitting next to me. I wished she was still talking about her day and eventually turning the radio knob up when a good song came on. My eyes lingered on the radio dash for a long moment before I eventually looked up at the green digital read out of the clock.

"Is that really the time?" I wondered before looking down at my watch to verify that it really was 9:26. I couldn't believe I had wasted so much time doing nothing. I threw the car in gear and drove back onto the street heading straight for the mansion. I didn't understand what had happened to the last two and a half hours. I felt in some distant way that I was losing my mind as I drove past the other cars out of the main city and up to the giant estate compound.

So many people walked the streets, all seeming to come from nowhere, while cars blocked the way and slowed movement down to a crawl. I was already running late—it was already five minutes to ten and I was far from where I was supposed to be. When I finally made it to the parking lot, there were cars seeming to cover every spot, like a mall parking lot on a Saturday, only bigger and even more congested. I parked almost a mile away from the entrance to the masquerade and had to walk the entire way. The mass of people crowded the way, some of them wearing elegant dresses and perfectly trimmed suits, though most were dressed like me, in regular clothes. I wore a long coat that came down to my knees and covered my simple collared shirt and much of my black pants. No one seemed to notice as I walked with them that I was a detective secretly watching every movement they made.

"Ticketed guests are allowed to enter the mansion over here," a voice said to a long line of people crowded at the entrance to the mansion's outer walkway. I couldn't help but curse the Captain for not telling me I would need a ticket, and wasn't sure how I was going to get in. I waited in the long line for what seemed like an eternity before I reached a giant man wearing a mask that said security.

"Ticket?" He spat distastefully in my face, most likely tired of hearing people complain about just the thing I was about to bring up.

"I actually lost my ticket. Is there any way you could look it up or something?" I tried to sound honest about the whole thing but I knew just by his body language that it wasn't going to work.

"Get the hell out of this line if you don't have a ticket. The other line will lead you to the outer courtyard."

I looked to where the man was signaling and realized that I was in the wrong line; the people standing with me were no doubt the richest of the rich. I immediately joined those in the right line and followed the crowd down a long narrow pathway. It curved around the mansion and seemed to be leading all the way to the back. The grass was soggy under my shoes but it was still lush and green. The clouds shook violently as a boom of thunder caused everyone to jump. It sounded like the rain was coming back.

After what felt like an even longer walk than the one from my car to the entrance to the grounds, I started to hear loud sounds, far louder than even the thunder. I stepped out into a giant open clearing and at first I couldn't understand what I was staring at. My heart started to bounce in my chest in fast unbalanced patterns; I could feel pure heat leaking up my spine and into my throat. All I could think was how this sight in front of me was a police officer's worst nightmare; or, more accurately, it was my own worst nightmare.

Two

The sky was an elaborate dance of clouds, stars, and moon. All seemed to fight one another for the spotlight, as if they were actors all begging for the most screen time. A flash of bright brilliant lightning shot across the sky, temporarily stealing the show from the other competitors. A slight breeze picked up in the instant after the lightning flash, and the grass seemed to respond by shaking the cold rain away. What should have been cold wasn't, at least not with so much going on in the back of Funny Bunny's mansion.

Every image, every person, every sound rushed my mind. Somewhere in the distance I could hear thunder, and I tried to focus on it to block out the sounds that swelled out in front of me. My eye danced back and forth behind my mask, registering every movement in split seconds. In the second it took my eye to take in the sights my hand reached down to feel the cold steel of the pistol at my side. My mind suddenly clicked, aware of the action I was about to take, and it stopped me cold in my tracks. I had to get a hold of myself; this wasn't just some party I was supposed to bust up. My mission was to watch out for the unexpected.

"Hey buddy, go ahead and make your selection of party favors." A tall man carrying a giant suitcase in both arms was standing in front of me; he had an oddly human looking mask that of course wasn't human at all. The mask was tan, almost the color of skin, and was covered in human looking hair that formed a mustache and full beard. The suitcase he carried was now opened up in his arms, a mass of needles, little bags, and pill bottles littering the case. It didn't take a detective to figure out this was a large collection of drugs, all of them ready for the taking.

"I'm fine for right now, maybe later or something." It wasn't really what I had planned to say but it was all I could manage, hoping to get the man away from me before I started arresting people. The man looked at me for a long time before he slammed the case closed and went on to find other customers amongst those who just walked in. After seeing the man I realized how many of these salesmen were walking the crowd, like hotdog vendors at baseball games.

A loud series of clicking sounds came from down the way, closer to the middle of the mansion than from where I was standing. Lights of all different colors shot out across the crowd, illuminating thousands of men and woman of all shapes and sizes, cheering at the tops of their lungs. A mass of different colors and styles of masks covered just about every square inch of the mansions giant lawn. Every kind of drug and alcohol in the world seemed to be available all on one spot, this spot. Scantily clad women were screaming for attention, exposing themselves further as their drugs started to kick in. A collection of ups and downs were passed around the crowd like candy: ecstasy, heroine, meth, PCP, LSD, cocaine, weed, mushrooms, and or course alcohol. It only took seconds to see an array of these items all in use, and another second to see why police had never come here in the past.

A giant balcony connected to the mansion was suddenly lit up by an oversized spotlight, showing the balcony to be more like a theater stage. The crowd roared again, this time louder than I thought possible. With a splash, loud bass music began to pump into the party, forcing every person on the lawn to bob up and down in a drug induced wave. I felt alone standing on the outskirts of the party, only watching the gathering of so many having the time of their lives.

Even with one eye it seemed as if I was the only one that noticed the giant steel gates that led to the pathway out of here, slam shut. They creaked and groaned until the black gates connected together and a giant lock was fashioned in place. The policeman in me thought directly about how many fire codes had just been broken. Again I looked at the crowd and could see the effects the drugs were having on many of the party goers. Some were off in the corner vomiting; others were swaying back and forth with the music in an unconscious dance. I could tell that many people were in danger here, either from overdosing or just getting hurt by their own craziness. I wondered all over again what I was looking for. From where I was standing everything looked suspicious.

The crowd's cheers turned from an endless low level murmur amongst themselves to a sudden wave of screams that centered at the balcony. The music changed to a low thumping sound, the bass still carrying over to the back lawn, creating the feeling that the ground I stood on was trembling. If I thought the cheers from before were loud, I was sadly mistaken; when a man walked to the front of the balcony the world went wild. He wore a perfectly fitted suit that had to be some kind of name brand as it appeared to be perfect in every way. It didn't take a fashion expert to note that the suit was probably worth more than my car. He had a golden watch that seemed to glint off sparks of light, likely the reflection of light touching the diamonds encrusted in the gold in the most dazzling way. Instead of a face I saw the rich man's mask and knew who the crowd was so interested in at once. The lights were all on him and for a moment the crowd and the music went silent. There was a microphone attached to his mask, much like the one a pop star would wear, and he spoke into it excitedly.

"It's Funny Fucking Bunny!" His voice echoed into the mike, spreading out all over the crowd like a cancer. Fireworks and music ignited the moment the words left his mouth and the crowd seemed to eat up each and every word, as if it were a prayer. The bunny mask covered most of his face but left parts of his mouth exposed. The mask was a brilliant shiny white and it too was encrusted with diamonds, as well as gold trimming, and had a red nose and the appearance of whiskers. The ears extended almost a foot above his head; they too were lined with bright yellow gold and glistening with diamonds.

"I am pleased to welcome each and every one of you to my party." Funny Bunny said to the crowd without giving any sign that he was going to speak again. Immediately the crowd had once more gone silent to hear the all-important words of the man they all idolized.

"Today is the kickoff celebration, the beginning of a series of parties that will dazzle each and every one of you. I will warn all of you to be cautious. If you have a faint heart you may want to walk away now before the parties get even crazier." Funny Bunny stopped on the word crazy and seemed to twitch awkwardly in front of the crowd, in some kind of comic spectacle. This continued until he was doing some strange dance that finished with a shot of strong alcohol, and a straight line of cocaine off the balcony post.

"Every god damned one of you," Funny Bunny said angrily to the crowd, looking at each mask like he was ready to start a

fight. "Better give a massive welcome to the lovely Rosie Rabbit!"
He increased the volume of his voice until he finished with a loud
yell. The crowd did as commanded, cheering and bouncing up and
down to the rhythm of the music and the approaching woman. An
elegant shimmering red dress barely contained the curves of the
woman who walked up and stood beside Funny Bunny. Her mask
was a similar bunny shape but was trimmed in pink and had bright
red rose colored cheeks standing out against the light. I couldn't
help but stare at her; even with the concealment of her mask I
knew underneath she was beautiful.

"It's such an honor to have each and every one of you here
today, on this momentous occasion. I love all of you," Rosie said to
the crowd and finished with a kiss by touching her hand to the lips
hidden beneath her rabbit mask and blowing it to the masses.

"Enjoy the party my friends and prepare yourselves to be
chosen to join the inside of the masquerade," Funny Bunny said
and motioned to the inside of the mansion, directly behind the rich
man in his wonderful suit. At that moment even I admired Funny
Bunny and wished I could be as care free and well-loved as this
man.

"Till we meet again my beloved crowd, and don't you ever
stop being funny," he said, raising his hands to the sky in a mock
god-like pose that the crowd seemed to love. Fireworks erupted
with the end of his speech and the loud bass pumping music
consumed the crowd as the spotlight shut off. Rows of rhythmic
light that danced with the music in a variety of colors started
shooting out like scientific laser beams. I hadn't realized how far I
had moved into the crowd until I noticed I was now right
underneath the balcony.

"Funny Bunny you're fucking awesome, please pick me,
pick me." A continues series of voices came from random locations

in the crowd, all of them trying to get noticed by Funny Bunny. With this new excitement things were starting to get confusing, so many bodies bouncing up and down. Voices came from everywhere and seemed to be inside my head as well as all around me. I tried to push out of the crowd but there were too many bodies all pushing back at me. I was trapped in a front row seat at the craziest concert of all time. I pushed hard and came face to face with this laughing joker mask, plumes of smoke pouring out of the mask's nose holes. A girl, probably too young to be at the party, grabbed my shoulders and tried climbing up so she could be one step closer to the balcony. I tore forward, pushing her off of me and turned to face her, nearly screaming at the sight of her mask, which was covered by a spider, as though a giant tarantula had made its home on her face. Her bra was loose and parts of her chest were spilling out in an unflattering way, only adding to the gruesome scene.

"Come on man, I'll make it worth your while, just help me reach the balcony," the tarantula girl said trying to sound sexy, but only appearing desperate and disgusting. Instantly I was dazed as a crowd surfer kicked me hard in the back of the head, blurring my vision and almost knocking me to the wet ground. I struggled to stand knowing full well falling down here might mean being trampled to death.

"Get out my way!" I yelled weakly at the mass of people in front of me, feeling a growing claustrophobia, but no one seemed to care, and no one tried to move. I felt a prick of pain in my shoulder that I couldn't define, and then the joint felt like it was droopy and numb. Enough was enough: I was finished dealing with this crowd and all of its pressures and pains. I turned and pulled the crowd surfer down, dragging him to the floor and causing a large group of people to fall over like dominos. I jumped over there fallen bodies and pushed through the next mass of people, knocking them out of my way in an angry bunch. A tarantula came into view and that same drugged out girl with no morals was right in front of me. Again she spoke like she had something to offer.

"Quite being such a square man, join the fucking party." I wasn't normally one to act with such aggression but when an animal gets cornered it can only react in the way of self-preservation. I reared back and punched that ugly spider right in the center, knocking it and the weird girl to the ground and out of my way. In that moment I couldn't help but feel the eyes on me; in some distant way I could tell that people were aware that I didn't belong there. I had this fear that most of the crowd knew I was a detective, and I knew if I was right, they would never let me out of there.

I could see the gate that led out of the mansion's back lawn—the only place I wanted to be as I pushed through the crowd. Covered in sweat, feeling fear and something close to frantic panic, I wasn't about to slow down for anyone. My heart was beating fast in a rapid thumping motion that was matching the beating of the loud bass music. I could see the edge of the lawn; from where I was standing I was only a few more feet from breaking out of the crowd. I was only steps from making it out of the mob safe and sound when I was pushed hard from behind. I tripped over my own feet and tumbled to the grass just outside of the crowd.

"What's wrong with you dude, having a bad trip or what?"

I turned and saw two obviously strung out guys, both bigger and crazier than I could ever be. The man talking looked like his drug of choice was steroids and he didn't mind showing it off. Without his shirt on you could see the definition of his muscles and the giant blue veins that stuck out all over, mainly on his neck.

The other guy was even more terrifying, and looked homeless with his ugly hair and stained clothes that bunched up all over him. He looked wet and moldy, like he had been sitting out mildewing over the last few years. His mask was plain, except for the dirt and grime that stained it, and the fact that it couldn't contain his ugly beard. Worst of all he seemed to be hiding a weapon by the way he kept touching something at the top of his waist band, beneath his shirt.

"You listening to me bitch or are you just a fucking idiot?" Steroids said before he ran forward full of aggression and no place to put it, besides in me of course. He kicked me hard in the stomach knocking me from my knees and down onto my back, where he attempted to climb on top of me. I may have been out of the game for a long time, but I still remembered the basics of survival: never let someone get one top of you in a fight. I rolled just in time and was back on my feet faster than the drug filled steroid man could register. I went after him and hit him hard in the side of the face, doing my best to punch through the son of a bitch. His head rocked back but it didn't do much good. He only looked happy to have someone to fight on this great night. His return hit sent me flying back to the ground—dazed and lost, I all but forgot what was going on around me.

"Is that really it, you've got to be kidding me," the laughing voice of the steroids man said from somewhere in the distance. I focused instead on the music—the steady thump, thump followed by the whine of some kind of electric noise that matched the laser beams. A steady trickle of rain was picking back up and absently I could hear the crowd cheer the heavens on, for more rain. My ears felt hot and my head was swimming but everything started to clear again as the steroid man lifted me off the ground back to a standing position.

, It's embarrassing of course for me to admit that this was how the fight went down, but it should offer a bit of proof to you that this story is true.

Everything was blurry again and I knew I was back on the ground but I didn't know how, when, or even why. Through my clouded vision I could see both the man who looked to be on steroids and the one who seemed homeless kicking at me while I was on the ground. At this point I was close to blacking out and everything was a little bit foggy. Still through all that pain and confusion I heard a voice—to me it was the voice of an angel.

"Back off, both of you. This man has been chosen by Funny Bunny." The voice was strong, defined, but clearly female, the voice of beauty incarnate. Through starry eyes I looked up into the pink rabbit mask and for a split second I pretended to see the face beyond the mask. While I couldn't see her actual face, I focused on the other great things about her, like the mass of curly dark brown hair, and her big green eyes, highlighted by pink makeup that complimented the mask she wore. Her long slender arms reached down to help me back to my feet and I saw the pink tipped nails at the end of each finger.

"Are you ok, can you hear me, are you ok?" Her voice repeated before I settled on her words and found clarity in them, which brought everything in the real world back. The music returned, and with it the crowd's chants and the steady droplets of rain that fell all around me. I knew Rosie was still talking but with all the sounds circling me I could no longer hear what she was saying, no matter how badly I wanted to. I knew, in some distant way, that my face was wet, but when Rosie started rubbing my face with a white handkerchief I realized it was more than water. I saw the steady streaks of blood on what used to be white and realized my lip was split and my nose bleeding. I worried that she wouldn't be able to stop the bleeding while I was wearing that damned mask.

"Come with me, I have been instructed to take you inside of the mansion." I finally heard Rosie this time but only because she put her lips close to my ear as she spoke. Her breath was hot against my cold neck and I felt shivers run down my spine. Two large men with the security symbol on their masks lifted me up and began dragging me away from the crowd and toward the mansion. With my body facing backwards as they turned me around to help walk me out of the mansions lawn area, I saw the homeless man's cold dead eyes. I knew he was smiling behind that plain mask, even more so when he drew a long curved knife from his waist band. He held it in the air menacingly, like he was trying to make a very serious threat clear to me. Before I could see anything more, the security men turned me around and led me straight into the mansion.

Everything was still floating in and out; something was wrong that I couldn't quite figure out, something I was having trouble understanding. I had been in fights before and none of them had left me feeling so disoriented and confused. My head was starting to ache to the sound of the bass music, even though I was aware the music had stopped. My mouth was growing dry and my throat felt so raw, it was all I could do not to cry from the pain of swallowing.

I wasn't sure how I got into the mansion. When my senses came back I was aware of all the bright fluorescent lights, and the clinking sounds of people eating dinner. I was placed in a red velvet chair that looked to be a vintage piece of furniture with its dark polished wood, probably worth more than six months of my rent. Within seconds I was brought a glass of water and a group of on staff nurses saw to cleaning me up. I was feeling far better but my headache was persisting and I still couldn't think clearly. I did my best to push it aside. I had a job to do, and now that I was inside the mansion, I felt like I was one step closer to completing my mission.

The floor was white marble and shined with the glow of the chandeliers golden light. A series of long oak tables with golden tablecloths draped over the sides filled the giant space. Each item I saw seemed far more valuable than the last. The faces behind their expensive masks didn't even bother looking at me across the way from their fancy dinner tables. I could smell the variety of foods coming from each table, a collection of fancy foods that were all but unknown to me, from specially cooked salmon to the roasted duck I could see at one table, untouched by the fancy eaters. Each suit and dress seemed to stand out more then the next; it was easy to see how the richest class of people competed with one another. Despite all I saw in those moments, I couldn't focus any longer when the form of Rosie came into view. She walked towards me, each step taking on a life of its own as her dress sparkled in the chandelier's light. In the well lit dining room of the mansion she looked even more beautiful than she did when she came to my rescue.

"Well, I can see you're starting to look better, but if you like I can get one of the limos to take you to your car?" I wanted to speak but something in my throat was preventing me, a mix of dryness in my throat and the nervousness I felt in her presence. When I finally found the words, they all came out in a confusing jumble, mumbled too quietly for her to even hear.

"No, I'm fine. You don't need to do that, but thanks for the help out there."

She moved her hand over her hip and I envisioned the eyebrow she was lifting in confusion at my jumble of words. I took in a deep breath and tried again. "Really, I'm doing okay now, but thank you for saving my ass out there. Things weren't looking so good." Rosie laughed—a slight sound that only lasted a moment but was enough to lift my heart; I didn't know why I was feeling this way.

"If you can stand I'll take you on a quick tour of the mansion," Rosie said as she held out her hand to help me up from the velvet chair I was resting in. Her hand felt warm in mine for the split second it took for her to pull me up, and though it left me wanting more, I let her go without showing it. She walked a steady pace about a foot in front of me, leading me down a small set of marble stairs and out into an open ballroom, with a massive twin staircase.

"This is the primary entryway but its size is perfect for a dance hall or a ballroom. The stairs go up to a series of bedrooms, offices, bathrooms, weight rooms, and Funny Bunny's personal rooms." Classical music was playing by a live orchestra that stood a step higher than the well dressed men and woman who danced to the sound of the music.

"All guests of the mansion are allowed to move freely around the home, except anything up the stairs is off limits." Rosie pointed up the stairs as she spoke, then continued walking leaving the masked dancers behind and headed into a long hallway with the same white marble flooring. On the walls of the hall were several paintings, or rather places where many paintings should have been. Instead each space held life sized images of Funny Bunny, his mask, his suit, everything.

"Rosie why are all of these pictures the same?" I asked, stopping in the center of the hallway, marking not only the paintings but certain side doors that Rosie wasn't mentioning.

"Good eye. Most of the guests I bring into the mansion don't even notice the walls they walk through. What I can tell you is that each of the paintings that were here depicted the family history, as well as the faces of Funny Bunny and his immediate family. Funny Bunny doesn't want to shy away from any of the masq policies and prefers to keep his identity secret." I took a long interested look at this, not just because I wasn't used to the masq polices but because it felt suspicious.

"Anyway if you just keep following me down this way," Rosie said before trailing off and turning back around, heading for the other end of the hallway. We came out into a giant room with glass walls completely lined with plants. Even the ceiling was made of glass that looked out on the cloud filled sky and the falling rain that was picking up with every hour. The floor was made of perfectly placed stone steps that continued to give off the illusion that you were outside.

"This is what we call the lounge area, and over there is the full sized heated pool, the hot tub room, steam room, showers, another weight room, tanning rooms, massage rooms, and of course full bar." I looked out on the pool which was the only thing she'd listed that I could see from where I was standing. I found it almost funny seeing all of these men and woman walking around in there bathing suits but still wearing their masks. This was the first time I had seen anything quite like that since I got out of the hospital.

"Come. I'll show you where everything is," Rosie said before she continued walking down the stone path where a giant bar and restaurant looking area came into view. The bar looked like something you would see on the beaches of Hawaii, with a roof similar to the skin of a coconut. The bar stools and other seats were brown and everything had some kind of tropical feel that encouraged relaxation. However, Rosie didn't walk over to the bar. Instead, she turned, and two double glass sliding doors moved open, leading into the pool area

Rosie continued to speak from over her shoulder, directing me to one thing or another, but I was too busy getting used to the smell of chlorine and the mass of wet bodies in the pool to listen. Brown doors at the back of the pool room opened up into another hallway that had doors on each side that were again all brown. The only difference with these doors was the glass circle at the top that allowed onlookers to glance inside as they walked by.

"On the left are the hot tub rooms as well as the shower and steam rooms." I looked inside the first window and saw a collection of bodies playing in the hot tub, naked except for their masks. I continued walking trying not to linger on the temptations of this place as the tour continued down the hallway of doors.

"To the far left side of the mansion there is a grand banquet hall but that's closed off at the moment. Tanning, massage and weight rooms are on this side and as you can see all of these rooms are considered free rooms, so anything goes." Underneath my mask I started to feel like it was my cheeks that were turning a rosy red rather than hers.

"That's about it unless of course you party; if you do I can tell you where to go and how to get anything you want." I thought about this for a moment, not wanting to believe that this was something my new found love interest was into.

"No, I don't, but thanks again for saving me from that chaos outside," I said, trying to control my strange behavior around this woman, which was so unlike me.

"Ok, well, I'll see you soon then. When you hear a message over the loudspeaker, head back to the entrance room. Everyone is gathering together at the same time to hear a speech by Funny Bunny in honor of our most prestigious guests." Rosie said this confidently but also in a way that reminded me of a zombie doing its master's bidding. I kept wondering if she was some kind of machine slave created just for the purpose of tricking men into wanting her. I knew it was a bizarre thought but watching her leave, it was the only thing I could think to clear my head of her.

My headache continued to grow worse and worse after Rosie left me in that hallway. I tried to sneak a peek back into one of the hot tub rooms but my head was aching too much to even enjoy that. I left the hall, walking straight past the pool and sat down at the bar, trying to clear my head in any way I could. Everything around me was growing fuzzy again; it was as if Rosie's presence was the only thing that was keeping me going. Without her I was in trouble.

"Straight vodka," were the only words I could manage when the bartender came over to take my drink order. I shot the drink back, barely tasting the warm liquid that ran down my throat and seemed to ignite my belly. I drank one after another for a short while trying to clear my head in some way, but it seemed to only work in the vaguest sense. My eye was starting to feel heavy and I desperately wanted to sleep. This night was far too much for my first day back. I reached for my wallet to pay my tab.

"No need to pay, friend. Everything here is free, compliments of Funny Bunny."

I looked at the bartender through weary eyes and put my wallet away only just understanding what he had said. My shoulder abruptly had this strange itch but when I tried to scratch it, I felt pain and a sore spot where a bump was forming.

"You don't look so good, friend. You may want someone to escort you over to the party side of the house. People over there are better trained to take care of overdose patients and you know other things like that."

My head was swimming, like I was inside of a fish tank trying to talk to the rest of the world from under the water. "I don't do drugs, don't even worry about it." I slurred the words wondering how much alcohol I drank in that short time. I didn't have much time to wonder about it, though.

"All party guests please proceed to the ballroom for a special meeting and speech by the one and only Funny Bunny." The intercom sounded and everyone started gathering their possessions and rushing for the hallway leading to the ballroom. Men and woman anxious to be the first ones there left their clothes and went in just swimwear. When I turned back to the bartender he too was gone, heading with the crowd in a surge for the entrance way.

Not having any other choice, I followed the rush of the crowd down the long hallway and back to the ballroom. People were pushing and shoving, moving so fast that I felt like I was running from the bulls in Pamplona. Just ahead of me I thought I saw the strange homeless looking man from outside—the one with the big curved knife—rushing with the rest of the crowd. I remember thinking how strange it was that he was able to get inside, but within another second the man was gone and I wondered if what I'd seen had just been a hallucination.

The lights of the ballroom were out, and only a long line of candles extending up the staircase were lit, giving the room an eerie glow. It was, I noted, the perfect dramatic ambience for Funny Bunny's speech, just what his guests would expect.

Somewhere in the distance thunder cracked just loudly enough to be heard amongst the hushed crowd. So many bodies were gathered together that no one could move comfortably and the room was growing warm from the tangle of body heat. In this dark, warm room my headache ceased and in that moment I wanted nothing more than to sleep.

A rush of wind came from the top of the stairs sending air touched by the moisture of rain tumbling down into the awaiting crowd. The cold air blew the candles out, and all went dark and still; in this moment I couldn't hang on any longer. The strange feelings I was having took hold and I fell into a deep sleep.

Lights came on, blinding me and the rest of the group gathered together in the ballroom. There'd been no warning as someone flipped the switch to the chandelier, illuminating everything in the entrance room of the mansion. My vision cleared. The tiny nap I had in the darkness had done the trick, and I was already feeling much better. At least that's what I thought until I looked down and felt my stomach lurch and my head start to throb again, this time in confusion. Face down in the center of the room, at my feet, was a body. A steady stream of red blood was slowly soaking the white marble floor.

Three

In my life I have seen death, both in the field of my dangerous occupation and in what was supposed to be the protection of my own home. Many crime scenes came to view in the flash of only a few seconds: the oddly strewn bodies on the floor, broken and exposed for the world to see. I recalled the way I always felt when looking down the tunnel of an impossible case that seemed to have no answers. If I had only been here to see who did this, then I could catch the sick freak and you can finally have the peace you deserve. Every detective has thought this at some point or another in his career; it's only natural to want closure for your victim.

Now I stood over the dead body of a man, who only moments ago had been alive and well. Under my watch, my suspicious watch, someone had been killed, and I didn't have the faintest clue as to who did it, when, or why.

After a rough shriek that came from the women closest to the body, a brief silence came over the crowd in the ballroom. The rain tapped steadily somewhere in the distance, high on the mansion's roof. Only just giving off that faint sound, like fingers drumming a table nervously in rapid succession. Even louder than the rain, the crazed partiers from the outside lawn were taking turns chanting and screaming for another audience with the enigmatic Funny Bunny. In the ballroom several people were backing up, getting farther from the body and closer to the exits of the large entrance room.

"Stop where you are. No one is leaving this room until we know who did this," I said out loud so that everyone could hear me nice and clear. I wasn't sure what I was doing just yet but somewhere inside I was still a cop, even if it had been awhile since my last crime scene.

"Yea well, what are you a cop or something?" some chubby man in a black tailored suit asked smugly from behind his pig mask. After he spoke several others began nodding and muttering in an agreement beneath their own masks.

"In fact, that's exactly what I am," I said to the mob, pulling my badge out of my pocket and showing it to the crowd. The group sighed and made a series of exasperated noises, showing clear hatred for police officers. The chunky pig man stepped closer to me, making sure I was paying close attention to him and his attitude.

"If you are a cop, why can't I see the policy mandated badge on your mask?" I couldn't help but think how ironic it was that this pig man was questioning whether or not I was a real police officer. Can somebody say bacon?

"I'm Detective Wink, just reappointed earlier today, so my mask hasn't been issued with the required badge, as of yet anyway. Now if that will be all, I need everyone to back up and give me a little room, but no one can leave until I know what happened to this man." The pig man snorted in anger but stepped back, and everyone else followed, giving me more room to check out the body. The man lay face down on the marble floor, his body twisted unnaturally in a half flat, half sideways position. I moved to a crouched position and pulled a small package out of my pocket with certain standard issue detective equipment, so that I didn't contaminate the body. I withdrew a small evidence bag from the package and wrapped my hand in it. Normally I would have a few pairs of gloves but it had been some time since I restocked my essentials package. After the necessary preparations I pushed on the man's shoulder moving him farther over on his side. The body lifted up with some effort revealing a tear starting just under the heart and going all the way down to the man's waist. It didn't take me much time to determine that the murder weapon was some kind of curved knife.

"You know, I can't be certain but I could have sworn, when the lights turned on you were the one closest to the body," the pig man said from his snout, still sounding smug and better than the rest of the people at the party.

"That's a mighty suspicious thing to say. Tell me friend what is your name?" I only asked this to put the pig man in his place; this crowd wasn't the sort to respect a detective. I had to stop this in its tracks, before others joined in and things got out of hand. The pig man only stared for a long minute before he stepped back into the crowd, muttering something I couldn't distinguish. I wanted to pursue him, but the body was a much greater concern and I didn't want to waste valuable time on some rich snob.

I closed my eyes and tried to remember any sounds from moments after the candlelight was blown out. Turned away from the crowd, I tried to envision something that I had missed, but nothing came. I really couldn't remember anything. I had been deep asleep for one reason or another and had failed the one job I came here to do, the job I was told to do. I couldn't waste anymore time trying to make sense of this all one my own—it was time to call in the police. I pulled out my cell phone and speed dialed the Captain, one of the only people I had left to call. While the phone was ringing I couldn't help but think how similar this crime was to the board game Clue. I was thinking the man, in the ballroom, with the knife. This wasn't the best way to think about a crime I should have prevented but I couldn't help that the thought came to me.

"Wink, this better be damned important. Do you have any idea what time it is?" The gruff voice of the Captain sounded even more thick and grumpy then it normally did.

"It is important sir; there's been a murder here at the masquerade." I had to be direct or else the Captain would have been even more annoyed. While I waited for the information to sink in, I looked all around the room at the faces, or rather the masks, of all the suspects. I looked at all that plastic, wood, metal, rubber, and whatever else those masks were made out of and saw nothing. I had no way to judge what the people in the room were thinking; their faces were just as mysterious as the murder.

"I see, so I guess suspicious was a bit of an understatement." The Captain tried at a joke but the situation I was standing in didn't really seem all that funny to me right now.

"I'll send some officers over," he continued. "Give me about twenty minutes to get there."

I could hear rustling and could tell the Captain was getting out of bed as he spoke.

"Wink did you see anything, or do you have any suspects?" I felt ashamed at the thought of telling the Captain I had fallen asleep at the only important moment of the night, so I left that out.

"Nothing concrete, but I do have someone in mind," I answered, as vaguely as I could. I did notice the crowd perk up and look at me when I said I had someone in mind, so while the comment didn't help me, it did at least scare the crowd.

"Good job, Wink. Keep everyone there, and don't let any suspects slip out. I want a crack at them tonight," the Captain finished. The click of the phone ended the call and left me in a room full of potential killers, and a dead body.

The sound of footsteps came from the top of the staircase, and then Funny Bunny and Rosie Rabbit rounded the corner and came into view, both looking cheerful and ready for the gathering. As they neared the bottom of the steps they stopped cold in their tracks and Rosie let out an awful cry of surprise at the wicked sight. The elegant woman buried her masked face into the suited chest of Funny Bunny and started to cry.

"What happened here? I knew my parties were to die for, but this?" Funny Bunny said while putting an arm around the shaken body of Rosie who continued crying in what was starting to sound like a strange way.

"Funny Bunny, I'm Detective Wink. I can't be certain what happened here but the authorities are on the way to investigate. This is an official crime scene and I'm going to need your cooperation in solving this case and will need you to remain in this room." I was so new to this I felt like a rookie all over again and with all the masks, I felt surrounded and alone.

"Detective, of course we will do everything we can to help this situation come to a happy resolve. I will end the party at once until this man's murderer is found. I have to say I am appalled that one of my guests would do such a terrible thing." I wanted to believe this Funny Bunny but I couldn't help but wonder if he was being serious, or simply sarcastic.

"Do you or anyone else in the room for that matter know who this man is?" Several gathered to get a better look at the man and immediately I felt claustrophobic. In addition to that, I felt fear that a man with a curved knife was still hiding amongst the crowd and would stab me at any moment.

"I can't say that I recognize the mask, but many people attend my masquerade party, so it's hard to keep track," Funny Bunny spoke as he walked back and forth on the large space of the staircase, just one step up from Rosie who was now sitting. No one else spoke in the ballroom; everyone remained silent and unsure of what to do next, other than to wait for the police. I knew I should take action and try and find the person holding the knife but being so recently reinstated, I wasn't sure if I was ready to handle the situation.

"Screw this, I didn't come here to stand all day and wait for the police. I didn't do anything so I'm leaving and that's that," the pig man said suddenly and turned to walk out of the ballroom, with several others muttering and following the fat man on his rampage out of the room.

"No one is going anywhere until the police get here and a proper search can be made to ensure no one has the murder weapon on their person," I spoke trying to sound forceful, making sure the pig man and the rest of the crowd knew I wasn't playing around with this.

"If you got something on me then arrest me, otherwise I'm outta here."

That was the final straw; I had to assert myself to the crowd or would lose my murderer forever. I left the dead body and made my way through the mass of people standing between me and the pig man, who had already reached the exit to the mansion.

"Sir, I will not repeat myself. Get back into line with everyone else or I will arrest you for impeding an investigation." The pig man didn't seem to care that I was telling him what to do, maybe because he'd done too many drugs, or maybe just because he was so rich. Or maybe because he was a murdering psychopath. I didn't know from where I was standing if this man was the killer or not and the way he was walking towards me, I was starting to feel very threatened. Despite my fear I didn't respond until the pig man stuck his hands in his coat pocket, for what I thought to be a knife.

"Don't move! Now slowly let me see your hands!" I called out, my voice echoing loudly in the giant ballroom. My pistol was in my hands and pointed at the pig man who had stopped dead in his tracks, his hands still in his jacket pocket. It felt good to hold the weapon; I hadn't used it for so long but here and now, it felt like it was meant to be in my hands.

"What are you going to do, shoot me cop? Is that why you needed to be reinstated—you spend a little too much time with your finger on that trigger?" The pig man was still trying to sound tough, though most likely now he was trying to keep up his image since he had started so much trouble. I wasn't going to shoot the guy unless I had a reason to, but without a partner there was no one else to force him to comply with me.

"Chops, for god's sakes get your hands up and do what the officer says," Funny Bunny said in a somewhat annoyed voice to the pig man, who was apparently named Chops. The pig man didn't waste any time pulling out his hands and dropping to his knees obediently. I walked over to him nice and slow, keeping my pistol available in one hand while I reached into his coat pocket. I felt around and couldn't seem to find anything, not even a flask or some cigarettes. It seemed the pig man was only trying to get a rise out of me with his attempt at grabbing something in his coat pocket. Still I didn't trust him, so I continued my search of the rest of his pockets and any other place I could feel for a hiding place. Chops turned out to be clean but that didn't mean he wasn't the killer. It only meant he stashed the knife somewhere in the ballroom.

"Now get back in line. It shouldn't be much longer until the other officers arrive." I holstered the pistol as the pig man got to his feet and ran back to where he had started. From there he remained silent. Only moments after this outburst, several police cars sounded outside, and then their bright lights came into view. The dance of red and blue traded places over and over again against the outside walls of the mansion, through the windows and into the ballroom. Several officers came inside and started searching all those present in the entrance room at the time of the murder. The Captain and a few other detectives arrived and started taking statements from those who had already been searched. Finally the techs arrived and went to work on the forensics. Blood splatter and forensic pathology would be done to determine what killed the man and how it was done, but I already had a good idea on that. The only hope we had of finding out who did this would be to find the murder weapon or to get some fingerprints.

"Alright, Wink, things seem to be in motion here. Why don't you tell me what you know about this mess," the Captain asked, but I was busy watching Funny Bunny talking to detectives on the other side of the room. I watched them all laugh and couldn't help but wonder what kind of a statement Funny Bunny was giving to cause the detectives to laugh so much.

"Unfortunately I wasn't able to see much Captain. I was in the room when it happened but the lights went out for a moment and I didn't hear anything." I wanted to focus on the Captain, give him my full attention at this moment more than any other, but I couldn't do it. I watched them let Funny Bunny go and couldn't turn away as he walked up the stairs and out of sight.

"Captain, why are they letting Funny Bunny go? He's a suspect just like everyone else," I asked before the Captain had time to respond to my previous statement.

"Well, from my understanding he wasn't in the room when it happened and besides we did a weapon search and he was clean. Plus he's been very helpful with giving his statement and letting us take over this place for the investigation," the Captain answered matter-of-factly, like he was trying to get it out of the way so he could get to what was really important. I tried to forget Funny Bunny and focus on what the Captain was saying.

"The thing is Wink, we've taken over forty statements so far and all of them match up except for one."

I became more interested in this, and even started to get excited at the idea of finding the murderer. "Some good news after all. So who is it? I'd like to get a crack at him down at the station, see if I can get him to talk."

The Captain had a strange look in his eyes, which were the only real parts of his face that I could see with his awful mask, with its golden star of the captain's badge covering his entire face. "Wink, the only story that isn't matching up perfectly right now is yours."   Astonished by this I froze in place looking at the Captain, for the first time in my life I was considered a suspect. "What do you mean? Do you think I'm the killer or something?"

Unable to comprehend what was happening, I was starting to feel hot; the prickle of fear and sweat lingered on my skin.

"According to the statements we've taken so far, everyone was gathered in this room for the meeting and speech by Funny Bunny. The candles were blown out and everyone went quiet, thinking this was all part of a stunt put on by Funny Bunny. In the darkness just about everyone heard some strange sounds followed by a peculiar groan of a man. They all say the groan sounded funny, like a joke meant to make everyone think there was a ghost floating among them. Everyone mentioned the noise, except you." The Captain was almost whispering now, not wanting to draw the attention of anyone else in the room, like it was our little secret. I didn't want to tell the Captain anything about my night and what had happened to me, but it was starting to look like I would have to.

"Look, Wink it's your first day back after some pretty traumatic stuff," he continued. "I understand if you weren't perfect out there. But I can tell you right now if this gets out to the other officers, you are going to be suspect number one, unless you tell me the truth right now." I considered my options for a few moments and decided to tell the Captain what had happened. I did my best to retell the story starting from my entrance to the party, going all the way to the ballroom and the dead body, this time including everything.

"Asleep? Wink, you have to be kidding me. How did you fall asleep in this room, with all these people?" The Captain didn't like this part of the tale but unfortunately it was the only truth I had.

Only at that moment did I realize how stupid I was, how insanely idiotic I had been not to notice something that should have been so obvious. "Oh shit, Captain someone must have already known I was a cop. Someone was trying to make sure I wouldn't see this murder go down." A light bulb came on above my head that was easily the size of the sun and again I couldn't believe that it hadn't occurred to me before.

"Calm down, Wink, and tell me what the hell it is your talking about." The Captain was growing impatient with me.

"The fight, Captain. Right before I started getting my ass kicked, I felt a prick in my shoulder, something that made me feel numb right away. After that I felt droopy and tired. Captain, I was drugged." I knew it was true: I had felt the pain in my shoulder just before I started feeling so strange.

"Don't you see, Captain, I thought it was because of the fight that I felt like shit, but it was because someone knew I was a cop snooping around and took care of it." I didn't know why I was getting so excited; maybe it was because I knew my name would be cleared. "Just get one of the techs to take my blood and get it to the lab for a drug test. That will prove that what I'm telling you is the truth." Even as the words left my mouth I almost regretted them, knowing how it would look if the test for some reason came back negative.

"Alright I believe you, Wink, but if you're right then someone planned this in advance and wasn't going to let a cop get in the way of things. Worse is the fact that either you are the world's worst undercover or someone already knew you were coming to the party." The implication was a frightening one, even with the little I knew about what went on in the department these days.

"Go get your blood drawn and I'll go gather up your two star suspects for questioning," the Captain said, putting a hand on my shoulder for a moment and then walking away to find the men I most suspected to be the murderer.

The tech didn't even bother asking me questions about the blood draw, but only bitched from beneath her mask marked by the medical symbol about how long this was all going to take. When it was done, I went to the other end of the ballroom where the detectives were taking turns questioning suspects. I wanted to catch up to the Captain and see if he had made any progress on my two star suspects, when a young detective got in my way.

"Hey, no one is allowed back here until their turn to be questioned. Now get back in line and wait your turn." I knew he was young by the sound of his voice, and I didn't know who he was, so chances were he had earned his detective badge within the last three years.

"I'm Detective Wink. The Captain is back there with my two suspects, and I need to see if I can lend a hand in the interrogation."

The young detective moved his hand but didn't step out of the way; instead he only looked at me for a long moment. His mask was all black but had blue veins spread out, starting at the eyes and going down to the cheeks. It looked like electricity sparking all over his face, and the blue matched with the color of the shield above his right eye.

"Fair enough, Detective Wink. Welcome back to the squad. I'm Detective Light," he said with new emotion, transforming from cocky police officer to co-worker and then on to overly polite friend as he continued talking. "I uh, heard about what happened to you. I can't pretend to understand what you went through but I am sorry that it turned out that way."

This was the last thing I wanted to talk about, and I tried to brush it off quickly. "Thanks. Anyway what is the situation so far— did you guys find anything I should know about?"

Light seemed okay with changing the subject. "So far we've found three knives, one of them on your prime suspect. All three will be going down to the station soon enough. Other than that we found drugs on every person at this little fiesta, but the Captain said not to worry about them. I guess it would take forever giving a hundred people minor drug charges, not really worth the paper work. Your other suspect, Chops, was clean but is definitely on something. My guess is he took everything he had when he found out you were a cop. Still, with that much aggression he's going down to the station for questioning, and we'll see what comes from that."

It was beginning to seem that Light would talk forever if I didn't stop him; he was just one of those people that loved the sound of his own voice. "Thanks detective, I appreciate your help," I cut him off before stepping past him and heading to the back hall where the Captain was just finishing up with the dangerous, homeless looking guy.

"Anything come out of this one, Captain?" I asked staring down at the man; I couldn't help but feel that he was the one who killed the man. He was the murderer.

So far, he's been talking absolute nonsense, so we'll just have to see what he has to say back at the station. The knife we found on him is more than enough to hold him until tomorrow, when this mess will be better sorted out. Why don't you head home, Wink? You look like shit and this has been one hell of a first day back."

I did feel tired, clearly an effect of the drugs I'd been injected with, but I wasn't ready to stop for the night. Besides, how shitty could I really look to a person who couldn't even see my face? "I would really like to help with the interrogation of this one, and that chunky asshole Chops, if that's alright Captain."

The Captain shook his head immediately, and I was starting to think he really didn't trust me anymore, after what had happened at the party.

"It's going to take a long time to get all of this sorted out and we can't go straight into interrogation until we question and search everyone. Go home and get some rest, and come in early in the morning and we can get started trying to piece this thing together." The Captain didn't give me any room to argue; just like that I was finished for the night.

I walked out of the hall and straight to the front door, so I could get out of the ballroom and head home.

"Hey buddy, do you need a ride to your car?" I turned to see Light standing close by; he had followed me to the door so he could offer up his services, in the form of a ride.

"No, thanks, I think I could use some time to think after everything that's happened." Light nodded before I turned and walked out of the mansion, through the giant oak wood doors. The stone was damp from the rain and small drops were still falling from the sky, giving off that smell in the air of the world being washed clean. The crowds were gone and the lawn was empty, except for the beer bottles and drug needles that were surly resting on the damp grass. Funny Bunny must have sent everyone home early, although it was closer to daylight than it seemed. Time had flown by since I'd arrived at the party; already I could see the bottom of the dark sky giving off that faint red glow. In only a couple of hours the sun would break through the ground and bring light to another day.

My walk to the car was uneventful but my mind was still working over the events of the night, trying to figure out exactly what had happened. Driving home was the same; I only went through the motions as I continued to think about what occurred in the ballroom after the candles went out.

I reached my apartment—not the home I used to have before the hospital. Home for me now was this ugly apartment overlooking the view of another, just as ugly. Only the window in my living room looked out on the sky; since I was on the top floor, the view from there wasn't bad. Still, every time I walked into the apartment I would grimace at the sight of the tiny kitchen and the one bedroom I had. Living somewhere like this was better than facing every hour of every day by the reminders that came from my home of the past, by the bedrooms of my past.

I undressed, almost unable to do so because of the sudden fatigue that washed over me at the sight of my warm blankets. I pulled the gray mask with the blood red tear from my face and placed it on top of my dresser, put my pistol beside me on the night stand and got down to my boxers for sleep. It was then that I saw something strapped to my leg just above the ankle, something I sometimes used for backup.

"I don't remember grabbing you before I left today," I couldn't help but say out loud to my lonely apartment, as I reached down to grab it. I pulled free the holstered object and held it out in the lamp light; the cold steel of a curved knife sparkled against the glow.

Four

Everything was turning and shifting in a constant circle, a seemingly never ending cycle of twisting vision. My head wouldn't stop circling the room, so I tried that old tick of putting one foot on the floor to gain some kind of balance over the world. The spinning I felt made me question whether drinking all that alcohol was such a good idea. Once the nausea came, first at my stomach, then all the way up my throat, I knew it was a bad idea. In the past I had dealt with hangovers, and even the effects of drinking way too much before going to sleep. This however was far worse than any of those nights, thanks to the mysterious drug leaving my system.

Somewhere near morning, I ended up on the bathroom floor gripping my stomach in an attempt to quell the pain. I was writhing back and forth, my stomach gurgling strange sounds and sending harsh chemicals into my throat. I can't be certain how many times I vomited in the early hours of the morning, the dark still conquering the city. All I know is far more than just the flat burger and stale fries came out of my body in an exorcist-like rush.

In my position I couldn't tell exactly when the ache started to slow down and I was able to think enough to get my mind off the pain. As I lay there on the bathroom floor, my thoughts wandered off and I couldn't help but think about her. For whatever reason it was difficult to see her face in my mind's eye, but I knew she was the one I wanted there to take care of me. I thought of her long brown hair that reached the middle of her back. I could see her green eyes full of excitement and passion for the life we couldn't wait to live. In my head she was standing over me in the bathroom rubbing my stomach, trying to coax the pain away.

"It's going to be fine and as soon as you feel better, we can do whatever you want." I heard her voice and let the soothing sound of it comfort me into a state of relaxation. Somewhere in between the bathroom floor and the dream I was having, the pain left me and I fell into a deep, soothing sleep.

A knock came from my front door and my eyes opened. My surroundings confused me, as I could barely remember ending up on the bathroom floor, but after a moment of listening to the knocking on the door, my memories started coming back to me. I got up from the floor, my bones popping and creaking like an old man's, though I knew it was only from sleeping on hard tile. I stepped out of the bathroom and heard my alarm going off; I had set it last night so I could make it to work early.

"You've got to be kidding me," I said out loud, hitting the alarm shut off button angrily and heading for the door to see who was there. My first thought was that the Captain had come over to my apartment after I hadn't shown up, and now would be angry at yet another failure. When I opened the door, however, I was surprised by my visitor. It was her.

"Jesus, you need to put some clothes on, and you can't open the door without your mask. Come on, detective, you're supposed to be upholding the law, not breaking it." She stood in tight jeans and an even tighter t shirt that showed off the bottom portion of her stomach. I glanced down, remembering the day we both got tattoos.

"What are you doing here, Danielle? I didn't think I would see you again after the hospital," I said, standing in the doorway in just my boxers, not even caring that my face was exposed to the world, or at least to the apartment complex.

"I've already seen you once since the hospital. Don't you remember anything? Get out of the way—we need to get inside before someone sees you and complains to the police." She stepped inside my home and shut the door behind her, only after making sure no one was watching.

"And what's with this Danielle stuff? You know we're not married anymore and you can't just use my real name." I looked at her mask and felt my stomach cringe, much like it did the previous night. I hated the idea that everyone I knew in life before what happened no longer had a face. Her mask only covered half of her face, starting at her eyes and surrounding the nose. It was sparkling white and had gold glitter streaks all over it, creating no pattern that I could distinguish.

"There is no way I can just forget your name and start using that fake one. It just doesn't feel right after all we went through together." I spoke honestly but I knew it wasn't going to work on her—she had this strong sense about her that commanded independence. I knew her well enough to know that she was scared of the dark, but here and now she was fearless.

"My name is Viola for the time being and you are Wink. End of story." Her attitude was there but it wasn't real. It was just this act she put on to make herself seem meaner then she really was.

"Well then, what is it that you stopped by for, Viola?" The words came out in a sarcastic tone that I made sure she would notice. With all the years we were together and then married, we both knew what to say and do to piss the other person off.

"I just thought I would come by and see how you were doing. I know you got reinstated yesterday, so I figured you would be heading back to work today." I watched her pink lips move up and down as she formed the words, and I just wanted to look at her real face.

"I actually started back last night but it wasn't exactly an easy first day back on the job." I walked away then, into the bathroom to grab my robe off the back of the door.

"Why, what happened last night?" Danielle or Viola asked in a concerned tone that hinted at what she thought of me working again. Since what happened to me and to the world, she had it in her head that I didn't have what it took to get back on the job.

"It's fine, nothing I can't handle." I wanted her to leave, annoyed by her presence in my place, and already late for work. It was funny how I could spend all night thinking about someone and all the good times we had, only to see her and remember all the things I hated about her in the first place.

"I just can't see how you can get back out there after everything that happened. I mean, don't you want to just get away from all those things that remind you—"

"There is no running from what happened," I cut her off, angry with her and all the memories she was bringing on. "Especially with this idiotic masq policy in effect. No matter where I go or what I do, it's going to be with me and hearing you talk about it right now, it's about all I can't do not to lose my mind." I was speaking through gritted teeth and I knew by now my face was red and I was only seconds away from losing my temper for real.

"Alright I get it. I was just coming to see how you were doing. I must have had a weird dream or something, because I was worried about you and wanted to make sure you were ok." I understood, of course, given my own dreams and the terrible night I'd gone through. Still, she was my ex wife now and wasn't the support I was looking for.

"I'm fine, except for the fact that I am running late for work." The statement hung in the air, while I waited for Viola to take the hint.

"Okay, I'll get out of your hair, but I want you to remember, I know what you're going through, so you better call me if you need to talk or need anything else." She was sincere in her commitment to make sure I was ok, but not sincere enough to keep our marriage together. At this point I had little patience for anyone in my life.

"Thanks, Danielle, I'll keep that in mind," I said just to humor her and get her out of my apartment and my life. We said our goodbyes and I let her out of the house, but as she left I couldn't help but feel this sensation of utter sadness that she was leaving me all over again. Some part of my head wanted her to stay so desperately, but the pain and hurt I carried wouldn't let me tell her anything close to that. Once she was gone I went straight to the shower and began my morning rituals so I could get out of there and off to work.

After the troubled night's weather, the sun was fighting back, pushing its bright rays here and there through the clouds. The rain had stopped for the time being, but the sky looked ominous. I pulled through the early morning traffic in my jeep, trying to keep my mind clear enough to drive, no easy feat in my mental state, not to mention the fact that I had only one eye and was wearing a mask. My intention was to head to the police station down on One Police Plaza, but there was something else I had to do first. I reached the building and pulled around to the back and parked, marking how grateful I was that I didn't eat breakfast that morning. I walked through the glass doors and down the hallway underneath the sign marked Morgue.

"Detective, it's been some time since I've seen you; I thought you'd transferred to a more peaceful division, with what happened to your partner and all." The morgue attendant was a polite older woman, and in a different time or place I would have known her name and face. Here and now I looked at the doctor's mask that covered everything besides her eyes and knew I would never see what was underneath it again. I avoided her remark about my partner and hoped she'd take the hint.

"Technically I'm no longer in any division. I was just reinstated yesterday." Though I had not yet officially been assigned to Homicide, it seemed I was destined to work with murder.

"It's good to have you back in any case. I was starting to get tired of explaining everything to all the new officers who come in here. But I guess now that we're meeting under these circumstances we have to introduce our selves all over again. So, hello Detective I'm Doctor Monroe. What can I do for you today?" In addition to being polite, I remembered that Doctor Monroe was also a little bit loony.

"For the time being I'm Detective Wink. I'm here because a man was murdered last night, he had a knife wound to the chest but I didn't get a good look at his mask."

"Ah yes, you must mean the gentlemen the Captain was so interested in. Come with me and I'll walk you through what we have so far." Monroe turned from her station and opened a door leading into the room where they temporarily keep the bodies on ice. She consulted some chart in her hands and then pulled open a steel door near the bottom left corner of the room. The cold air rose from its chamber and for a moment floated to the ceiling, as if it were a ghost escaping from this world. The wheels spun and the table the man lay on was pulled all the way out until he was right in front of me, dead and exposed.

"You have got to be kidding me, this can't be protocol." I stared down in annoyance at the body.

"Oh, yes, it's all part of the masq policy: the victim of a crime must remain masked until all information can be determined or until a family member comes to claim the body."

The man on the table was pale white from the cold and from death. His chest had a long curved gash that went all the way down to his belly. He was tagged and ready for his funeral, except for the mask he had been wearing at the party. It was all silver and had a red painted eye piece, with screws and bolts placed all over, giving it a robotic feel.

"How in the hell am I supposed to solve a murder when I can't even see the victims face?" Again I felt like this was all some kind of sick joke, and I wondered how the world could be at peace with everyone hiding their faces.

"Unfortunately that's the way we have to do it. We won't even know his name until the masq code gets back from government headquarters confirming his identity. However, for the time being until we get the test results back on everything and the name, I can tell you what I know." In that moment I actually thought Danielle was right: I couldn't adapt to this new world of strange crime investigation. I'd been a cop for most of my life and already knew how things were supposed to work; so much had changed in my absence, it just seemed impossible.

"Alright, just tell me what you know so far," I managed to say while still staring at the dead man's mask half lost in my own thoughts. Monroe flipped through the pages of her clipboard until she found what she was looking for and then began to read in a monotone voice.

"John Doe is approximately forty years of age. Cause of death was a deep puncture wound to the heart. He tested high for blood alcohol content as well as various other forms of substances that have yet to be determined. DNA results came back negative for anything but his own tissue; fingerprint analysis came back with nothing as well." Listening to the information provided by Monroe I realized that I already knew just about everything that she was reading. Without DNA evidence and without the knowledge of the man's identity I couldn't see how I would go about solving this case.

"Basically our guy was no saint, though I doubt any of the people at that party were sober, so it doesn't really help that he was drugged off his ass."

Monroe stopped reading and looked at me from above her doctor's mask for a long time, and I realized I must have sounded very rude.

"Look Detective, whoever did this had a reason to kill this man; this wasn't just some random drug kill. If it had been, the killer would have stopped at the heart. Instead he continued all the way down to the stomach, either to make sure the man was dead or because he had a lot of anger against that man." I smiled with my eyes at Monroe—in only a moment she had cleared up everything that was troubling me. My thoughts had been stuck on how I could solve a murder without a face, and now I knew exactly what would bring this case out to the open.

"Motive—that's how I can solve this thing. I just have to find out why someone wanted to kill our man, and then all the other pieces should fit together from there." I laughed at little at my own stupidity: motive was police academy 101 and I had overlooked it because of a mask.

"Thanks, Monroe. Keep me posted if you find anything else out about our Vic," I said while walking away from her. I didn't even give her the time to answer before I was out the door and on my way. Suddenly I thought of something that wasn't really important but I turned around and poked my head back in the door anyway, so that I could ask.

"When I first walked in, how did you know it was me?" I saw Monroe smiling beneath her mask; I could spot the happiness coming from her just by looking at her eyes.

"Sometimes, Detective, seeing a person's face isn't the most important thing. Given whom you are and the job you're trying to do, maybe you need to take notice of the things that set people apart, besides their faces."

This didn't really answer my question, but I left the room and went on my way somehow satisfied by her response.

Looking back, I realize that I'd failed as a detective once again. I knew there was a meaning in those words beyond the question that I asked, but I didn't pay attention to them as I should have.

I didn't waste any more time, and headed straight to the station, figuring that I was already in a world of trouble for being so inconsistent. Still I was less afraid of the Captain and more interested in the case and how I would go about solving it.

*****

My mind was lost in the images from the previous night as I drove from the morgue to the police precinct. I knew I was missing so much from that night but instead of focusing on what I knew, I lost myself in the depths of what I didn't know. Over and over again I would picture the ballroom and all the people inside of it and what I thought happened when the lights went out. I went through several scenarios trying to get a clean image of who killed the man, but only ended up with the same conclusion each time. It was simple: the only man that could have drugged me and ended up killing in the ballroom was the homeless guy. I needed more facts before I could make a proper conclusion but I just couldn't stop thinking about the ballroom.

I pulled into the back parking lot designated for employees and headed straight inside. For the first time I took comfort in my mask, as I knew the bulk of the force wouldn't recognize me and therefore wouldn't bother me. I didn't have anything against any of them, but I already knew all the questions they'd ask, and I already knew I didn't want to answer any of them. I wasn't lucky enough to slip inside completely unnoticed, though.

"Detective Wink, I was starting to wonder if you were going to make it in today. I could use some back up on the interrogations from last night." It was Detective Light, and it seemed like he had been waiting by the elevator for me to show up.

"Yeah, I got a little snagged this morning, I thought I would check up with the morgue and see if they found anything on our Vic." The last thing I wanted was for Light to think I was damaged and unable to do my job, so I made sure he knew I was working. I tried to say this quickly and keep walking, as though I was busy and had things to do. But Light had his own ideas.

"I'm just getting back on an errand. We can ride up together," he said happily as he pushed the up arrow next to the silver doors of the elevator. I wasn't thrilled about this and remained quiet, only smiling at him as we waited for the elevator.

"So during your interrogations were you able to come up with anything?" I asked as soon as the doors shut and the elevator started its climb to the third floor. I would have rather gotten this information from the Captain but I was afraid of the approaching awkward silence, so I asked anyway.

"So far we don't have much of anything, and we only have two suspects left in the interrogation room. Your friend Chops got out first, thanks to his lawyer who argued that we couldn't hold him just for being annoying. The other was let go because his knife was a short pocket size, far too small to inflict the damage we saw."

I didn't like that Chops was able to walk out of the precinct, but he never really was my top suspect anyway. "So tell me, is my prime suspect still here?" He was the only one with the weapon and the opportunity; he had to be the killer.

"Yeah, that punk is still here but it's like talking to a mental patient. I doubt were going to get anything out of him." In some way I was happy that Light and the others had failed on breaking the homeless man; that meant that it was my time to shine. The elevator opened and we walked out of the box and straight to the back of the office, where the interrogation rooms were.

"Don't you want to check in with the Captain or something before you get started on these losers?" Light asked after taking a step ahead of me, preventing me from getting any closer to the rooms that looked onto the suspects through one-way glass.

"The Captain trusts that I can do my job. I'll speak to him after I find out why my suspect killed a man last night." I didn't have anything against Light but I was already starting to get annoyed by his constant need for attention, like a neglected dog.

"Just tell me which room my suspect is in." Light pointed to the steel door on my right and I didn't waste any time in walking right past him and into the room. Everything was plain and cold on this side of the room, but my attention was focused on the man, rather than the area. The glass protected me from sight but it left him exposed, sitting with his head down on a black table in the all but empty room that was just big enough for the suspect to feel trapped. I wasn't getting any answers just watching him, though, and I knew it was time to get to work, when of course Light entered the room.

"Hey, I wasn't trying to bust your balls out there; I know you've been at this far longer than I have and you know what you're doing. Hell I'm just a rookie—the only reason I'm even on homicide is because I have family up the chain of command and I got hooked up with this early. I'm just trying to get on your good side; everyone in this precinct already thinks I'm a joke." I didn't have time for a heart to heart with a rookie cop everyone hated, but I still felt a little bit sorry for the guy.

"Forget about it. I know you're just trying to do your job, and it's not a big deal. Look, if we can figure out this murder then we can both get back in the good graces of the department, so let's just focus on that." Just like a puppy waiting for approval, Light changed from a sad man to a happy one—if he had a tail he would have been wagging it.

"Sounds good, Wink. I'll work on the other guy while you try your hand at this freak and then we can go from there." With such a range of emotions, Light gave me a funny feeling, but I couldn't figure out what I was sensing with him. One second he was on his way to tears, the next he was cocked and ready, already giving out orders to a senior officer.

"Oh, and here is the file we put together so far on your suspect." Light handed me a plain manila folder. As soon as I took it the detective was gone, just like lightning. The file had a picture of the knife and the results of the forensics—only the suspect's DNA and fingerprints were found on the weapon. He was thirty-two years old, blood type A-positive, and had no real address to speak of other than his childhood home. It wasn't much to go on, but I did at least find out his name, other than that I read the statement he'd made to the police, but none of it made any sense." Only the other cops hadn't known to ask why he had drugged a detective earlier that night.

I closed the folder but kept it handy in case I learned anything else to add to the document. I also knew that just carrying a folder put a little extra fear in the suspect, making them believe you knew more then you actually did. I was through waiting around for an answer, I wanted to get in there and push the homeless man until he cracked into a million pieces. Before going in however I had to put my pistol on the desk, just to make sure the suspect didn't get a hold of it. Without further delay, I entered the interrogation room and began my performance.

Five

"Good to see you again, Rex. It's been a whole night since you and your buddy jumped a police officer in the midst of a drugged out party." I wanted to come off as nice but at the same time get right to the point of what I wanted to know. Rex kept his head down, not even stirring when I entered the room. His appearance hadn't changed much since last night, though with his head down on the table it was hard to get a good look at him.

"Rex, I'm not going to waste my time trying to talk you into confessing something that you didn't do, so all I want to know is why you drugged me last night. That whole murder business may not involve you, but right now the whole department thinks you're the killer. How are we supposed to know if it's you or not when you won't even talk?" Finally the head resting on the table lifted until it made eye contact with me, and I looked right at a blank mask. Rex still didn't say anything; he only stared at me through his protective layer of mask. Dirt and grime still caked the mask but now his facial hair looked hot and sticky, clinging to the stains on his mask.

"Look, I know you don't want to sit in jail until we catch the real murderer, so why don't you just start talking and we can work something out." I wasn't trying to press the murder for the simple reason that I didn't have enough evidence; I thought I would start small and work my way up. Still the cold eyes only watched; occasionally he blinked but that was all the movement I could get from the homeless man.

"I won't sit here and pretend you can't hear me. This is your last chance to say something or I'll start taking this interrogation old school." At this Rex turned his head awkwardly to the side, his gaze never leaving mine.

"The maggots just dance in the rain." At first I wasn't certain what he'd said but after a moment of rethinking what I just heard, I knew I was hearing gibberish.

"I'm not stupid, Rex; I already know that you're not insane. You might be a little out there, and probably really wild but the one thing you're not is insane." I let out an awful sigh now realizing what kind of wall I was up against; at once I understood what Detective Light was talking about. Light had said the man was crazy but I didn't buy into it. I just knew he was faking, and that he knew something about last night.

"Lambs to the slaughter, that's all we can be, that's all we are," Rex muttered from behind his mask and I had to resist the urge to break it off of his face. I was starting to get irritated so I just let out a deep breath, sat still, and tried to calm down. The room was all white and had no windows; it was becoming hot, which was all part of the interrogation. The idea behind a no torture society was to find other ways to get someone to talk, but torture in one form or another seemed to get the best results. The heat was meant to slowly bother a person until they wouldn't want to sit in the room any longer. Another technique was to leave someone alone for long periods of time, until the walls started closing in and loneliness took over. Another was to leave someone in a room without food for long periods of time; it was funny how much someone would talk just to get a decent meal.

"Tell you what, Rex, if you quit this bullshit crazy person act I'll hook you up with something good to eat. I know you don't like jail house food; it's never all that great and you probably haven't eaten all day." The homeless man perked up like a starving animal but while the offer caught his attention, it didn't get him to agree to anything.

"What do you say, how about a large pepperoni pizza and any other toppings you might like? Just say the word Rex and I'll get right on that food order for you. The only thing that's stopping me is you." I couldn't see his face under the hair and the mask but I knew he was licking his lips like a wolf readying itself for an easy kill. I watched him for a long time, waiting in silence for him to say something that proved he wasn't insane. Again his head went to the side, an indication that he was going to speak.

"Even the cows walk with the sheep to the slaughter house."

"God damn it!" I yelled smashing my fists hard on the table before I pushed back on my chair hard and stood up, knocking it over with a loud crash. I watched my hands reach across the table to grab the little freak by his collar, so I could beat the answers out of him. The man didn't fight back as I jerked his head up to face me. Rex only watched from behind his mask, didn't even blink at what I was about to do to him. I stood like that for a long time ready to beat the piss out of the little shit.

"I get it Rex: you can't just tell me what I need to know because you don't want to go to prison. Eventually Rex you're going to break and you're going to tell me what I want to know. It's only a matter of time before you slip up in this crazy act." I let go of

Rex and he dropped back onto his chair with an awkward plop. I didn't sit back down but I did pick up my chair and set it back where it was supposed to go.

I knew that I couldn't hurt the man without losing him forever; some court lawyer would make sure his client walked due to unlawful interrogation. Instead I decided I would have to get Rex on my side. "I understand that you can't trust me Rex. Hell, I even get the acting crazy bit; I have seen it work in the past." I thought it would be a good idea to tell him more about my life in order to get him to understand my situation so that he would come clean himself.

"I'm going to tell you a story, Rex. There really isn't much else for you to do in this room so you might as well pay attention and maybe you'll have a change of heart." Rex was still trying to play like he was nuts so he didn't give me any indication that he understood what I was saying. Still my gut told me this guy was only playing stupid and that he would eventually break.

"Some years back my old partner and I were working this case that involved some crazies who killed a lot of people. At the time we didn't really know what we were up against. All we knew was that this small convenience store was full of dead bodies. There were two dead men, three dead women, and even one dead kid, a boy about eight. All of them were stabbed to death and each one of them had been robbed of what money they had. You see we didn't know what had happened at the time but it didn't take long to track down the killers." I emphasized words like killer, and dead bodies, to see what kind of reaction I got from the homeless man.

"Not only were the bodies left penniless but the women had been desecrated after death—it was a gruesome sight. My partner was all about stopping things like that; she had spent her entire life trying to make the world a better place. Some might have called her a bit of a hippy. I know I certainly did, but she only wanted the best for the world. When she saw those bodies I thought she was going to break apart right there on the crime scene. However she held it together and did her job just like the rest of us." I was getting off the point of my story but it felt nice thinking about her like this. So much had happened it was hard to give her memory my time.

"Chloe was a strong person but that day she broke, even if just for a moment. After the crime scene I heard her crying but I never actually saw it. She would never have allowed me to. After that she became obsessed with the case and just wouldn't stop digging for anything that would lead her to the killers. I tried to help her but there wasn't a lot I could do. Her special interest in the case made it something she had to solve herself." I could picture her clearly in my mind as I spoke to Rex, and I realized that the story had become more real for me than for him. She was taller than I and probably had more muscles as well; although she wasn't a beautiful woman she had a presence about her that at times made her appear much more attractive than she actually was: one minute she seemed average looking, and the next she looked more like a supermodel.

"Anyway, Chloe discovered that one of the dead women had a child earlier in her life who wasn't really a part of the woman's life. It turned out her son from long ago had a mental condition that made him criminally insane. Only weeks before the crime he had escaped from an asylum. You would be surprised how easy it was to find him once we had an image and could ask around about his whereabouts. Thanks to an eyewitness, we learned he was hiding in some old meth house outside of the city limits." For the first time since I started my story I saw Rex twitch in his seat and upon further inspection I saw his hand shaking. The homeless man grabbed his hand to stop it from shaking and after that he went right back to his blank stare.

"We busted into the abandoned house and saw far more horrors then either of us wanted to see in a lifetime. Apparently this mental patient didn't escape alone and his two friends were just as crazy as he was. I don't want to recount everything I saw but I will say there were twenty two bodies in that house, most of them woman and children. The three insane didn't come quietly and we had to kill two of them and wound the other to stop them. The woman's son was alive and eventually told us the story of how he escaped and the things he had done." I sat back down in the chair and waited for a long time before speaking again, more for my own sake than for Rex's.

"That man did things to his own mother that I won't even repeat. That day I looked at a truly insane person and saw nothing in his eyes. After that experience Chloe and I always knew when a person was faking insanity and when was the real deal. Rex, I can tell you right now that you are not that sick man who sat across from me in that same chair years ago. When I look into your eyes I can see there is a person inside, someone that isn't capable of such horrible things." Seconds raged on for centuries after that statement as we sat in the hot interrogation room looking at one another.

"What happened to your partner?" The voice wasn't disturbed, and it didn't sound crazed and it didn't say random words that didn't make any sense. Rex sounded even more reasonable than I thought he would, and I wondered what had happened to make this man so disturbed looking.

"She took a bullet to the face a few years back, she died instantly," I said to Rex, keeping my voice low, hoping none of my colleagues were listening from the other side of the glass. Rex nodded from behind his ugly mask and I wondered what kind of emotions displayed on his face. I wished I could see it just for a second.

"I've told you a story, so it's your turn now: tell me the story of what happened last night." Again Rex nodded but it didn't last too long before it looked as if he was gaining some level of his composure back.

"I didn't do anything last night. I just happened to be in the wrong place at the wrong time, same as everyone else there."

I didn't lose my temper, but only nodded; I knew he was already breaking and piece by piece he would give in. "I don't care about the murder right now. The only thing I want to know is what you saw last night and why you drugged me at that party." The silence in the room seemed to suffocate us both. I could see in his eyes that something was there, something human, that wanted to admit to everything. When I tried to focus beyond that stare and beyond the silence, I swear I could hear Rex's heart beating.

"I, uh, don't know anything about that, I already told you." I could feel the uncertainty in the air; I knew he was only moments from revealing everything. All I had to do was find the right button to push and he would crumble to the ground.

"Rex, there is no reason to keep this up. Just tell me what you know, so you can get out of here and get back to whatever it is that you like to do." Rex looked back and forth like he was making sure no one was listening and then he sat up straight clearing his throat, readying himself for speech. I heard his mouth open and the first words begin to form, when the door opened behind me and the voice of the Captain filled the room.

"Detective, I need to have a word with you out here." Rage pumped in with my blood and pure adrenalin shot out like a wildfire, consuming everything. All I wanted to do was turn around and smash the Captains face in for ruining everything. I was so close to success I couldn't stand it. However, somewhere beneath the anger, I knew I couldn't lash out no matter how tempting it was. I guess that's how you know the difference between those who can control their anger and those who can't.

"Right away, Captain," I managed to say before turning to follow the Captain out of the interrogation room. I had to leave Rex behind for the time being, despite how close I was to breaking him. I shut the door behind me and looked up to see the Captain, Detective Light, and another man carrying a suitcase.

"Wink, this is Barrister. He is here to represent Rex." Barrister the lawyer was a tall man with a mask that looked something close to a vampire. It was pale with fangs sticking out for all to see just above his real mouth. The bloodsucker was a walking cliché—name, teeth, profession and all.

"It's great to meet you Detective," the vampire said and I reached out to shake the hand he offered, even though I didn't want to.

"Sorry, Wink, but we have to cut him loose. We've held him as long as we can," the Captain said in a regretful tone while Light shook his head behind both men.

"What do you mean? This is our guy! You can't let him just walk out of here—if he leaves now we may never get another chance at this."

"Look, Wink, it's not up to me. We've got no witnesses, no forensic evidence linking him to the crime, and we can't be sure that his knife is a match for the murder weapon. Until we have some hard evidence, we have to deal."

Barrister nodded at the Captain and walked right passed me to inform our murderer that he was to be set free immediately.

"I'm sorry man. I tried to hold him off as long as I could." Light was trying to console me in his puppy dog manner, but it only caused me to get even angrier at my situation.

"This is a bunch of bullshit. I was this close to breaking him. I had that son of a bitch." I emphasized each important word making it clear that I didn't want to be followed this time by my puppy dog. I pushed passed Light and headed out to the main area of the office and immediately noticed my old desk was being used by someone else. Hot with rage, I was extremely close to quitting my job right there and just moving on with my life. Somehow, though I managed to keep my cool.

The rest of the day was uneventful as I sifted through statement after statement trying to find some evidence or even a tiny clue. I set up a temporary office inside one of the mission rooms amongst the white boards and plastic chairs. I went over photos of the dead body and tried to see something beyond what I saw at the scene. But for every twenty minutes of actual work that I did, I spent forty minutes thinking about the people in my life who were dead. The story I told Rex was true and with it came memories of those I had lost. My only visitor the rest of that day was the Captain, who stopped by to give me even more bad news.

"Look, I know it's rough Wink but you're going to get used to all the politics of police work again, and eventually you won't get so hung up on something when it doesn't go your way. I'll see about getting you a desk set up for tomorrow, but in the meantime keep working this case wherever you have to." The Captain was getting on my nerves more than ever, but I told myself it was just because it was my first day back. I didn't answer him but only nodded, no longer caring about much of anything, until he spoke again.

"Oh, and you can't be running around without a partner. It just isn't safe. Starting tomorrow you and Detective Light will be partnering up." This was the last straw. I didn't want to replace Chloe, especially with that puppy.

"Captain I think I want to work alone for awhile. I'm just not ready to have some kid following me around." Somehow I knew it was a false hope that the Captain would hear out any of my requests, after what happened at the masquerade.

"Look, both you and Light need a partner, so now you're together and that's that." The door shut and I was left in the mission room for the rest of the day, happily alone for now. I continued to obsess over the papers and the file put together from the night before, but there were no answers to be found. I was back to square one and more helpless than ever. Already I was on my way back to another breakdown.

Later that night I sat on my couch playing with the tear in the armrest, while I stared at the pile of mail I had brought in upon arriving home. I left the mail, not wanting to open up any bad news, but that didn't stop me from continuing to think about it. Finally I turned on the TV, an attempt to forget about everything going on in my life. I barely even registered what was happening on the screen; instead the images I saw were flickering inside of my mind. I remembered meeting Chloe for the first time when she came to homicide so many years ago. She had been fresh from vice and only got the promotion because of a lucky bust she had made over some drug exchange.

A new show flicked on the TV, interrupting my memories, and for a moment I took some time to notice it.

"This is the true story of eight strangers picked to live in a house, all of them wearing a mask. Find out what happens when people stop being polite and start being real." The title of the show—The Masq World—appeared after the opening along with the logo for MTV. A group of scantily clad men and woman started prancing around the house wearing only masks and bathing suits. I watched for another moment but it wasn't long until they started fighting about some relationship, so I tuned it out. I went for the remote but instead reached for my drink as my mind drifted back to Chloe.

The apartment was quiet and still, but outside I could hear cars driving by, people yelling, and the occasional drift of music from some apartment below. The world was moving all around me, even in the dead of night. It was growing late and eventually I went to my bed, though I can't be sure exactly when. The last thing I remembered was the TV showing the group from The Masq World off at some club having the time of their lives.

"It wasn't fair that you died and I didn't. God, I wish it had been me," I said to the empty apartment and to what I hoped was the ghost of my partner Chloe. When she joined up they made me her partner, since I was very unsociable and she was easy going. I'm the kind of person who just likes to go to work and get the job done; I'm not all about hanging out with coworkers. Because of this, I never had a partner for more than a month before they would inevitably ask to be switched. When Chloe showed up at the department I didn't want anything to do with her but she broke all my barriers down within a week. After that I couldn't help but open up and let someone from work—Chloe—into my real life.

"What would you do if this was your case? What if you had missed a murder while standing only a foot away from the killer?" I asked even though I didn't expect a reply from her ghost. I tried to think like her; she was always a better detective then I. Closing my eyes I pictured her back at the office wearing the strange clothes that never looked like they belonged on a detective. Everyone always assumed at first that she was a hippy and that wasn't far from the truth, only her appearance meant a lot more than that. The reason she seemed that way was because she cared about the world and thought being green was important.

"You have got to be kidding me, what the hell are you wearing?" I remembered kidding with Chloe at the sight of her strange purple dress thing that had a black belt and these fat sleeves. She only made her big eyes even bigger and made a face like she was going to kick my ass.

"I just thought you would be ready to do some work, not go out for a night on the town." She shook her head like she had a thing or two to teach me.

"Actually this dress is going to attract far less attention than what you're wearing. Hell, you might as well wear a sign on your face that says cop." We were standing in front of some club where, according to a tip we'd received, the murderer we were looking for was hanging out. From what I remember of the case, we'd learned that the killer was a middle aged woman who killed people who looked like her husband. She knew that killing him would only land her in jail, so to get out the aggression she had, she would kill lookalikes.

"Detective, do I have to remind you that it's always the details that count in a case. You should really do your research more and read everything that's placed in front of you." Chloe thought she had one on me this time because I hadn't read the details about what kind of a place we were going to.

"You know I hate shit like this, so why do you think I would read something that is only going to remind me of bad news?"

Chloe raised an eyebrow before turning around and heading into the club, where we would ultimately catch the lookalike killer.

I wasn't asleep or dreaming; I was deep in thought trying to remember every single detail about the night we caught up with that killer. Chloe had known everything about the club we went to, so when we got inside no one expected her, including the killer. Chloe was able to gain her trust throughout the night and was about to close the deal. But the lookalike killer spotted me and knew instantly I was a cop and tried to escape. Only thanks to Chloe she ran off with a detective to get away from me and ended up spilling everything to Chloe.

"Read everything that's placed in front of you," Chloe had said on that case and for some reason it seemed to ring true even here and now. I abruptly knew why it was so important and all at once I jumped up from the bed throwing my covers to the floor. I stepped past my mask and half ran around my bed to get out into the open area of my living room. I can't be certain what time it was but I had left the TV on and The Masq World was still running, probably reruns. Even with my excitement at realizing what I was trying to avoid, I still felt like turning off the TV first before I flicked the light switch on.

"Let's see if my subconscious is making up for my weak detective work." It was a stupid thing to say standing there alone in my apartment but for some reason I needed my own approval of the situation. I grabbed the stack of mail off the coffee table and started flipping through it, feeling for what I had felt earlier when I grabbed the stack out of the mail box. Underneath a bill for the electricity I felt the thick larger envelope with the black permanent ink on the front. I ripped open the top and pulled out a dazzling card, with a white background and sparkles that immediately caught the attention of my eye. The picture on the front was of two plain masks dancing back and forth with one another, as if they were alive themselves. I opened the card and saw the address and time for an upcoming event and marked the signed name. I dropped the envelope and saw those bold black letters again, and this time I read them, making them real.

"Invitation." When I'd picked up the mail earlier I had to have been looking at those bold letters but for some reason I hadn't wanted to know it was there. Another masquerade party—this one was themed as a dance—was going to happen the next night. I remembered how Funny Bunny had remarked at the opening party that it was only the first of many. The first party had only been the kickoff and now they wanted me to come back and make sure everyone was safe from the mystery murderer, who was likely to strike again. This time I would be ready for him. I looked down one last time at the signature of Funny Bunny and then glanced again over the bold letters of the invitation.

Six

Dreams are a strange thing: when they wanted to come you have no choice but to let them. My mind had spent so much of the day thinking about the past that when I finally fell asleep that night, they came at me with perfect clarity. I do not want to relive the horrors of the night that ruined my life, but as I remember my dreams, I have no choice. Though it's hard for me, I know that if you're listening to this report, and need to know me and understand the things I did, then you have to hear the truth.

It was before the masq policy was enacted, before all the talk about how the government was going to fix the crime wave sweeping the nation. Crime was at an all-time high and detectives like Chloe and I were working around the clock, trying to do everything we could to help others. In those last couple of years I can barely remember the number of killers we put away. The sad truth was that, though we put away so many people, we only caught about one in every ten of the murderers in those days. It was hard to keep up and even harder finding people you could trust.

I spent so little time at home the last two years; I was working constantly since there was no one else to do the job but me. Chloe and I had obligations to fulfill and because the crime was rising it meant our obligations were days long. Time for both of us and just about everyone in law enforcement was spent working, no matter the cost.

It was already hard to be married to a police officer and even harder when that officer was a detective who was always needed for high profile cases. My marriage was already in shambles, and just needed one last push to knock it over the edge and plunge it into darkness. The increase in the crime wave was that very push that led to Danielle divorcing me before I even had the time to register what had happened. I loved Danielle but over time it had become a distant thing and in the end we fell into the cliché of drifting apart.

The streets Chloe and I worked day and night to protect were starting to get cleaner, but still the higher ups weren't seeing any changes. To them things were only getting worse. Assassinations were at an all time high as masked individuals were coming out of the wood work and shooting important people. It wasn't long until no President, no judge, not even the mayor of a city was safe. When the crime wave was at its worse, both the President and the Vice President were killed in rapid succession. All the mask-wearing criminals were getting away with shooting high profile men and woman in important positions. From where America was standing things were only going to get worse before everything fell into total anarchy.

It was during that time when my life changed forever. The country was still deciding what to do while not even one politician was willing to step out of his home to try to govern the country. The government of the United States of America was at a standstill, and it wouldn't be long until other countries made a move while we were weak. This was the world in which I lost my wife, and my whole life began to fall apart.

After the divorce the only thing in the world that mattered to me was my daughter. Calliope was five years old. She had short brown hair that Danielle always put into pigtails that seemed to suit her perfectly. She stood shorter than most kids her age but had a round face with big blue eyes that at certain times looked dark, almost gray. In the wreckage of my life she was my light at the end of the tunnel. Despite the crime wave, the busy hours, and the divorce, I knew that at the end of the week I could see Calliope. I would have done anything and everything for her and my greatest wish is just for one more chance to save her.

I didn't learn all of the details until later, after I had recovered. A couple of criminals who Chloe and I pissed off at some point in our careers started following us around. Once they knew where we lived, they decided it was time to get vengeance for whatever it was that we did. It was a dark night and I was busy putting Calliope to bed. I remember reading her Green Eggs and Ham by Dr. Seuss. I finally got Calliope to stop giggling and close her eyes as I read the story out loud for her.

"I do not like them, Sam-I-Am. I do not like green eggs and ham." Around the time I was reading these words, someone knocked on my partner Chloe's door. It was one of our first nights free at home and when she opened the door, she wasn't prepared in any way.

"You do not like them. So you say. Try them, try them and you may." Chloe was shot in the face and killed instantly by two masked individuals. She was found by the police later that night, a hole at the top corner of her head, right at the hairline.

Later that night after Calliope had just fallen asleep, I was at work in the kitchen making sure everything was clean for Danielle when she picked up our daughter. A loud knock came at the door, followed by two more. I stopped what I was doing and went over to look out the peep hole. I was used to people coming over even later than that—usually just Chloe coming to talk about a case. I know now that I left my gun in the locked drawer of my office, where I usually kept it while Callie was home.

I pushed my eye up to the peep hole and didn't see anything. At the time this didn't strike me as odd, so I opened the door all the way in one motion. Both men were wearing masks that I only just got a glimpse of. I saw a pistol about a foot from my face and I had no time to react. I heard the bullet but I didn't see it. In some strange way I felt it enter my eye but I didn't feel any pain. The force rocked my head back and the last thing I saw was my daughter Calliope standing on the staircase, a stuffed Care Bear in her hands. By whatever chance fate had to offer, I was standing in the perfect position for the bullet to hit my eye, part of my head and continue its descent. The bullet was lined up perfect and finished its run by burying itself in Calliope's chest; the bullet hit her dead center in the heart, killing her. I remember all that blood, the blood on my face but more importantly the blood on the staircase. Oh god, if only she hadn't come down to see who was at the door. If only she hadn't taken the bullet that was meant for me.

To this day I don't know who killed my daughter, all thanks to the masks my enemies wore that day. I hate anyone who hides there face behind a god damned mask and will never forgive myself for what happened.

I was in a coma for almost three years. The bullet had done significant damage but it hadn't been enough to finish the job. While I was recovering my daughter was buried and I never got to see her again, in life or in death. The hatred Danielle had for me slowly faded away and now she pretends not to curse me for getting our daughter killed. As soon as I was able I started looking for the people who shot Chloe and my daughter but it was impossible. Not only had it been three years, but in addition the world had changed, to me in the worst way.

While I was out the assassinations went from bad to worse and just as predicted America was one step from total anarchy. Already parts of the US were falling apart from riots and uprisings as gangs struggled for territory. The police were too afraid to make a stand while every criminal was wearing a mask. Several people stepped up to take over as President of the United States, only to be gunned down within a week.

People started claiming that threats from other countries were on the horizon and by the end of the year everyone would be enslaved by our enemies. This only pushed the people closer to joining in with the growing gangs and criminals so that they would have some kind of protection. If there ever was a time in our history when our country was in danger of falling apart, it was then.

No one can actually take credit for the idea, but rumor has it a group of congressional officials who were in hiding finally decided on a solution. If the people weren't safe from masked criminals, then it was time to join them and make all of America wear a mask. I wasn't there to see the faces of all the criminals when they went out and saw everyone else was wearing a mask. I can imagine the frustration as everyone was given a new identity and the masq policy went into effect. Each mask was given a certain serial number and only the higher ups of society could access that kind of information. With everyone wearing a mask the crime rates dropped, ultimately down to numbers we had never previously seen in our history. America changed overnight and the world I woke up in was a very different place, for more reasons than one.

I heard one story from those early days of a group of bank robbers who pushed through the doors of a bank, pulling out their weapons as they came in and pointing them at the people inside. Normally with their faces hidden and the citizens' faces exposed, the criminals could judge the level of fear. This time, though, everyone inside of the bank was wearing a mask of some kind, and they all just turned and looked at the criminals, safely hidden from behind masks.

"Get on the ground; I want everyone to put their faces against the floor!" Yelling, the head honcho moved from person to person making sure the people knew he wasn't just joking around. When he turned to look at his men he saw that many people were still standing amongst his own soldiers and he couldn't tell who was who. So many masks were bearing down on him, it made the criminal feel alone in his bank robbery.

"I want everyone that isn't one of my men to get on the ground, or I will start shooting." He made his words very clear and expected obedience from the frightened people in the bank, only they weren't all that frightened. No one moved; if anything more people stood up, no longer afraid, no longer willing to bow to the threats of a thief. The leader went to open fire lifting his tactical 12 gauge shotgun up and into the firing position. Only he stopped there, as he really wasn't sure who were his men and who were ordinary people.

"Guys, make yourselves known if you don't want me to shoot you." Immediately, everyone in the building started holding up their hands, begging not to be shot by the leader of the criminals. The man in charge of the operation couldn't figure out how he would go about robbing a bank when he didn't know who was who. Finally he made a decision; it was the only thing he could think of at the time.

"Guys, take off your masks. It's the only way were going to know." The team of crooks pulled off the masks and pointed the weapons at the crowd, now taking control of the situation. With their masks off the team of robbers were able to subdue the people, get the money, and take off before the police arrived. Too bad for them everyone saw their faces, and within two hours all of the robbers had been caught and the money returned.

This was just one example of a story I'd been told when I tried to argue that the masq policy was a stupid idea. I objected that the robber would know his team by their weapons, but apparently it didn't play out that way. The truth was that the masq policy worked in many ways, but most importantly it had stopped the crime wave problem in its tracks. I still can't see how all of civilization wearing a mask could fix crime, but I guess you never know what's going to work in the world today.

I got up from bed unable to sleep after thinking so much about that night and all the politics that had gone into developing the masq policy. It was times like this I wished I smoked just so I could have a habit to focus on.

The clouds still clung to the sky, and seemed only moments away from sending rainfall down once again. The moon was back there somewhere, but it was hard to see amongst its blanket of clouds. Calliope was dead and gone and I was all alone, without even my partner. All the people I cared about were gone in one form or another. I reached up and touched the rough spot where my eye used to be, my constant reminder of all the bad things that had happened. Despite the cool night air, my apartment felt hot and stuffy; if I didn't have to work in the morning I might have went out for a walk just to get some air.

"Callie, I'm so sorry I let you die. It's my fault." I buried my face in my hands; I just couldn't accept that my daughter's big smile full of tiny teeth was gone forever. I felt trapped by her death when I was alone, and would never forget that I didn't get a chance to say goodbye.

"It's my fucking fault!" I stood up and grabbed the nearest thing to me, a lamp, and threw it with all my might against the wall. The plastic thing crashed into the plaster but it didn't even break, only bounced and then fell to the floor, not even close to my desired effect. I was beyond anger at that point, feeling something closer to a deep frustration because of all my failures.

I didn't have any hope of getting to sleep after all the bad dreams and terrible thoughts that followed me everywhere, so I turned on the TV not to watch but only to leave in the background as I tried to focus on something else. The TV was still set to MTV, and I left it where it was. I walked over to my kitchen counter and sat down on a bar stool, pulling my work bag out and setting it on the table. I didn't have a desk or even an office anymore so I decided this would be just a good a place to work as anywhere. I dumped out a series of files that I had gathered since the murder and started going through things. But even as I tried to work, the TV caught my eye and I started watching what appeared to be a music video.

A group of masked men stood in a room of photos too small to see from where they're standing. One singer, a man wearing an all blue mask with a number three on the side began screaming into the mike. The rest joined in the song and I saw a series of masks, one all white with a white hood pulled over the top, another with blood smeared under each eye. I saw the words in the corner identifying the band as Hollywood Undead and I couldn't help but get into the lyrics of the song. The music video held my attention until the camera zoomed in on the photos all over the walls, depicting only people wearing masks. That video stayed with me for some reason; I just couldn't get over all of those faces on the walls, each of them wearing a mask.

I went back to the files on my desk and started looking over the papers, trying to find something that I had missed when I had first looked at them. I still put my money on Rex, so I grabbed his file and looked over his past arrests and the statement he gave the police. There was nothing in the statement. It was complete nonsense, I knew, and yet I read it again anyway. The only charges he had on his arrest record were a few low level drug charges, nothing violent and nothing that proved anything. No DNA had been found on the weapon linking Rex to the crime. From where I was sitting this case was looking more and more like it had reached a dead end.

*****

I awoke that morning with my face planted on the pages of files that were strewn out all over my kitchen counter. I blinked the sleep out of my eye while sitting up, and felt pain in my back from sleeping in such an awkward position. Still, the fact that I had fallen asleep was good news to me; for someone with issues sleeping is good no matter where you get it. I quickly got ready for the day and I ran out the door and back to work. I didn't have any breaking news on the case, but I did want to talk to the Captain about the invitation I had received.

The police station was a brand new building that stood out amongst the tall structures like a shiny new penny. I went inside and straight to the elevator, hoping I could get in to see the Captain before anyone—mainly Light—got a chance to question me about last night. I also hoped that with my new information he wouldn't notice that I was late to work yet again. The elevator doors opened and standing right in front of them was, of course, Detective Light. I just couldn't catch a break; no matter where I went I seemed to run right into the detective.

"Wink, I was starting to wonder when you would make it in. The Captain wants to see both of us in his office." I stared at the puppy and for the first time started to wonder why the detective was always there, seeming to follow me around.

"What are you doing standing in front of the elevators?" I hoped this would send the puppy into the corner, whimpering as if he had just been scolded by his master.

"Actually I was just heading down to help out my old department with a case. I guess my old team just hasn't gotten used to the fact that I don't work for them anymore, you know what I mean?" If I could see beyond that blue lightning mask I would find a giant smile, something cockier and more confident than a puppy could ever be. Something struck me as odd with the detective, but I didn't know what. He just seemed to change so often it was hard to pin it down. I nodded to what Light said but didn't press any further. I didn't want to know any stories about his rookie days pulling people over and issuing DUIs.

"Is the Captain here right now? I actually have something I need to talk to him about."

"Yeah, he's in his office. Come on, we might as well knock this out now that we're together." I made a face at this comment before I realized it, but then remembered that I was wearing a mask and could make faces at anyone I wanted. The realization didn't bring the comfort it should have, as it also meant others were undoubtedly making faces at me.

We walked down the hall and knocked on the door before entering the Captain's office. He held up a finger letting us know that he needed another minute to finish what he was working on before he spoke to us.

"Wink, Light, it's good I have you both together because I want to make it official," he said when he finished what he was doing. "As of right now you are partners, which means each is responsible for the other, so I want you to watch each other's backs." I didn't mean to but I let out an awful sigh, having all but forgotten what the Captain told me the other day about the upcoming partnership.

"Look, no offense to Light, but I'm just not ready for a partner yet. Just let me work this masquerade case first and then we can talk about partnering up." Again I was arguing and the body language coming from the Captain demonstrated pure anger at my insubordination.

"Wink, I didn't want to have to say this but the performance you gave on your first night back was terrible and I don't want it happening again. The only way I can make sure I am doing all that I can is to give you a partner. It isn't up for discussion. Now, both of you get the hell out of my office before I start getting really pissed." I turned to Light and saw that he wasn't even paying attention, but was instead just looking up at the ceiling. Again something struck me as strange, as I wondered why Light would act like he didn't care about the Captain's authority. Still I didn't have time to think about it, so instead I turned back to the Captain to tell him about the invitation.

"Before we go, Captain, there was something I needed to talk to you about first."

"Well go ahead, what is it?" The Captain turned off his angry mode and I had to wonder if the whole thing was just some kind of act he was putting on for showmanship.

"Last night I got this in my mail box and I think the killer is going to strike again." I dropped the invitation on the Captain's desk and noticed that now Light was interested, as he stepped forward to look at the glittering object.

"So what makes you think this mystery killer is going to do it again?" I watched the Captain speak and as he did I had to wonder why I was so sure the murderer wasn't finished yet.

"I can't say for sure, but the way the murder happened, it just seems to me like things are just getting started. And if this killer is ready to get his hands dirty again, what better place than at the mansion where he got away with it the first time?" I felt certain of my words while the Captain looked over the invitation. I turned to see Detective Light starting at me in such an awkward fashion, like he was deep in thought trying to figure something out.

"I don't know, Wink, if the killer knew who you were the first time, it might be best if you don't go walking into some kind of trap. Do you even know who sent this?" The Captain said trying to sound concerned for my safety.

"I guess I'm not sure, but I would assume it's a good will message from Funny Bunny." It made sense to me and the Captain and Light nodded in agreement.

"Look, I'll bring Light with me. He may not have an invitation but maybe we can work something out. Or even better, he can stay in contact and if things get bad, I can just call him and he can run in and assist me with whatever the situation may be."

The Captain kept looking at the invitation for a long time until he finally spoke again, this time in understanding. "I do think your right: the murderer may try something at this masquerade. You can attend this little party, but keep Light close by. Like I said, I do not want a repeat of last time."

I nodded, now excited by the prospect of what I could uncover at the next party. I walked out of the room ready to hear an earful from Light, only he didn't come out of the room with me. I turned to look through the window of the Captain's office, only to witness the blinds being pulled shut. Whatever it was they were talking about, Detective Light or maybe even the Captain didn't want me to be a part of it. I saw a familiar body working away at his desk and decided I would do some of my own talking.

"Hey, buddy, how you doing? It's been awhile."

The big man with the beer belly looked up at me from his desk. I started to remember what his face looked like and decided that the military green war paint of his mask was a definite improvement.

"I'm doing fine, but since when did we ever talk? From what I remember it was Chloe who always did the talking, not you."

I had forgotten how rude he could sound, but I did remember that he usually never meant anything by it. "Well, now I've got to do the talking for myself. And since we're talking, I could use some information."

"What is it that you want, exactly?"

It was becoming apparent that talking to me was only a reminder of the dead, as though I was the embodiment of all those who had passed on. I realized since I had come back to the station I hadn't really talked to anyone I knew from before. Maybe I really was a ghost in the station, someone others thought was untouchable.

I pressed on with my question anyway. "I just want to know about Light. One minute he seems like such a rookie, and then the next he's acting like he knows a little too much. What's his deal?"

The big man coughed before he leaned his head down and started talking in something close to a whisper. "All I know is that he's some hotshot no one wants to partner with. I heard that he's crazy, and being with him you might as well turn in your letter of resignation."

This didn't tell me much, and I knew there was always some crap rumor about the new people. I was looking for something more. "Has anyone in the department partnered with him yet?"

"No, he just got here the Friday before you came back." The big man laughed before he got up from his desk and walked away. Then the door to the Captain's office opened and Light walked out staring at me the whole way as he strolled back to the elevators.

As I watched him walk away, I heard something but wasn't sure what—my mind was so focused on the detective and the mystery surrounding him.

"I'm sorry what?" I said turning away from Light and looking right at the Captain who was standing close enough he could sneeze on me.

"I said, your new desk is that one, over by the drinking fountain." The Captain pointed to the corner desk that was opposite to where my old desk had been.

"Oh, thanks." I wanted to ask about Light and why they had talked so much after I had left the room, but I froze up and the

Captain just walked away. Something was going on; I just didn't know what, and I didn't know how I was going to find out.

I organized my desk and got my files in order, but I didn't stay at the station long, I wanted to try and get a few more hours of sleep before the next party. Before I headed home, though, I made sure to restock my investigation supplies, just in case I needed them, and I dropped by the armory and picked up a backup clip for my 9mm berretta, just in case. The masquerade was a dance theme and absently I wondered if Rosie Rabbit was going to be there. This time I wanted to dress a little better for the event, now that I knew what to expect. Except I didn't really know what to expect, at least as far as the killer was concerned. I knew it might be the only chance we had to catch whoever it was, since the evidence we currently had was crap.

I waited until Detective Light came back to the office, which was just after lunch time, before I gathered my things to leave. I wanted to go over some details with me new partner so that when the time came we would know what to do.

"Hey, Light I'm on my way out of here, so I'll see you at the masquerade. I just wanted to get your number so that I could call you directly if something went wrong."

"Oh, yeah, of course." He wrote down his number. "Also I drive a silver Bentley if you need to find me in the parking lot for some reason."

I took the number and wondered briefly how the hell my partner could afford that car. "Alright I'll be on the inside of the mansion. Stay close by partner." This came out sounding strange and insincere, but I just wanted to get away from Light as fast as I could. I headed to the elevator, pressed the button, and stood waiting, the whole time trying to think soothing thoughts and realizing how badly I needed some sleep.

As the doors opened Light walked up behind me and said something that chilled me to the bone and ruined my nap before I even got home. "Watch your back, Wink. If the killer does strike again, there's a good chance he'll come after you. Just stay alert if those lights go out."

Nodding my head I stepped into the elevator and headed home.

Seven

The wind whistled through the tiny opening in my window, invading my thoughts. The night was warm and the cool breeze from outside had been the only thing keeping my apartment from becoming sweltering. In and out of sleep, I had shut the window when the noise from outside became more annoying than soothing. Now it stood only an inch open, just enough to create a steady whistle that disturbed the silence.

"Screw it; I guess getting up now is as good as any other time." I pulled my weary body from my bed and went over to close the annoying window. I stopped and looked out over the darkness, and all the lights that prevented it from consuming everything. Tonight I had a masquerade ball to attend. Somewhere out there amongst the darkness a killer was waiting for the perfect moment to strike; something told me tonight was the night.

A military jet caught my attention and I watched it move slowly across the night sky, as it took on the appearance of a shooting star. It made me think of the military and how effective the masq policy had been on making our army an even stronger presence in the world. The few wars that have been fought since the masq policy was enacted had all been tilted even more so in our favor. There was something powerful in a group of men and woman wearing camouflaged masks as they ran at the enemy. Fear could always be seen in a face, but in a mask the cringe of terror, the pout of grief, the emptiness of loss, and even the signs of weariness were hidden. While wearing their masks the military became more and more like a well oiled machine.

I could picture that military, out in some remote jungle or desert, crouched at the ready to face another enemy, a sea of bodies peering out from behind masks that not only served as armor but would strike fear into the hearts of the enemy. Shots would echo out marking the beginning of the battle and the enemy would show its weaknesses in their faces. I could see the blood that stained the masks of the army, our army. But more than anything I could picture an endless victory at the hands of the military without a face.

After slamming the window shut, I got a glass of water and tried to ready myself for the upcoming masquerade ball. This didn't just involve my appearance, but was more a mental state, an awareness I would need for success. Though I will admit that my appearance did seem pretty important, since this time I didn't want to seem like such an obvious outsider. I pulled out my suit. It was the only one I had and I didn't even want to think about the last time I had worn it, but as I unzipped the protective bag I couldn't help it.

"You didn't have to do this, Danielle; I was fine coming here on my own." I was standing on a field of endless grass surrounded by the people who cared about me and what I was going through. I was wearing my all black suit with its barely visible stripes. Underneath I wore a white buttoned shirt with a high collar that wasn't complete without my gray tie, the tie that matched my mask. I complemented the suit with a pair of dress shoes that squeaked when I walked.

"She would have liked us to be here together, so we are."

I looked away from Danielle and stared at the grave stone that marked the resting place of my daughter Calliope. It was funny to think about all the movies I had seen, with all those dismal funeral scenes with the rain falling dramatically. I stood over my daughter's grave on a perfectly sunny day, the kind of day I should have spent with Calliope at the beach. I touched the grave stone and walked away. I just couldn't go on looking at the gray stone slab that was supposed to be my daughter.

"Are you okay, Wink?" Danielle asked when I turned to walk away. I had no intention of telling my ex-wife anything near the truth. I hated her just as much as I did everyone else in the world. There wasn't a way I could express how I truly felt. Even after the mock funeral that Danielle had put together, it just wasn't enough to let her in.

"What the hell do you think?" I managed before walking away from the headstone. To this day I have yet to return to the gravesite.

I finished the thought as I finished the last button of my suit and was happy to leave the gloomy memories behind and begin my night. I fastened the gray mask with the bloody tear over my face. As my emotions were hidden away I left the past and shifted into work mode fixing the 9mm Berretta into place underneath my suit jacket and pocketing the essential detective's package. After one last glance in the mirror I ran out the door, down the stairs, and out into the windy night air.

I hailed a taxi and hopped in, making sure to give the necessary directions as I did. I knew Light would have his car and I didn't want to deal with the hassle of driving and trying to park when I got there. I didn't get half way through the address before the cab driver waved an understanding hand and started driving. It was no mystery that Funny Bunny was having his famous series of parties, and the cab drivers were familiar with the location. I relaxed in the back of the cab, sitting back and drinking a bottle of water while I waited to arrive. The driver turned up the radio and I could hear news reporters talking about the same old shit.

"Everyone is waiting on edge to hear if the masq policies are going to be extended for another term, even though the answer is so obvious. The preliminary votes are in and the people of America need to stop worrying about it and just accept that the masks are here to stay." The man, host of some cheesy late night talk show, was arguing with a caller over the phone about the masq policies.

"Well then what about Face? These people are breaking the law running around without masks on. I want to know what the government and the local police are doing about these disturbers of the peace." The caller was even more annoying than the host and I was starting to wish I had chosen to drive so I could shut the stupid thing off.

"There is no real difference between Face and the hippies that protested Vietnam back in the late 1960's. The government will deal with this group in the same way and eventually they will all fade away. It's not like they have any real say over what happens."

I could see the mansion and couldn't believe how happy I was to see something I had been dreading all day. I felt inside my jacket and pulled the invitation out, making sure to keep it handy for my arrival. I looked up at the taxi driver in his mirror and took in the sight of his mask, only just realizing how strange it was. It had three faces, one on each side and one at the center, each of them different. The center was something close to a child's face and on either side were the faces of a woman and a man.

"You want me to take you to the front entrance?" I heard the driver ask but couldn't tell out of which mask he spoke. I noticed he had an ominous tone to his voice and understood why he was making me so nervous.

"Yeah, the front's fine, just right over there."

Three face nodded and I sat back to get my wallet out so I could pay the man. The car came to a stop in front of hundreds of people all walking across the street to enter the party; I didn't want to wait in that creepy car any longer.

"This is fine," I said pulling my wad of cash out and paying the man according to the meter. I opened the door and stepped out onto the cement and got ready to walk the short distance to the entrance. The crowd had made it across the street way and the way was clear for the cab, but he didn't drive away.

"Good luck, Detective Wink," I heard and turned to see three faces for only a second before he sped off, squealing his tires and leaving me with new questions. How the hell did he know who I was, and was that some kind of a threat? More than ever I was worried about what Light said and couldn't help but wonder if I really was the next target. Still my curiosity was stronger than my fear, and more importantly, I knew I had a job to do.

I stepped into line and waited for the familiar security guard to hold out his hand and take the invitation, allowing me to go directly into the mansion. He somehow seemed to remember me.

"I already told you, if you don't have an invitation you need to go around to the back of the mansion."

I didn't like that everyone seemed to know who I was while I didn't know anyone, but at least I had an answer for the guy this time.

"Here, this is all I need to get in right?" The big man checked the invitation and waved me through, no longer caring to tell me what was what. This time I didn't have to wade through the crowds of people and try to survive the madness of the lawn. I stepped inside of the mansion and immediately remembered the image of the dead man lying on the marble tiles. The memory was something close to a flash of horror, but was gone almost as soon as it appeared. The image cleared and instead I saw a host of beautifully dressed men and women dancing back and forth in what looked like an intimate slow dance.

"Detective Wink, it's so good that you were able to make it to my masquerade ball. I had wondered if you got my invitation. I know how busy you police types can be." Funny Bunny's voice came from right behind me, but when I turned to see who was speaking I had to look twice just to be sure it was him. Even with the time I had spent at his mansion I never actually had much of a chance to speak with my host.

"I wouldn't miss something of such great importance." There was some kind of a sarcastic battle taking place between us; on my side the false appreciation covered my real purpose at being there. I can't be sure what Funny Bunny was trying to do, but it seemed clear he wasn't really happy to see me there.

"Well, you'll have to join in the dancing. I'm sure there are quite a few ladies who wouldn't mind taking your hand for a dance." Before I could respond the man lifted both of his arms and women on both sides grabbed a hold and they walked away.

"I'll have to speak with you later Detective. If you don't mind I have a crowd to entertain." I nodded to the back of the bunny mask and walked over to snack on a few of the food items that were placed out in buffet style. Every kind of food you could imagine was lined up against the staircases while waiters walked around in white suits handing out glasses of champagne. I had no choice but to turn down the offer. I had only one intention at this party and that was to keep my senses and make sure I caught the killer, if he even appeared.

"Well look who it is. What's wrong, didn't ruin enough of my life? You need to come back and torment me all over again?"

Turning toward the snarky tone I recognized, I thought for a moment that an actual pig was sticking its face in the mash potato bowl, but of course it was just Chops, the pig man. "Be careful there, Chops, you don't want to slip and drown in that gravy you're so in love with." The pig man stepped away from the buffet line and looked at me past his gravy covered snout, that same anger in his eyes as our last encounter.

"You listen to me, Detective, if you don't watch what you say around certain powerful people like me—"

"You'll what Chops, you'll kill me? Is that what you're going to say, because I think that could win you another night in jail just on suspicion of murder." The pig man stopped what he was saying and instead grabbed a turkey leg and walked away.

"Yeah, that's what I thought," I couldn't help but mutter as Chops went all the way to the other side of the ballroom, keeping his distance from me. I watched the dancers for awhile and wondered how many of them knew they were dancing in the very spot where someone had been murdered just a few nights ago. Almost all of the women wore poufy dresses and as they spun around it became almost impossible to see anything. Though I tried to focus on individual dancers, through the mix of flying dresses and masked faces I couldn't distinguish anything. My phone started vibrating and I knew that it would be Detective Light calling to check up on me. Though I didn't want to talk to him, I also didn't want him to come running in and ruin everything, so I answered the phone to avoid any problems.

"Everything is fine in here Light; I'll call you if anything comes up."

"Wait, I just wanted to let you know who I just saw entering the party." Suddenly the music got louder, something close to wedding music, and everyone stopped dancing and starting looking around. Light continued talking but I wasn't able to hear him over the loud music and the murmur of the crowd.

"Alright, I got the message; I've got to let you go—something's about to happen." I hung up the phone even though I hadn't heard anything Light had said. I knew his information would be just as useless as he was. A light beyond the twin staircases turned on and I saw a balcony stage. I could only assume that this is where Funny Bunny had intended to make his speech at the last party.

"Greetings, my prestigious guests of the grand masquerade ball. I hope you haven't been partying too hard because the dance is about to get even crazier." Funny Bunny spoke to the crowd like they were his disciples and once again I couldn't help but feel a little bit jealous. Another light came on the crowd went wild at the sudden appearance of Rosie Rabbit. I realized that I was as happy as anyone to see her again, and have to admit seeing her again was another motivation for me to return to the parties.

"I would like to introduce my VIP guests, starting with the lovely Rosie Rabbit," Funny Bunny continued.

Rosie bowed her head to the crowd and performed the gesture of blowing a kiss that was becoming her trademark. More spotlights turned on and the crowd went insane with excitement at the sight of the other VIP guests, who I didn't recognize at first.

"Standing on my left and right I would like to introduce P Feather and Eli Phaunt." After hearing Funny Bunny say their names I remembered the man and woman as two of the hottest new actors, who I'd seen on TV. A large spot light turned on and the twin staircases were illuminated and more famous masks could be seen standing above the crowd.

"And finally it is my pleasure to introduce to you the entire cast of The Masq World," Funny Bunny yelled like a boxing announcer, letting his words extend and inflect at the end. The group of famous actors nodded and waved and did all sorts of gestures to signify they loved their fans.

"Now I want every one of you to pair up and prepare for the dance competition. The top winners will get the chance to dance with the celebrity of their choosing, so give it everything you got." Immediately men and women were scrambling to their partners, preparing for the dance of a lifetime. When the numbers started to dwindle down some of the men started pairing with one another, not caring about dancing with a man if it gave them a shot at the prize.

"I personally will judge your performance, with the help of the celebrities of course, so I want everyone to focus." The spotlights on the stairs and the balcony shut off and the dance floor of the ballroom lit up brightly in the chandelier's glow. I tried to see the masks of the famous people but they were shrouded in darkness, and it was just too damn bright where I was standing.

"Everyone has to have a partner." I turned and saw Rosie Rabbit standing in front of me questioningly. I looked around and saw everyone in the entire ballroom had a partner. Even the pig man was standing with something close to a pig woman. I was the only one in the ballroom standing alone; I hadn't realized I would be forced to participate.

"Why don't you dance with me, Detective?" She held out her black gloved hand and I could only stare at it for the longest time. Eventually I took hold of her hand and she led me to the center of the dance floor, which was the last place I wanted to be. I didn't know the first thing about dancing, but I could bullshit with the best of them, so I decided just to wing it and see what happened.

"Is everyone ready because the dance contest is about to start," Funny Bunny spoke from the distant shadows, though my attention was elsewhere. Rosie was wearing a red dress, like last time, only this one was poufy like the others and surrounded her knees in sparkling red. The dress was strapless, and showed off a little bit more than I was ready for, and when we got close together for the dance, I couldn't help but shoot a glance downwards. Hand in hand I held her close and prepared myself to follow her lead. At least, I hoped she would lead, sensing that I didn't know what I was doing.

An ominous music began with the strumming of all kinds of strings and the patter of a constant drum beat. The song was obviously slow but still held a steady beat perfect for a fast moving dance that still had the element of romance. A female began to sing and I couldn't tell if it was one of the guest celebrities or just a recording. Once the woman began to sing I recognized the song immediately and almost laughed out loud at how perfect it was.

The song was the main theme from the Phantom of the Opera, a play that was all about masquerade parties and a ballroom dance just like this one.

I felt her hips begin to sway and the rhythm of her body became obvious and I easily followed her movements; I was right in thinking she would lead the way. All of the bodies dancing in the ballroom were moving right alongside us and I became one with the music and her body. A male voice came into the song next, giving the song an eerie touch, and the bodies in the room seemed to slow down in perfect harmony to the sound of his voice.

"Those who have seen your face, draw back in fear," the female voice sang following in perfect rhythm the voice of the man, and with it our bodies did the same. My hand rested on the top of Rosie's shoulder and I couldn't help but run it all the way down her side. As we executed a difficult dance move, something felt so comfortable between Rosie and I, almost like we were meant to be dance partners.

"Your spirit and my voice in one combined; the phantom of the opera is there, inside my mind." The voices sang together in a romantic yet eerie duet that pulled me, and everyone one else on the dance floor, in. The beat of the music picked up and with it so did the dancers, the women spinning faster and faster, blinding me where I stood. A constant flash of dresses whirling out of control seemed to obscure everything else. The greens, blues, reds, blacks, and whites of the fabrics blocked out the world as the strange dance took hold. In that sea of colors, in that sea of dresses, I lost myself in the arms of the radiate Rosie Rabbit.

"Sing, my angel of music!" the male singer yelled out and the female complied, issuing a series of notes too beautiful for words. Her voice reached new heights and the beat of the music picked up. Somewhere amidst the music and the dancing and the multitude of colors, I saw something moving with the crowd. It was hard to see but clearly was out of place; for that one split second I saw the face, or rather the mask, of pure evil.

"The phantom of the opera," the female continued to sing, intermingling her high-pitched voice with the beat of the music. The wicked mask was black with think bloody tears cut into it. Black horns sat atop it, giving the appearance of a demon. As soon as I glimpsed the mask, it was gone, leaving me wondering if it was ever really there. Meanwhile the singing turned to screaming, ending with a sound high enough to shatter windows. All of the dresses on the dance floor were spinning and it started to sound like more than one woman was screaming in the chaos. A sudden hole appeared in the wall of spinning dresses, as though someone had fallen down. The song ended, but instead of clapping or cheers from the crowd, the people on the floor began to separate.

"Oh my god what the hell happened," I heard someone say. I looked down to see blood once more moving across the white marble floor. The crowds continued to move until I could see the form of a woman in a green dress with golden trim on the bottom of the skirt and across the bust. She was on her back and a red gash was visible starting at her chest and reaching all the way down to her waist. Her mask looked like a tribal tattoo and went down both sides of her face, leaving the center of her face visible.

"Everyone get on the ground, on your knees! There is a killer here." I pulled my gun as soon as my mind registered what happened and tried to see where that wicked mask had gone. Everyone got down on their knees and all of the lights came on, and I could see all of the famous people standing close to Funny Bunny. I tried to see if anyone seemed suspicious, but of course everyone was wearing a mask and waiting for me to find the killer. Again I had missed what happened and the killer was either gone or was sitting amongst the other partygoers. I pulled out my phone once it became clear there was no way for me to identify the killer.

"Light, we've got a 217, I repeat we have another murder inside the mansion."

"Shit, I'm on my way."

"No, I need you to call for backup and check for anyone suspicious trying to escape the mansion."

"Alright, I got it." As Light finished talking I heard the sound of him opening the car door to head outside to look for the killer. I shut the phone and yelled up to Funny Bunny now knowing that everyone respected him and would listen to what he said.

"Funny Bunny, I need you to keep everyone where they are until I can figure out what the hell is going on."

Funny Bunny nodded and immediately began telling the crowd to remain where they were until the police took care of things. I went over to the body and inspected the wound, though I didn't have to get very close to see the job was the same as before. The green dress was stained a dark red and I knew the woman was dead.

This time the crowd didn't give me any trouble—even the pig man remained in his corner until the police arrived. Light stayed outside until the police got there, but unfortunately he didn't see anyone suspicious leaving the mansion. Again the police began the routine of statements and searches, but nothing was turning up. This time the Captain ordered all the guests on the lawn searched as well, but otherwise the investigation proceeded the same as with the first murder. It looked like it was going to be a long night.

"I can't believe it happened again and I didn't see anything," I said to Light. He only nodded, and I felt a tension in the air, as though the young detective was disappointed in me.

"Look, there was nothing I could have done. There was too much commotion going on, and I couldn't see anything."

Again he only nodded, and looked like he was deep in thought. I could only assume that he was thinking about how bad this all looked for me, once again. A regular officer walked over to us then and spoke to Detective Light, loudly enough for me to hear.

"We found him outside; we have him in custody now."

Light said something that sounded like 'good work' to the officer, and I suddenly felt out of the loop.

"Who did they find?" This case was getting away from me at every turn; what should have been obvious was again something that I missed.

"Didn't you get my message, from when I called you earlier?"

I thought back to the phone call it had been too loud for me to hear. "I heard parts of it but it got so damn loud in here right when you called, I must have missed something."

The officer standing by developed a red flush starting at his neck, most likely extending up to his cheeks. I could only assume he was thinking about me. Everyone thought I was some giant joke and that it was my failure that was letting this killer escape. I knew then that my days were numbered as a detective if I didn't find a way to solve this case.

"What I was trying to tell you," Light continued, "is that I saw our little friend Rex enter the party. I called so you'd be ready for him." He let out an awful sigh, like he was talking to a disobedient child. I knew, though, that what had happened wasn't entirely my fault; beyond that I hadn't seen Rex anywhere near that dance party. Still, I remembered the wicked demon mask that had flashed into my line of sight for only a spit second, and I had to wonder if Rex had simply changed his mask before sneaking inside and taking care of business.

"I get it, Light—I haven't been up to par lately, but I feel like I'm starting to catch on. Just let me have one last crack at Rex before everyone else destroys all the work I put into him. I know I can break the guy. I just need you to keep the Captain off my back while I do it." The other officer had already left, so it was just me and Light. I had to play the partner card even though I didn't really know my partner that well yet.

"Okay, Wink. I'll give you one more shot at interrogating the punk," Light said and then put a friendly hand on my shoulder. "See you back at the station," he continued and then walked away. It seemed, unbelievably, that the disappointment he had expressed only a moment ago was gone, and he was already back to his happy, friendly self. I watched him walk out the doors and suddenly thought I knew a little bit more about my young partner. I knew a lot about the way the police force worked and Detective Light was definitely out of place in it. I had to wonder for a second whether Light had more to do with the things that were happening, more than I could ever imagine.

Eight

"Where is he?" I sounded angrier than I meant to and the police officers sitting behind the desk jumped at my startling entrance. I knew Rex had been brought down to the station and I had no intention of waiting for his paper work to interrogate him.

"I'm looking for a man named Rex," I continued. "He was just picked up outside of a mansion." Both officers glanced at one another and then started flipping through papers to find out what I was talking about. There was a reason these two cops were working the front desk.

"Come on guys, he's a suspect in a major murder investigation. There can't be many of those going on right now." That did it. One of the cops nodded and headed to the back to get Rex, while I filled in the check out forms.

After watching Light leave the mansion, I had done the same thing. The last murder had taught me one thing and that was this killer was too careful to leave anything behind at the scene of the crime. If I was going to catch the murderer I would need to take a different approach than before. That meant rushing to the interrogation room before anyone else ruined my chance at the man who was now the number one suspect on everyone's list, including mine.

"Alright, here he is Detective; I'm officially releasing him into your custody."

Rex looked up at me as the officer pushed him over to me, handcuffs still tight on his wrists. I grabbed his arm just above the elbow, nodded to the officers and led him out of the room. I didn't say anything yet, only pushed him along until we reached the interrogation room. I sat Rex down in the chair, and then left him alone in the room while I went out to the staging room to watch him for a few moments from behind the glass. He kept his head down in the practiced fashion of someone who has seen a lot of interrogation rooms. I removed my 9mm pistol just in case and went back inside the interview room, ready for round two. Before I began I removed the handcuffs that were tightly binding his wrists.

"Hello again, Rex. It was only a matter of time before we ended up here together again. This time no lawyer is going to save you; now that you're the prime suspect we can hold you for quite some time." Rex wasn't playing crazy this time and at the sound of his long stay with us, I saw his body flinch in fear. I knew a lot more about Rex now and I had a feeling about where this interview would end up, but I took it slow, easing him into it.

"Rex, I hate to tell you this but you're the man we like for two major murders. That's life on the inside of a prison, Rex. You need to give me something that will save you from a lifelong sentence. Tell me what happened at both parties and you might have a chance." I was bullshitting of course—we didn't really have anything that could pin Rex to the crimes but he didn't need to know that.

"I, I can't say anything," Rex stuttered and then starting shaking his head, obviously afraid.

"Rex, the way I see it, there are two different kinds of people in the world. One group I like to call impulse thinkers: these are the minor offenders who only commit small scale crimes. The impulse thinker might steal something, or get caught with some drugs. The biggest crime an impulse thinker commits is usually a quick robbery of a gas station or a liquor store. Most of the time impulse thinkers won't kill someone unless it happens in the heat of the moment, or just a straight out accident."

Rex seemed transfixed, as if he were trying with everything he had to pay attention to what I was saying, no matter how difficult it was for him.

"Now," I continued, "the flip side of this are the deep thinkers. Most deep thinkers don't commit minor offenses; most don't commit any crime at all in their lifetime. Chances are you won't catch a deep thinker with a bag of dope and you won't see him holding up a random liquor store. If a deep thinker does commit a crime, it's usually serious. These end up being high profile murder cases, like those committed by serial killers, or major shootouts at places like schools or hospitals. Deep thinkers might also commit crimes that require a lot of planning, like an elaborate bank robbery." Rex continued his steady gaze, blinking his eyes only occasionally, but never looking away.

"Now you might be wondering what the point is of all this. The point is, Rex, you are not a deep thinker; you are obviously an impulse thinker. The murderer, on the other hand who has killed at both masquerade parties under the watch of a Detective is most likely a deep thinker. You have a clear chance right now to come clean and tell me what you know, because you won't have a detective backing you up for long." I could almost see Rex begging to say something, but an obvious voice in his head was holding him back.

"Last chance, Rex, to say something helpful or I won't back you when you need it most." I was back to where I was before, only seconds away from Rex breaking and telling me everything.

"I just can't, you have to understand, I just can't say anything." Rex lowered his head once more and I knew he wasn't going to continue without some incentive. I wanted some kind of lead, some kind of answer to go on and if that meant I had to play dirty, then so be it. There was something I noticed the last time I interviewed Rex and this time I was going to put it into practice.

"Fine, if that's how it's going to be, just sit tight, Rex, and I'll be right back." I left without saying another word, closing the interview room door hard behind me. I walked to the elevators and pushed the button to take me to the basement. For what I was about to do, I didn't want any one standing by so I had to hurry. The doors opened and I gazed out on the dark room, which looked something like a warehouse. There were tall beams molded out of the cement that housed long plain sections of space that created shelves.

On top of the first beam, the word "Files" printed in clear, bold letters covered the top of the first beam, giving any one who entered an indication of where they were heading. It took me a few minutes to find what I was looking for amongst the clear plastic bags and the cardboard boxes containing files.

A second section of the basement was separated by a giant locked door that required a badge number to enter. The sign above the door read "Evidence." I entered my badge number and stepped into the room full of guns, drugs, and cash, among other bits of evidence. Everything was organized by category and then by case. I found what I was looking for in a matter of seconds and I didn't waste any time putting it into my pocket. Cameras were of course placed in the room but I knew exactly where the blind spots were, as any experienced officer would.

I know what I did that day was illegal but I needed something to go on and from where I was standing it was the only solution. I reached the interview room housing my suspect in record time and was happy to see no one had come looking for him yet. With my new secret weapon hidden in my pocket, I was confident I could make Rex talk all night.

"Alright, Rex, we don't have a lot of time so I'm only going to give you this offer once. I am proposing that we make a trade. I'll give you what I have in return for information about both masquerades." Rex looked at me with confused eyes, seemingly wondering what I could possibly have to trade with him. I reached into my pocket and pulled out the clear baggy keeping it cupped in my hands so only Rex could see what I had.

"Ok, I'll tell you everything I know." Rex was practically foaming at the mouth, and I knew the new look in his eyes meant he would tell me anything I needed to know. I recalled the last interview we had and how Rex reacted when I mentioned the word meth. It was an addiction for him and he would rather go to prison then give up even a small amount of the drug.

"Start from the beginning, Rex. Tell me why I was jumped by your steroid-popping friend outside of the mansion."

Rex fidgeted in his seat, no longer content to keep his head down and out of trouble. "Give it to me now and I'll tell you everything, just give it to me now." Losing his focus, he only could think about the drug and how badly he wanted it.

"Rex, I need you to keep focused; you can have this as soon as I have the information that I want. I told you we're making a trade. Just relax and start talking. The sooner you do, the faster you get the stuff." Finally my voice broke through and Rex calmed down a little bit, if only to get to his meth faster. After a moment of silence Rex started talking, not as confidently as before but more in a whisper.

"I really didn't know who you were or anything at the time of the party. I just wanted to get inside of Funny Bunny's mansion. Once you're inside everything is free and you can have all the drugs you want, it doesn't matter how much." I remembered when I had tried to pay for alcohol and the bartender had told me everything was free.

"My buddy, we call him Flex, came over and said he was given an offer for an invitation to the inside of all of Funny Bunny's parties."

I all but laughed when I heard the steroid man went by the name of Flex. Flex and Rex—just perfect.

"Anyway he said that all we had to do was take care of someone and then I could have access to the rest of the parties. I was given a small syringe with some strange liquid in it. I couldn't tell you what it was, I only did what I was told. My plan was to distract you with my girlfriend so I told her to start climbing all over you and to just start bothering you." The spider on the young women's face that had scared the crap out of me was all part of a larger scheme, then. I wasn't surprised.

"I injected you with the stuff but you were moving so fast I couldn't be sure if I got it all in. We didn't want to fail after coming so far, so Flex attacked you. After that Rosie came and took you. Right after that a man in a demon-looking mask dropped off the invitations for all the parties."

My mind raced back to the mask I had seen for a split second mixed in with the crowd of dancers. It had to be the same person, someone in the shadows orchestrating everything. "Tell me more about this demon masked person." I had to find out more about the man who just became the real suspect number one.

"I didn't know the guy and I only saw him for a moment when he dropped off the invitations. The only thing I remember is how wicked the mask looked with those bloody cuts on the face and the black horns on top."

I could only conclude that the wicked man had been watching my moves from within the crowd; he knew I was a detective and knew I would get in the way. This mysterious case was getting worse and worse the closer I got to the truth, and I still had a ways to go to unmask my villain.

"Something else isn't making sense to me—why the hell were you waving that knife of yours at me?" If I could see Rex's face underneath the mask I am sure I would have seen something resembling blushing embarrassment.

"Honestly, I'm not much of a fighter and I didn't know who you were, so I just thought it would be best if I let you know not to mess with me later, when I was alone or something." Shaking my head I almost couldn't believe how far from the truth I'd been at that first party, but now I at least had something to go on.

"So tell me about the grand ball and what part you played in the murder that happened there." Rex seemed confused; even though I couldn't see his face I could tell he was wondering what I meant.

"I was just showing up to use my invitation; I don't know anything about the first murder or the one that just happened. I already told you everything I know."

"Alright fine, so your buddy Flex, it sounds like he had a longer conversation with our demon friend. Where can I find him?" I was jotting small notes down in a notebook, trying to keep any details that might mean something later. I noticed that it seemed to be bothering Rex.

"Look, I don't know where he lives or anything. If you haven't noticed, I don't have much of anywhere to live myself." I had a lead but I wasn't going to get anything else on the subject out of Rex. Drugs or no drugs, he obviously didn't want to get anyone killed on his account.

"I'm guessing the reason you don't have a home is because of the meth. You know some time in jail might end up doing you some good."

"I can stop any time I want and I plan on doing it soon. My son is going to be six soon and I want to be clean for his birthday. It's the only way my ex will let me see him and all." I cringed at this new piece of information and memories started flooding my brain of Calliope, making it hard for me to function.

"What school does your son go to?" I managed in-between my struggling breaths, if only to keep my composure in front of Rex.

"I don't know the name of the place but I do know that he will be finishing up kindergarten soon." Rex's son was the same age as Cali when she died, and in my mind I imagined them in the same grade together.

"I need you to sign a statement of everything you told me, Rex, and I have to charge you with assaulting a police officer, if only to help get you clean. I want you to consider this the last drugs you do. Get clean for your son, Rex; you don't know how lucky you are to have him." I tossed the baggy across the desk and into the junkie's hands, assuming he would snort the stuff right away. I shut the door to the interview room and leaned against the door not even realizing the eyes that were on me. Someone had been watching the interrogation.

"Don't worry, Detective, I won't say anything about this. Sometimes you have to get the information any way you can." I looked up to see the blue lightning mask; my partner was standing next to the glass, where he could see and hear everything.

"Thanks, Light. I need to get out of here. Can you get his statement down in writing before he loses it? Also I need someone to start looking into finding Flex. He's a big guy, looks like he's on steroids or something. Someone at the parties has to know him. Arrest Rex if you will, I'll do the paperwork later charging him with assaulting me at the party." I felt weak in the knees and just wanted to get out of the police station. I wanted to avoid all the questions about the grand ball.

"No worries, Wink. You've already done the bulk of the work. I can take care of the rest."

I nodded at Detective Light and then headed out of the room and straight out of the police station, feeling suddenly like I had to get out of there.

I couldn't shake the feelings I was having after leaving the station. I went home and tried to get as much sleep as I could but only ended up tossing and turning through the night. Once morning arrived I knew I had no choice but to go where my mind was forcing me, to acknowledge the thoughts that had bothered me all night. I didn't want to go parading around an elementary school, but I just had to go see where Calliope used to go. The school wasn't all that far from the police station so it really wasn't out of my way. I pulled into the parking lot, passing under the sign that said Adam's Elementary in dark bold letters. I parked the car and headed into the building, making sure to check in at the front office before I walked in. Nowadays schools don't care much for middle aged men walking around, which is a good thing.

"Hi, my daughter used to go to school here. Would it be alright if I got a guest pass?" I asked the elderly woman on the other side of the desk, making sure she could see my badge as I spoke. The woman's dark rimmed glasses were built right into her mask, and she peered at me through them as if trying to understand a silent secret.

"That's fine, officer. Just sign in on this sheet and bring that card back when you're through," she said, pushing a card towards me with the word guest written on it. I signed the piece of paper, which seemed strange because all I wrote was Detective Wink on the page. I nodded to the woman, picked up the guest pass, and connected it to my shirt before walking into the school.

While it may seem to you that this portion of my story doesn't exactly pertain to the case, you have to understand that my state of mind is very important, and that Calliope was a major factor in the choices I made.

I walked by the lunch room but didn't see any children, as it was still a little early for the kids to be eating lunch. I walked on until I reached a row of classrooms for some of the older kids, the fifth and sixth graders. I looked into one of the rooms as I walked by; there was just enough room to see through the window at the top of the door. Around thirty masked kids sat in their desks, some paying attention, and the rest goofing off in one way or another. The teacher, a young looking woman with a purple flowery mask was going over math problems on the white board. There were so many little masks looking around the room it was hard to distinguish them from each other. I had to wonder how many of them would make faces while being punished by their elders. One student turned and looked at me with those big blue eyes but I couldn't see any joy in them. Instead I saw something closer to terror. I pictured a small girl afraid of the things she doesn't understand, afraid of how it felt to sit in a classroom without a face.

"Can I help you with something?" I turned around and saw a big man with a pot belly, wearing a suit and tie that matched the pattern of his striped mask.

"Sure, can you tell me where the kindergarten classrooms are? It's been some time since I've been at this school." The man eyed my mask and then looked down to make sure I was wearing the guest card before he nodded and answered my question.

"Follow this hallway to the end and then take a right, and then straight ahead from there. You can't miss them."

I nodded and thanked the man before starting down the hallway, all too aware of the eyes on my back. Though the directions were correct, something about the man bothered me and I couldn't help but remember the pig man with his smug attitude. I knew it was next to impossible, but still there was a chance that Chops, the pig man, was the teacher I had just run into.

Once I reached the kindergarten side of the school I remembered it clearly and knew right away which classroom used to be my daughter's. I touched the door and looked inside; for a split second I almost walked in thinking it was time to pick up

Calliope. This was a foolish thought because most of the time it was her mother that picked her up, not me. Still, being in this place, it was difficult to understand that the person I knew was dead, that I would never see her again.

I looked at the tiny bodies of all the children and again grimaced at the site of so many masks, some of them flat out disturbing. I looked over and saw Calliope's old teacher walking around the room complimenting the kids on their finger paintings. I could only see her back but still I was sure it was her. She wasn't a good looking woman, but she was skinny and dressed oddly enough that she stood out in a crowd. I remembered her pinched face that made her look like she was eating something really sour. The teacher turned around and I looked right into the face of a mask that resembled a female version of Buddha. I wanted to leave but it was too late, the teacher had seen me and was now walking over to the door.

"I'm sorry. I don't recognize you, but maybe you've changed your mask? Which student is yours?"

I looked at the Buddha face and didn't know what to say. I could only stare at her, feelings as though I was in some other dimension in which Calliope was still alive.

"Oh, I'm sorry," she continued. "I just assumed you were one of my student's parents. It's hard to tell with all the masks. I'm sure you understand."

Finally my mind returned to the situation and I was able to answer her. "Actually, my daughter was once one of your students. Her name was Calliope, and she passed away a few years ago. I just haven't been here since what happened and I couldn't help but stop by and see where she used to go."

The teacher took in a breath and let it out as if she had been waiting for this day for a long time and now that it was finally here she didn't know what to do. "I do remember Calliope. Her unfortunate circumstance has made her quite memorable in my mind. In fact I still have a few of her things if you would like to take them."

"Really, after all of this time, you still held on to some of her things?"

"After I heard what happened I didn't want to bother you or your wife. I waited for some time and then when I did try to get a hold of someone there was no one to return my calls. It felt wrong throwing her things away so I just kept them in a small drawer. Let me get them for you." The teacher went back into her classroom and I waited in the hallway trying not to look at all students who were now watching me.

"Here you are. It's not much but it might mean something to you."

I took the stack of papers from the teacher's hands and held them tightly but couldn't bring myself to look down. "Thank you for keeping her things, it does mean a lot to me."

The teacher nodded and underneath that mask I could still picture that puckered face, only now it was smiling. The door shut and I backed away from the door so I could have some privacy while I looked down at Callie's things. The top item was a purple Care Bear bag, with a zipper on the top that opened a pocket with crayons and colored pencils all loosely scattered inside. Underneath was a large piece of red construction paper and on it was a drawing of a house with some grass, a tree, and a sun with a smiley face. A white page was next and on this were a series of alphabet letters that went in order from aA to bB and on to cC. I flipped the page to see what was next, only there wasn't anything else. In that moment I felt my heart start to ache: for a split second it was like she was alive again but now I only had some paper and pencils. In my moment of panic I dropped to the floor and dumped her bag of crayons on the ground. I sifted through them trying to find something else to hold on to, something that would be new in my eyes. I started smashing my fists into the ground crushing the crayons and breaking the pencils in a fit of rage. Things were about to escalate from there when my cell phone started to vibrate in my pocket and I was able to pull it out and answer.

"This is Wink," I said calmly just managing to contain the rage that was brimming at the surface, like a pot of tea starting to boil over on the stove.

"Hey Wink, it's Detective Light."

It was the last name I wanted to hear. "I'm a little busy, what is it Detective?"

"I just got a lead on your steroid man. Meet me at Day and Night Fitness and I'll explain everything. Do you know where it is?" Light's words broke me free of my rage and replaced it with a purpose, to find the killer.

"Yeah, I know where it is. I'll be there in less than twenty." I hung up the phone and as I did I found something taped to the bottom of the purple pencil case. I pulled off the tape and removed the letter C from the bag and held it in my hand. The C was colored purple and had lines of glitter going up and down it in colors of green, pink, and blue. Inside the curve of the C was the name Calliope written in bold red marker. The C itself was laminated and felt hard like a credit card, and most importantly, it gave me something to hold onto.

I put the C in my vest pocket to keep it close to my heart and then went to work picking up her other things. On my way back to the car I dropped off the guest pass at the front desk. I did this all in a state of complete awe, feeling as though the moment had helped me let go of Callie a little bit more. I guess having something she made helped me to picture her with me, rather than gone.

I was through letting other people die under my watch; it was time to step up my game and catch the killer who so far had left no trace. I jumped into the driver's seat of my car and started off for the gym and the only lead I had, the laminated C gripped tightly in my hand.

Nine

The gym came into sight but before I even pulled into the driveway, I spotted Detective Light waiting patiently by his expensive car. Getting out of the car, I looked at the gym and realized it had been some time since I had actually been inside of one. I stepped over to Light and waited for him to tell me what was going on, but he stayed quiet, forcing me to ask.

"So where did you get this lead on our steroid man?"

Detective Light slipped something into his pocket and then turned to talk to me; I couldn't be sure what it was he had. "We were going through previous statements and started calling up some of the people we had on file until we got something. Apparently someone remembered Flex from this gym. The guy wasn't sure where Flex lived, but he is sure that he had seen him several times at this gym." Light seemed pretty excited over something that was more of a possible hunch than a lead. Still it was something to go on, which was more than I had at the time.

"Alright, let's go ask around and see if we can find out anything on our big friend." I turned from Light and started walking into the building, not really sure if he was following. I wasn't really sure if I even cared, though I did know that having a partner was always good when you didn't know what to expect from a situation. I couldn't help but glance back as I entered through the glass doors of the gym, just to make sure Detective Light was right behind me.

"Detectives Wink and Light," I introduced ourselves to two women standing behind the counter. "Do either of you have time to answer a couple of questions?" Both women wore masks with the logo of the gym on it, though one had an obvious twenty years on the other. I wondered if the workers before me were mother and daughter.

"What's this all about?" It was the older lady who spoke after stepping a full foot in front of who I assumed was her daughter. Her voice sounded irritated and I guessed I would be too if I had to deal with police barging in and bothering the paying customers.

"Nothing that involves your fitness center, so you don't have to worry. I only want to know about a particular man who may have visited this gym on several occasions."

"I can't say that I know the customers all that well. I only meet them when they sign up. Hell, after the first day I don't even look at them—they just come in, swipe their cards and get to working out, you know how it goes."

I could tell this woman wasn't going to give me anything, though that didn't necessarily mean she was trying to protect someone. You would be surprised to see how many people lie for no good reason; sometimes it's just to get back at the police in one form or another.

"Look I understand you're busy, so I'll just get right to the point. I just need to know about a regular customer of yours who goes by the name Flex."

"Nope it doesn't really narrow anything down for me; you have to understand this is a gym so lots of guys go around using names like Flex." I wanted to rip that mask right off of her smug face, just so I could get a better look at her and her sarcasm.

"If you could, ma'am, just try to remember, he's a big guy with lots of unnatural looking muscles, like he may be on steroids or something." As soon as I finished my sentence, the woman responded with what sounding like a scripted line.

"Day and Night Fitness does not condone the use of muscle enhancing drugs such as steroids, nor are we libel if any customer chooses to partake in recreational drug use."   Sometimes I wish I had the power to just get people to talk; it's amazing how people clam up around the police. "I never said anything about your gym being involved in steroids. I am only trying to solve a murder case and that is the best description I have of the suspect in question. Now, try to think if you could, and just give me any information you have. I don't care if hundreds of people come to mind. I just need to find this man, so anyone you think of would be a great help to us." At the end of my speech I focused in on each word using careful emphasis to show the woman how irritated I was getting with her.

"I don't appreciate that tone, officer. I already told you that I don't know anything about your suspect in question or whatever you want to call him."

"You might have seen him outside with a homeless looking man who goes by the name Rex. Is any of this ringing any bells?"

Behind the woman her daughter flinched—I could tell by the movement of her hair line behind her mask.

"Wait, I think I might—" This time it was the daughter that spoke, only her answer was brief because her mother silenced her immediately.

"Be quiet. You have nothing to say to the police officers, now get back to work. The tanning beds need to be cleaned." I wasn't about to lose the daughter just because the mother was trying to hide something that was starting to sound more and more like a drug case.

"Go ahead, please. Whatever you have to say could be very helpful in solving some serious crimes." I watched the brown eyes of the daughter look at me and then her mother, before she shrugged and walked away.

"I'm sorry, Detective, but my daughter is only seventeen and I am not giving the police permission to speak with her about this or any other case. Now if you'll excuse me I have other things to do. Good luck with your investigation, Detective," the old bitch said before walking away from the counter, leaving us with absolutely nothing.

"So what the hell do you think about all that, Light?" I realized that I had been doing all of the talking and Light hadn't said one word to help coax the mother into talking.

"I think that obviously the daughter knows something, but since we can't talk to her we need to figure out another way to get answers."

I glared at Light and was about to criticize his words with some snappy remark, when he just walked away. He'd spotted some guys working on the bench press and went over to see if they knew anything. I followed, shrugging my shoulders, realizing that it wouldn't hurt for the kid to take some initiative.

"Excuse me gentlemen, my name is Detective Light and I was wondering if I could ask you a few questions."

The man spotting the lifter nodded to the young detective but didn't pay much mind, as he was so distracted with what he was doing.

"We're looking for a man who comes here often. He's large, but not in the healthy way, and others have described him as being on steroids. He goes by the name Flex and has a shady homeless looking friend who he would hang out with outside of this place." One man grunted and the other shook his head, not even giving Light the time of day to help out. Detective Light wasn't happy and started into the men with all the regular police jargon.

"Both of you need to be aware that if you are hiding this information from the police you will be charged with impeding a criminal investigation." I stopped listening around that point but Light was just beginning with these guys. He didn't like to be ignored. While he continued talking, I focused on the words of three young guys just coming off the basketball courts.

"Yea that chick who works here dude, the other day she came into the locker room completely naked except for her mask." His friends were calling him a liar and making jokes about how he was banging the gym owner's daughter. I had no intention of missing a chance like this to get valuable information.

"Detective Wink," I said, stepping up to the group of men. "If you have a moment, sir, I have couple of questions." The laughing friends stopped in place and looked at me, each one of them taking turns pointing to see who I was talking to you.

"Yes, I'm actually speaking to you." I indicated the guy who had been bragging about his sexual exploits with the gym owner's daughter.

"First off, can you tell me how old you are?"

The young guy coughed through his limited edition ESPN football fan starter mask to clear his throat. "I'm twenty-three, officers." Light had finished scolding the other men and was now joining in with the conversation, just in time.

"I just spoke with the owner of this establishment and she told me that her daughter happened to be underage, seventeen I believe she said."

The guy swallowed hard and tried to talk but fear was getting the best of him and his words were failing him.

"That's fine if you can't speak up right now maybe you'll feel a little more talkative down at the station. We can chat for a long time on the subject of statutory rape."

"Wait, that girl is not seventeen. I know for a fact that she's at least nineteen because she's been going to college for two years now." The words came rushing out because of fear, and I knew he was telling the truth.

"Did you hear that, Detective Light? It would seem the only real liar of this establishment is the owner. Thanks for your help kid, and don't worry, you're off the hook." After a sigh of relief the kid walked away as fast as he could, and his friends followed at the same speed.

"Here's the plan: since we can legally talk to the daughter I'm going to the tanning beds so that I can ambush her with questions. When the mom comes to defend her daughter I want you to slap her with the same crap you were pitching to those muscle men a second ago."

Light didn't seem to need the low down. He had a handle on things; I could see it in his eyes. "Lead the way, partner," he joked from behind his mask, taking pleasure in the mocking words that made it clear he was my partner. I shook my head and walked around to the front desk and right past the mother, who was watching our every move. I couldn't see the look on her face, or how fast she came around her desk to catch up to us but I knew she was on her way. Light slowed down to run interference while I turned the corner into the tanning section of the gym. The two sides of the hallway were both lined with doors and I had no idea which room the daughter was in.

"What is it you think you're doing? I never gave you permission to go back there? The tanning beds are currently closed for cleaning." I could hear the mother talking but I didn't pay much mind. I was buys looking into the first tanning rooms for the girl. The mother did the job for me, though, and the girl came bounding out at the sound of her mother's angry voice.

"Hello again, miss, could you kindly tell me how old you are, and do me a favor and don't lie?" She was startled by my question but probably not as startled as the boy was when I asked him the very same question. Her voice was low and scared like she wasn't trying to get her or anyone else into trouble.

"I'm nineteen, but I never said I was younger. It was my mom and she was only trying to protect me—please don't arrest her or anything." Her voice grew louder with each word and finally she ended on a high pitched annoying sound that didn't help her case.

"Alright, just calm down. Your mother decided to impede a criminal investigation by lying to the police. Now if you want me to help her then I need information from you that is actually going to help me." The girl was nodding before I even finished talking; if she knew something she was going to tell me.

"I know you recognized who I was talking about when I mentioned the homeless man who spent some time with the guy I'm looking for. Tell me what you know about Flex and his friend, starting with how you know them both."

The girl sniffled and reached under her mask to wipe away what I assume was a tear before she started to talk. "Look I didn't mean to get involved with them; it's just my ex-boyfriend use to deal a lot of drugs out of the gym while I was working. So I just happened to find out that Flex would buy a good amount of steroids and that creepy Rex guy would buy meth." It was strange how someone who seemed so innocent could be so well connected with the worst kind of people.

"Alright, so where's this boyfriend of yours? I wouldn't mind having a few words with him if you don't mind." That was clearly the worst angle I could have taken because the girl backed up and didn't say a word. Apparently she didn't know or thought it was best to keep her mouth shut. I tried again.

"Honestly, I could care less about your boyfriend. I'm only interested in Flex, and if you can tell me where I can find him, I won't dig into your life anymore."

"I don't know where he is right now but I do know where he lives. Sometimes we would drop the stuff off at his house, after I got off work." Finally we were getting somewhere; with an actual address who knows what we could find out from this guy.

"Let's hear it, but I warn you, if you lying I'm going to be right back here and this time I'll be pissed."

The girl gave me the address, including Flex's apartment complex and room number. I left her there and walked back out into the open entrance area and saw the mother handcuffed and sitting in her chair.

"She didn't really give me much of a choice; want to bring her in for resisting?" Detective Light was getting a real kick out of the job today and wasn't taking crap from anyone.

"If you really want to, but I do have more important things we can do. The girl gave me the address of our suspect." I was getting used to this mask thing, and could actually see a smile on Light's blue lighting mask.

"I'm going to let you off with a warning this time, just don't let it happen again ma'am," Light said with a smile as he removed the overly angry mother's handcuffs. I could hear her mumbling from where I was standing so I was sure Light got an earful of her attitude.

"Alright, let's get out of here, partner."

Getting to the house didn't take very long, and with my car coming up the back and Light's up front, Flex couldn't have slipped out unnoticed. We met in the stairway and went up to apartment twenty-three with our game masks on. We didn't joke or play our usual back and forth game. In that moment we were just detectives trying to do our job, and that meant closing in on this all important suspect.

"Open the door, police; we need to have a few words with you!" I yelled into the door after a series of powerful knocks that no one could ignore. The bronze numbers rattled against the ugly green door as I started another series of angry knocks on the wood. Light and I listened for moving feet or closing doors or even the hushed whisper of words. We listened hard and didn't hear one sound from the inside of the apartment.

"This is Detective Light. Flex, we need you to open the door immediately!" Light tried his own words and powerful knocks at the door, but we were met by more silence. I looked down at my feet and saw ugly rips in the brown carpet, right at the edge of the door, I assumed from a couch or a table that was dragged carelessly into the apartment. Looking down, I also noticed the large gap between the floor and door; it was abnormally large for an apartment's entrance. I motioned for Light to stay on the door while I crouched down to have a better look of the apartment.

"Sir, we will not ask again, this is your last chance to comply with the police department and open your door." Light continued his threats as I got into position and looked into the dingy surroundings of the apartment. Before I could even register what I was looking at the smell of shit and rot punched me in the face. I felt my body expel two heavy dry heaves that threatened to empty my stomach out onto the scratches in the floor.

"On my count" I said standing up and drawing my pistol in one sluggish yet practiced motion. I expected Light to have some reservations with I was asking him to do, but instead he drew his gun and got into position. I lifted my finger and motioned one, two, and finally three before I kicked in the door to the apartment.

Clearing a room properly is an art form; when done properly it will keep people alive. As first man in I scanned straight and then stepped to the left only getting a brief view of the room and making sure no one was in it. I stepped into my corner keeping my weapon trained on the possible entry ways into the room. Detective Light stepped right where he was supposed to, keeping his eyes on the same location and remaining in the safety of the right corner. I moved into position outside of the first door that came into view which was on my left side. I lined up with the door frame as Light continued to watch the other doors and give me appropriate cover. Pushing the door in, I saw nothing but a dirty bathroom that was almost bare, besides the empty pill bottles on the floor. I didn't even see a shower curtain or toilet paper, but it smelt like it was used often enough.

"Detective," Light whispered from where he remained on the outside of the room watching the other door, which led into what I assumed was the bedroom. I stepped out and got a better view of the room, though I wish I hadn't. The carpets were shaggy yellow and showed off a multitude of stains for the world, or rather for me, to see. The couch was half ripped up and there were dirty plates strewn about, many of them still full of rotting food.

"Detective," Light said again, this time pointing to his ears and then back at the bedroom door, which was slightly ajar. This was his way of indicating that he had heard something, and meant it was time to get focused again. This time I stood secondary as Light reared up and then pushed in the door. The smell was the first thing that greeted us and it was impossible to ignore. That same stench of shit and decay, the only smell that you can't really define without calling it what it is: death.

"Guess we found steroid man, but it looks like he's no longer suspect number one," Light said as I stepped into the room and witnessed the horror that was Flex's addiction and demise. Drugs lay all over the bed, which didn't look like it had been cleaned in months. I saw the metal bed frame and knew it had made those cut marks in the doorway. Flex's eyes were rolled back in his head and he had a pool of white vomit leaking down his chin.

Marks from his drug overdose spread out all over his body and it looked like it was more than just steroids that did this.

"Looks like this is what I heard." Light pointed to the open window on the left side of the bed where streams of flies went in and out and the occasional car made too much noise. The smell was still there but somehow my nose grew numb to it and soon after the rest of my body went numb too. This was the only lead we had and there it was in bed, completely dead.

"Here, look at this. These confirm the statement Rex gave us." Light handed over a stack of five open envelopes, invitations to all the parties, even the ones that hadn't happened yet. I opened them and scanned each one until I become familiar with them. Once these landed it evidence it would be hard for me to look at them whenever I wanted to, so I memorized the set.

"The first one is listed as the welcome party, the second is of course the grand ball, and look: the third one is called the underground party." I felt the silver writing on the card and saw that the party was coming up soon, in only another few days. Another party meant another chance for me to get my hands on the killer in the act.

"What about the last two?"

I flipped over to the other cards and scanned them as well, filing them into my memory. "The fourth one is called the festival, and the last one is the grand banquet." I knew it would be difficult to catch the killer in the act, since I had already failed twice. But if Funny Bunny was going to go through with the parties there was a strong chance the killer would use them to strike again, which meant I had to try to stop him.

"Are you alright, Wink? Come on, let's get out of this stink— I think it's making us both sick." Detective Light called in the death and we both waited for the police to show up and take care of the ugly part of the job. We looked over the apartment for clues but there wasn't much hope; the guy seemed to be a junky in the worst way, the steroid-infused muscles were only the half of it. I didn't have much to say since I couldn't stop thinking about the underground party and wondering if all the same masks would be attending.

"There isn't much to do here; it looks like we're going to be back at square one with this case."

After hearing Detective Light's obvious statement, I took another look at him, wondering why none of this seemed to faze him. It was as if he was watching for my reaction to see how I felt about it, rather than showing how he felt. I didn't voice my suspicion but kept it to myself; I wasn't sure what I felt about the man but it wasn't good.

The rest of the time I spent in the apartment passed quickly, as I watched the police show up and start taping the crime scene off. Next I watched investigators come in and take photographs of everything from the body to the rotten food on the couch. Medical examiners came and took samples of everything while the police went door to door to collect statements from neighbors. Forensics came for their evidence and eventually I watched the coroners show up for the body. Everyone assumed it was overdose, but I still wasn't sure if foul play hadn't taken place here. The thoughts I was having were far too jumbled to make a decision now though, so I decided to just wait for lab results.

There were so many moving parts to this case but something told me it all came back to the masquerades and the colorful invitations. I closed my eyes and looked them over in my mind one last time before leaving that apartment forever.

1. The welcome party.

2. The grand ball.

3. The underground masquerade.

4. The festival

5. The grand banquette.

Ten

A few days later, I finally heard back from the lab on the blood work they'd done on me after the first party.

"Reports show that you had Flunitrazepam in your system, which if you don't know is the actual name for rohypnol," the technician informed me. So I had been roofied like a common college girl, and the alcohol had made it worse I'm sure. No wonder I had been so confused and tired at the party.

"That means that someone was on to us from the start. The killer of the masquerade parties not only had this planned from the beginning but was ready to deal with any police," I informed the Captain, while at the same time noticing that he seemed a bit strange, I could tell he knew more about this then he led on, and had to wonder what he was hiding.

"It would appear that way, but without any concrete evidence we can't say what the killer knew or planned in advance."

I was starting to really hate those scripted sounding answers that seemed designed to protect the speaker, no matter the circumstance.

"I'm not buying it, Captain. What is it you're not telling me?" This was a brave move on my part—not only had I failed at every turn during this case, but now I was calling my superior out.

"Honestly Wink, I'm under strict orders from above not to relay any information about the murders to anyone, including my detectives."

I stood alone in the office looking at the mask of the Captain feeling as helpless and as frustrated as ever. "I'm the lead detective on the masquerade murders. If you can't tell me then how am I supposed to solve the case?" I approached the situation calmly; I knew I was already overstepping, so I at least needed to sound controlled in my objections.

"It's not really up to me. Since the masq rules went into effect there are a lot of things I have to do to protect the identity of the victims." It clicked for me just then; I knew what the Captain was hiding from me and the rest of the team working the case.

"You know who the victims are! Is there a match, does it give us a lead on the case?" I couldn't ask questions fast enough, but each one was answered with only a shake of his head.

"I'm sorry Wink, but for right now I have to follow orders and keep all that information confidential. When the time comes I will inform you of everything I know, but until that happens I would suggest forgetting this case and working on your other ones." The Captain was referring to my current case load which was reaching upwards of six unsolved cases. But the rest of my cases weren't even homicides, and I couldn't bring myself to focus on such minor crimes.

"I didn't come back to solve anything but homicide cases. It's what I did before and it's what I want to continue to do."

"Detective, you need to get on board with the new practices of this department. Since the masq policy took effect all detectives help with whatever is necessary. There just aren't enough murder cases to solve anymore. You have been briefed on all of this and I don't want to hear anymore. I will inform you, when I can, of any updates on the masquerade murder case." The irritation showed in my superior's voice and I decided I would have to drop all the questions and demands for now. I left his office without responding. The Captain's lack of information disturbed me, but with no other choice but to wait for the answers, I headed for my desk.

I flipped through the case files as I had the previous couple of days, mostly just looking at the clock and waiting for the end of the day. I couldn't focus on anything but the masquerade murders. Today was Thursday and we had discovered the underground masquerade was coming up next Friday night. Just knowing the next party and possible murder was only a day away, I couldn't think about any of my other cases.

"Hey, Wink, I just wanted to compare notes on what you thought of the Wilson case."

I looked up at Light and, just as I had over the past couple of days, I told him I still didn't have anything. I would give him these quick answers and then look back down at my files just to get him to go away. I still didn't feel comfortable around my partner, especially after the way he reacted to the death of our only lead.

"Well, just let me know when you think you've got something on it," Detective Light said before walking back to his desk most likely annoyed with my lack of interest.

I realized as he walked away that the more interest I took in the regular cases, the sooner the Captain would bring me in on the masquerade case again. "Fine let's see what's going on with you, Wilson," I mumbled while pulling out the Wilson file and beginning my initial scan of the case.

Mr. Wilson arrives approximately at 9:15 at the Masked Beaver, a strip club located downtown. At around midnight Mr. Wilson goes to leave the strip club only to discover his car is missing, presumably stolen. Police arrive at the scene of a possible grand theft auto, soon after the midnight call from Mr. Wilson. During routine questioning Wilson confirms that he doesn't have a second set of keys and that his current keys are still in his possession. Wilson also swears he locked the vehicle before he entered the strip club, and there is no broken glass or signs of damages left at the scene. In addition there are no eye witnesses or cameras or anything containing significant evidence.

I flip through the papers scanning for something important that didn't come out during the initial report of the crime scene. The first thing I notice is the declaration from the insurance company, stating that the car would be completely covered under a theft. From there I make notes of all the finances that are readily available of Mr. Wilson. Based on what I can see he is unemployed and can no longer afford that car. I realized Light must have come to the same conclusion, so I decide it's about time I make things right with my partner, for now.

*****

I know this story isn't really about my day to day police work, but I think it's important for you to know that I had several successful cases since my return to duty. That case ended up being quite easy when we found Mr. Wilson's car in a buddy's garage. A simple grand theft auto case became insurance fraud pretty fast.

There were other cases that I went through during that dry period and most of them I solved successfully.

The Captain did take notice that I was doing much better, not only working with my partner but completing my other cases without complaint. And the next Friday before the underground party he called me and my partner back into his office.

"I was debating whether I should take you off these masquerade murders, seeing how personally involved you've been." I wanted to cut in right there and start defending myself but the Captain waved a hand and stopped me before I could. It had been in the back of my mind that the Captain was going to take me off the case, and I'd already decided to quit the force if he did.

"However you've shown me over the past week that you can still handle real police work, so I'm going to keep you on as lead detective."

"I appreciate it Captain, but does that mean you can tell me more about the victims?"   Again a shake of that masked head. "What I can tell you is that we're going to have a lot of undercover police at this next party and that I want you and Detective Light to be there as well."

Light didn't have any reaction to this, so I continued questioning the Captain. "Do you want me to assemble a team Captain?"

"No, I want you and Light to be separate from the team I will be assembling. We can't afford to miss anything and I don't want you all worrying about one another."

"So where exactly is this party being held?" I asked before the Captain could continue.

"It's in the basement of Funny Bunny's mansion."

I had the invitations committed to memory and could still picture the silver engraving of the card. While thinking about the card I suddenly had another question come to mind. "Wait, how are we all going to get in with only one invitation?"

"I went ahead and had some of our people make up exact copies of the one you two found in that apartment. Funny Bunny and his hired hands won't know the difference between the real ones and the fake ones."

It seemed as though all the pieces were falling into place and I felt good about our chances to finally catch this killer.

"Anyway you both know what time it starts, so make sure you get there on time. And if something does happen, don't let the murderer get away this time."

I ignored the angry Captain act and Light and I left his office.

****

I put on a good face, or rather a good mask, while I was at work but in the comfort of my apartment I couldn't help but feel overwhelmed. My job demanded so much of me, and just coming to terms with the new world I lived in and all the masq policy rules made things even more difficult. I had to just sit alone and try to analyze each problem and get a grasp on what was happening.

To begin, there were murders happening all around me and for whatever reason I was involved from the very start. My Captain was hiding information from me for reasons I didn't understand. At the same time I didn't trust Detective Light; no matter how much he tried to act like a partner, I knew something was off about him. And to make matters worse I had to fight through the background noise of my life: my missing eye and more importantly my missing daughter.

Interrupting my thoughts was the ring of the phone. God I hated the phone. It was a wonder I never smashed it to pieces against the wall. Still I picked it up, answering with an annoyed "hello."

"Hey, come outside."

Just three short words, but they were enough to make my stomach cringe. It was funny how an old loved one could change your thinking so quickly. Only seconds ago I'd been lost in the crime scene and the difficulty in solving a crime without a face. Now all I could do was run to the mirror to see how I looked, realizing as I did that of course looks didn't matter with the plastic on my face. I walked out my door and down the apartment stairs to the outside courtyard area.

"Viola, I didn't think you were going to be stopping by here anymore." If I could have seen her face I might have witnessed something close to hurt, though that wasn't my intention.

"Well, everything is still pretty new to you and I just thought it would be nice for us to meet once in a great while. You know, just to help you adjust." It didn't take a detective to read the lies from the mouth of my ex-wife.

"Why are you really here, Viola?" I kept wanting to tell her how much I missed her and how happy I was to see her; instead I remained cold and distant, safe.

"Fine, you caught me. Honestly I just was thinking about Callie and that of course led me to thinking about you and I just wanted to remember you both. I guess it's just easier to remember her when I'm around you, do you know what I mean?"

Knives couldn't have cut me on the inside deeper than her words. I swallowed hard. "Yeah I know what you mean," I managed to squeak, though the response seemed inadequate. I suddenly felt exhausted; the situation demanded too much of me mentally and all I wanted to do was sleep. I was thankful that Viola finally broke the silence because I just didn't have it in me to do it myself.

"So what are you up to tonight, any exciting police business?"

I was about to shake her off with something stupid about solving murders when she cut me off and kept talking.

"Wait, let me guess, you're solving the murder of a prostitute who was found dead on the side of the road?" I understood the mocking joke about the fact that, at some point in my career, I was always trying to solve the murder of some prostitute.

"No, but if you must know, I'm attending another masquerade to try and stop this killer. He seems to like to strike in the middle of these things." Viola didn't seem very interested judging by the way she was fiddling with the bottom hem of the designer shirt she was wearing. I suddenly noticed how nicely she was dressed and wondered how she could afford the designer outfit she had on.

"Well I'm guessing you're going to catch this guy tonight. You weren't good at a lot of things but one thing you were amazing at was catching the killers of the world." This was more sincerity than I could remember ever hearing from Danielle, especially about the job that was responsible for so much of our pain.

"It's been a bit of a challenge, but I guarantee with all the police that are involved in this one, the killer will be lucky not to get noticed in the first five minutes of this thing." Confidence I didn't know I had surfaced in that moment and all that worry about the underground party melted away.

"I guess a good luck is in order, but I know you don't really need it." I had all but forgotten how much I missed the woman I had married not all that long ago. There was a level of comfort that would always exist between us and I guess I wanted that comfort right now. I knew it was impossible; too much had happened between us, even before the tragedy, but still I couldn't help but think about it.

"I can tell you're doing a lot better since we last talked," she continued. "It would seem you're getting used to this whole mask thing."

Moments ago I was about to ask her what she thought about us maybe sitting down and talking, over dinner or something. I was about to try and rekindle a dead relationship, but what she said tore me away from that thought.

"I haven't really thought about it," I said, but on the inside I was wondering when I had stopped complaining to myself about every little masked detail. At first it had made me sick, at first it had been one of the most disturbing things in my life. Now I was growing used to it, becoming accustomed to not seeing faces.

"It's good to see that you're coming around," Viola said, but I was busy thinking that my daughter was killed by a masked intruder. That my partner was shot by the same masked intruder. And that I was shot in the face by a man wearing a mask.

"I'll see you later, Viola. I have some things I have to do before I can leave tonight." The fact that I was growing accustomed to this madness was making me sick, but even worse was that I hadn't even noticed.

"Alright, I'll step by again in a while just so we can catch up. Take care Wink."

I headed back up the stairs to my apartment without even looking back at the woman who was once my wife. It was difficult to wrap my mind around the fact that I was so used to everyone in my life wearing a mask. I vowed right then and there that I would never fully accept the world as it was but that I would only adapt to survive.

I prepared for the masquerade in the regular fashion, by checking my pistol and the ammunition as well as the knife strapped to my leg. I dressed to the best of my ability, not wanting to make it obvious that I was police. Still, people knew who I was because of the last two masquerades, so there was only so much I could do. The only real addition to my ensemble was the laminated C that I tucked into the vest pocket. The reminder was enough to give me comfort and confidence not to fail my daughter again. Every murderer that was allowed to walk the streets free was somehow connected to her death. I guess that's the real reason I decided to go back to my job, the real reason I was committed to catching the killer.

I headed out of the apartment and back downtown to the mansion, only this time I wasn't going to be inside or even outside the mansion. This time I was going to be underground where the killer would have nowhere to run, and unfortunately neither would I.

Eleven

At the mansion things looked similar to the last two times I'd been there, only this time the outside was silent and the inside was dark. A giant set of stairs were opened up, to the left of the main door. It reminded me of a bomb shelter the way the double doors swung open from the bottom and rested on the grass. Looking down, I couldn't see anything but the darkness below. I was already frightened of the killer lurking in the shadows.

"Take your ticket stub, you might need it later," one of the well-dressed bouncers said to me before handing back my invitation that was now missing a chunk. I put it into my pocket and started looking around for the hundredth time for my missing partner. We had agreed to meet outside of the mansion but there was no sign of him around. Crowds of people were walking down the stairs and I still waited, hoping to see that blue lightning mask, but he was nowhere to be found. After waiting for awhile I decided if he was going to be late we were just going to have to meet on the inside. I wasn't about to miss everything just because Light didn't show up on time.

I entered the underground party by walking down the stairs into the darkness. Each step I took everything became blacker, until I couldn't see anything but a faint flicker of light in the distance. There was nothing but cold stone as I set foot on the bottom floor of the basement, and the light flicking in and out. I expected cold but instead felt a rush of heat as I walked inside of the party. The dull thump of loud screaming music became immediately apparent and each step brought me closer to the sound.

"Yea that's him, he's the one." I heard whispers but when I looked around all I saw were stragglers, eagerly waiting for the moment they stepped into the real party. This place was already intoxicating and I couldn't help but become aware of my own paranoia. The music grew louder and the flicker of the strobe lights became my whole world. First I saw three people dancing in rhythm with the steady flicker and the hard rock. Next I saw twenty more all doing the same thing, their masks moving in and out of sight under my watchful eye. I came out into a giant clearing and saw the mass of bodies, moving in seizure to the music, many of them jumping up and down, taking turns slamming into each other in exited rage. The mosh pit was already extremely dangerous; I could see spots of blood being rubbed into the stone floor.

"AAAAAHHHHHHHHH" The singer screamed into the microphone so loudly I had to turn all of my attention to the band that was performing center stage. All black masks covered their faces, each of them painted with long white teeth and x's for eyes. The lead singer wore a mask of opposite colors, all white with black teeth and x-shaped eyes. Looking beyond the band I saw their name written on a banner in clear bold letters, and on the drum set on stage: Mushroom Head. The band continued to scream and pump the crowd up into a state of absolute fury.

"Party favors!" a man called loudly right behind me, but when I turned to see who it was the salesman only apologized and quickly stepped away. I recognized the mask and the suit case and remember the drug pedaling servers from the last masquerade. My assumption that people were going to better recognize me was an accurate one. I glanced back at the band and the crowd of people going crazy and decided I would avoid the area.

A familiar face, or rather a familiar mask, came into view of my peripheral vision. I turned and saw the pig man Chops walking by with two women under his arms, far too skinny to be with him. He walked away from center stage in an entirely different direction, toward another set of rooms that I hadn't previously noticed. I didn't really think he was involved in the murders but the smug pig was someone I would go out of my way to torture.

"How are you doing, sir?" I asked mockingly once we were far enough away from the music for him to hear me.

"Officer, I hadn't expected you to continue attending these events."

"I hope those girls are of age, Chops, for your sake—and it's Detective." I didn't wait for a reply, but just continued on into the next room, leaving Chops staring after me.

The kind of masks I saw in the next room would give you nightmares for a month: skulls, stitches, and blood, their wearers in shimmering bodysuits, and all of it glowing eerily in the black lights scattered around the room. People here swayed off beat to the music blaring from center stage in a familiar drug-induced daze. I didn't linger in that area long, but only glanced at each mask just to be sure that wicked one wasn't in the room with me. When I nearly ran into a werewolf as I turned the corner I should have felt scared but instead had a stupid thought: if this is how people dress every time they go out, what happens on Halloween? Is that finally a day where we can go without our masks?

I walked down a hall and just when I was starting to feel disoriented from being in this underground maze, I came to a room lit by normal fluorescents. Only when I stepped inside of the well lit room I found out there was nothing normal about it. Mirrors covered every surface, from the walls, to the ceiling and even the floor.

"Detective, I was hoping I would see you again." I knew who it was before I even turned and saw the beautiful Rosie Rabbit standing beside me. She wasn't wearing an elegant red dress as she had before, but she didn't look any less stunning in her new outfit. Tonight she was wearing a denim mini skirt with black boots that matched the half shirt revealing her belly. The name of a band was inscribed in blood red letter across her chest and the rabbit mask seemed different this time, though I wasn't sure how.

"Rosie, I was wondering if I was going to see you here. I mean, this place is huge." I was trying not to come off like a school girl excited to see an old friend but it didn't really work. Before I could even continue talking I did something that as a man I couldn't really avoid in a room with mirrors on the floor. I glanced down quickly just to sneak a peek up her mini skirt and when I looked back up she was staring right at me. Embarrassed, I tried to come up with a conversation piece to save me, but, flustered, chose the one topic I wanted to avoid.

"So this room of mirrors is pretty cool." I could only imagine in that moment that I seemed more like a pervert partier then the detective I was supposed to be.

"Yeah, I think Funny Bunny had it made with men in mind," Rosie said and moved her head in a motion that made me look to her left. I saw three other women walking around the room in skirts that were a lot skimpier then Rosie's. I was thankful that

Rosie was willing to laugh with me in the conversation rather than making things awkward.

"So do you have any leads on those horrible murders that have been happening?" Rosie sounded very concerned and I wanted to tell her that we had the guy, but truthfully we didn't have anything.

"Not yet, but were getting close. It won't be much longer before the killer is behind bars." I kept second guessing myself and right then I wondered how ridiculous I must have sounded claiming we were about to catch the killer.

"Did you see center stage yet?" Rosie asked and I nodded, not really sure what else to say. Or maybe I just thought I was better to stay quiet then say something stupid.

"Come on, I'll show you. Trust me, you're not going to want to miss the headliner of the show tonight." Before I could say anything Rosie took my hand in hers, something else I was growing accustomed to at these parties.

We reached center stage just as Mushroom Head finished their set and headed off stage. Soon after the stage was full of crew members, several of them running back and forth setting up the equipment for the next band. From the look of things the show would be starting soon. I was about to say something to Rosie while I had the chance and the stage was quiet but I of course was interrupted. Funny Bunny took the stage, as he always did in these moments, demonstrating his love for the dramatic.

"Hey, I have to go to the VIP section; Funny Bunny will be waiting for me up there. I hope I'll see you around Detective." And just like that the amazing Rosie Rabbit was gone again. I knew I wouldn't have any other chances to see her, since I was going to close this case tonight.

"Greetings, ladies and gentlemen! I just want to issue my thanks to one and all for attending yet another amazing party of mine. Tonight I invite you to get crazy, tonight I want you to go nuts, tonight is the night to get dirty. While you are with me in the underground I want you to forget the problems of the world and simply enjoy the night." The crowd roared at the sound of the offer, eager for the chance to lose themselves in the madness, if only for one night. I didn't roar, I didn't boom, I didn't even cheer. I was distracted by the moment I was waiting for, the moment the killer showed his mask.

"Now for your enjoyment and for your pleasure, I give you Slipknot!" Funny Bunny echoed out to the crowd and the gruesome looking group walked out on stage. One wore a mask made all of steel, with crude cuts in the bottom to give off the feeling the wearer was not from this world. The eyes and cheek bones tightened in and looked out at the crowd with a gaze of pure anger. Another was symbolic to Jesus, with a crown of thorns, only the image it gave off was of a twisted nature. One looked like an escaped mental patient, with straight jacket-like straps that held the mask together. Next there was an all-black mask with giant pins that reached out from all sides, each at least a foot long. More masks came into view: one with a long nose and sickly looking skin, another resembling a crazed clown, and one twisted looking, disproportionate mask with one eye bigger than the other and an empty hole for a mouth.

"Enjoy the show, and don't ever forget who brings this all to you, Funny fucking Bunny!" The crowd yelled out to the man and with that he left the stage for the VIP area, to watch the frightening band scream the world awake. Slipknot started in with the guitar and streams of fire started to shoot out around the band. The performance would clearly be an amazing spectacle. I however stopped looking at the stage; all of my interest was on the crowd. If the killer followed his own pattern, then chances were he would strike at the height of the show. I scanned every mask looking for wicked to show some sign of moving amongst us.

 I glanced over and saw Funny Bunny cheering with the crowd and I saw the man not just as the party planner but as the partier. It seemed there were more sides to the refined man then I had originally thought.

"I did my time and I want out," Slipknot sang and I could see with my peripheral vision the eruption of flames and fireworks. The crowd was sucked into the show but I couldn't even look. I had to find the killer before it was too late. Every mask melted into one another, as I tried to locate something out of the ordinary. But in a concert like this, it was hard to distinguish what was considered ordinary. I focused on the world around me and tried to pick up on something that would help me find the killer.

I stood there for what felt like a long time, but returning my attention to the show, I could hear the first song was still going on. Even though I was trying hard to pick out something different, I almost didn't react fast enough when I finally noticed it. Someone was moving through the crowd but not towards the stage, not to get a closer look or to be where the action was. Someone was pushing to the side as if they were looking for somebody; this person was moving away from the action.

My body shifted into motion and I started pushing people out of my way. I was trying to be graceful but with time running out I had to hurry. I stumbled and pushed past all the bodies as the song was coming to the end and I could just see the killer up ahead. It had to be the killer. I reached the area I'd last seen him, but I couldn't see any movement, or anything out of the ordinary. And then it happened: the stage lit up bright as a flare, bright as your first glance at the burning sun. Every person looking at the

stage was immediately blinded, like when you get your picture
taken in the dark and the flash temporarily shrinks your pupils. I
was looking away and still everything became blurry and difficult
to see in the haze of bright light and startled bodies. Then I saw,
unnoticed by the crowd, the knife in the chest of the victim, the
victim I had been looking for. I saw the glazed look in his eyes, not
from the show, not from the blast of light, but from death.

"Get out of the way!" I tried to scream but no one could hear
me over the loud music and the noise of the crowd. I pushed
through just in time to see Wicked pull out the knife and look at
me for a split second behind the red devil mask. The killer started
to run and no one noticed what had just happened. In fact the dead
body didn't even fall over, but instead clung there, resting on all
the other bodies pressed so closely together.

I felt for my pistol but there was no way I could get a clear
shot through all the people, so I just continued pushing through
with my weapon in hand. I couldn't see that well with only one eye
and pushing through like this was causing me to stumble and trip
over all the bodies in the crowd. I was losing ground on Wicked
and fast. If I didn't pick up speed I was going to miss which
direction he went after leaving the crowd.

"Not this time, I can't let him escape, I won't let him
escape," I muttered, motivating myself to push even harder than
before, no longer caring what happened to the people I smashed
into. I started kicking out legs and stiff arming people out of my
way; I was picking up speed and gaining ground on the quick
moving killer. A giant man with a mask full of piercings got into my
way and I rammed into him with all of my might. The man backed
up a step and then with a smile came right back at me, apparently
thinking it was all part of the mosh pit game. If I wasted precious
moments getting knocked to the floor by this guy I was going to
lose sight of the killer for sure. I lifted my gun and with a half jump

I pistol whipped the guy hard on the back of the head, with enough force to knock him on his knees.

"Sorry," I called as I continued pushing through the crowd with as much force as was necessary to keep up. I witnessed Wicked come clean of the crowd and head for a hallway, and I knew I hadn't blown it yet. I kept up and was only a few steps behind the killer, but I was afraid of losing him, so I lifted my pistol as I ran. We were both in the hallway now, leaving the crowd behind. Wicked turned the corner quick and I almost lost my footing doing the same. I hadn't run this fast in my whole life, but I wasn't going to let the killer get away for anything. I wanted to shoot, but only to wound him, just enough to stop his running—a clip in the leg would have been perfect. Still I tried to follow some kind of police protocol, so I didn't just shoot wildly at the killer as we ran.

"Stop where you are or I will shoot!" The killer didn't even flinch, and I did my best to line up the shot with his leg. The gun went off and I heard the bullet bounce off stone—a missed shot that cost me precious time. I lost a few steps on Wicked and he used them to turn the corner fast and open a door before I could get there. He didn't shut the door behind him and I was afraid he would jump out with that knife as soon as I walked in. So instead of bolting inside, I slowed down, got my bearings and then prepared to clear the room.

I took a breath and then stepped into the room, sticking to the art of what I knew best, making sure to check the sides before exposing myself. I didn't see anything but darkness waiting in the corners of the stone room. I examined everything in the room to make sure there were no hiding places; once I felt safe I walked in keeping my gun trained out in front of me. Straight ahead I could see another room connected to this one, at the end of which the killer sat crouched against the back wall. I could tell by the red glint of the demon mask that he was sitting there, waiting for me. I knew I had him right where I wanted him this time; there would be no escape for the killer. Excited and ready, I bounded into the room and came face to face with his mask.

Unfortunately for me, that's all it was: just the mask well placed in the corner as the perfect distraction. I felt the slash in my hand before I even registered that it had been cut open. I dropped my pistol and turned to face the killer, only to receive a harsh boot in the chest; I fell backwards onto my back dazed and half expecting death. Instead of the stab I was expecting in my chest, I saw the killer's back as he leaned down and picked the mask up off the ground. It was too dark and the killer was turned in just a way that I didn't see anything revealing and once the mask went back on I was too late.

"Who the hell are you anyway?" I figured if I was going to die I at least wanted to know who was about to kill me. Instead of answering, the killer turned to me, wearing all black and that red demon mask. I could only stare at the knife, which moved at me in the darkness. I could just make out the line of fresh blood on the blade, my blood. I scooted to the back wall and tried to think of something I could do to defend myself. Instead I froze, gunless and wounded and most importantly, alone.

Twelve

I knew in just a few more seconds I would be dead, but I remembered something in that moment: I had a knife of my own. It wasn't the giant heart piercing tool in the killers hand but I had a knife just the same; I could defend myself. That's just what I did. Moving my hand quick and clean to my leg, I pulled out the backup weapon. I held the knife out in front of me, inexperienced but ready to cut my mark into the man who was about to end my life. Then something strange happened, something I hadn't expected.

"Well go on if you're going to do it," I said sounding far more confident then I actually felt. The wicked mask turned its head and looked directly at my loaded pistol on the ground. Based on my quick judge of the distance, I realized the killer could have my pistol in his hands in mere seconds. I hoped to do something brave before I died, like throwing my body at the killer and trying to wrestle the knife out of his hands. Instead I watched the killer walk over to my gun put one foot on it and slide it backwards and out of the room.

"So that's how it's going to be then? Fine but I won't make it easy for you," I said, realizing that the killer wanted to kill me up close and personal, knife to knife. I might get my wish after all. I started sliding nice and slow up the cold stone, using my back so that I could keep my weapon at the ready. I reached a half crouched position when the killer started stepping back, keeping a close eye on me with each careful step. Just as I reached a standing position, the killer reached the entrance to the small back room we were in. I thought I was going to have a knife fight for my life but I was mistaken. The killer stepped back one last time and closed the door, never pointing the wicked mask anywhere but at me. I saw the cold steel door slam shut and become one with the rock wall of the basement mansion.

Fear is something that you can't quite explain. In my lifetime I hadn't really known a lot of personal fear for my safety. I had a bullet go right through my eye and almost kill me, but I didn't really have time to feel the real fear of the situation. Even up against the Wicked killer I hadn't really felt afraid; it was more of a helplessness then anything. In addition I was frustrated beyond belief with my own stupidity and the fact that I had failed once again.

I reached for the door handle only seconds after the killer had closed me in, but only to find what I expected: the door was locked. I yanked on the door, I shook the handle, and I even tried prying the lock open with my knife. Nothing worked. Other than the door that led into the room, I couldn't see anything but stone— the room was a dead end. I felt the walls looking for some kind of switch that would magically open up another way out of the room. After wasting time on this I decided the best course of action would be to find help. I pulled out my cell phone and dialed Detective Light's phone.

"Hello?" I asked because I didn't hear any ringing and just assumed Light had already answered the phone on the first ring. Then I noticed that I had no service in this tiny basement room. To make matters worse I now looked at my recent calls and saw a series of missed calls, first from Light and later from the Captain. I had put the phone on silent earlier that day and didn't bother turning it back on. I switched over to the text message section of my phone and read a message that Light had sent me earlier that night.

"Wink, security is on to the fake tickets, they're not letting anyone in without a real ticket." I read this and wanted to smash my face against the door, if not to break it open than to get some sense back to my foolish mind. I had been the only detective on the inside once again, only this time the police and my partner were on the outside wondering where I was. I read the next and last text message on my phone with more regret and longing than I thought possible.

"Did you make it inside? We can't get in and no one can reach Funny Bunny. Where are you Wink? The Captain is starting to ask questions." Things were looking worse and worse in my situation and I was starting to wonder if I even wanted to get out of the locked room. I used the light from my cell phone to again try and find a hidden switch of some kind, hoping maybe I had missed something when feeling along the walls. I looked over the walls and saw smears of blood all over the stone in long messy arcs that went from wall to wall and in every direction. I remembered the stinging pain in my hand and looked down at the slice across my wrist and palm that I had made worse by feeling for a way out. I ripped off a piece of my shirt and tied it around the cut to stop the bleeding. I went to work looking over every inch of that tiny black room still searching for a way out.

It had been some time since I was locked in that room and now I didn't have the energy to try anymore after so much futile effort. The only option left was to bust my way out. I couldn't tell you how many times I rammed that steel door in an attempt to break free. The door didn't even budge and my arm was starting to feel like it was broken. I was winded and without any ventilation coming into the room I was starting to feel hot and tired. My spirit was broken and I gave up, sitting down to get some sleep.

I was drifting away from the scene of what would be the most pathetic death of a man, who had come back from the grave missing an eye. I was trying to picture the scene of the murder, the one that I had just witnessed. Something had been out of place, besides the shift in the crowd that had led me to the killer. I could picture the crowd, the band, and even Funny Bunny bouncing up and down like a real rabbit exited for the show. My ideas were beginning to form; they were coming together, they were becoming something. I looked up at the wicked mask in my dreams and it was as if I was looking right into the face of a demon.

"Hello, Wink, can you hear me?" I woke up from my dream and couldn't see anything but the dark stone room I had fallen asleep in. For a moment I thought I heard Light talking to me but after a minute I just figured it was part of my dream.

"Detective Wink, can you hear me?" That time I was wide awake and what I was hearing was Light on the outside of the room, yelling for me. I went to yell and felt a touch of embarrassment that held me off for just a moment longer than it should have.

"Hey I'm here, I'm inside this room!" I yelled as I stood up from the excitement of being let out of the stone coffin that was becoming hotter by the second. I felt my head swim with the rush of standing up and for a moment I couldn't see anything but spots in front of my eyes.

"Hang on, Wink; it's going to be just a second we'll get you out of there." The idea of getting out seemed impossible when only moments ago I resigned myself to dying in that room. Now that I was moments from getting out, I felt panicked and rushed like I couldn't stay there any longer.

"Alright, I got it," Light said as the door to the small room twisted open; within seconds I was blinded by a series of flashlight beams. I tried to explain what had happened but instead the police officers grabbed a hold of me and dragged me straight out of there. Only a short time after being found I was sitting in the back of an ambulance being taken care of by a medic. Everything was moving so fast and I was in and out so much that I couldn't tell up or down for the rest of that night. My hand was bandaged, I was given pain medication, and was even hooked up to an oxygen machine for what seemed like hours. It was all very confusing and I couldn't get my head on straight enough to explain what happened. I shouldn't have tried so hard because the time for explaining was coming soon and it wasn't going to be fun.

I came out of the up and down blur in the bed of what I thought was a hospital. I saw white everywhere from the bed sheets to the cabinets. Sun light was squeezing in between the curtains, and with one look I could tell it was some time in the early morning. My hand was clean and bandaged and I was feeling surprisingly good, considering I was in the hospital. It all didn't really seem necessary; I didn't think a little cut on my hand would need so much attention.

"Here you are, Detective. Get dressed the Captain wants you downstairs." A nurse stepped in from out of nowhere and put the clothes I was wearing from last night on the bed. I knew the Captain wouldn't be happy about how badly I had screwed up so I didn't waste time asking questions, not wanting him to get even angrier. I dressed quickly, putting on the ripped and blood stained clothing from the night before.

"Come on, Wink, you don't have any time to waste." I looked up and saw my partner, Detective Light, the man I now saw as more of a friend then an enemy. In a way he was responsible for saving me and that was enough to change the way I felt about him. I finished putting on my jacket and then followed Light out of the room and into the dull gray of the police station. I wasn't aware of the medical bay that was at the police station; in fact I didn't think I had ever been there before that day. We went straight to the elevator and as soon as the doors shut I launched into my explanation of the previous night.

"Look, Light, you have to know how close I was to—"

Light lifted his hand, cutting me off before I could even get started with all that I needed to say. "I would save it if I were you; the Captain is waiting to hear this."

Things were starting to make sense: I was about to be put in the hot seat and would have to explain my way out of trouble. The doors opened but not on our floor of the homicide offices that I was becoming so familiar with again. Instead we were on the top floor, the executive side of the force, where all the big wigs and politicians were. No one ever wanted to end up on that floor, unless of course it was time for a promotion. I watched Light navigate through the top floor like it was his home turf, once more with my suspicions about him. How fast I could go from trusting someone to thinking they were the enemy, how fast indeed.

"Alright here we are, Wink. Good luck." I wanted to respond angrily, but thought better of it when the doors opened on a room full of men and women.

"Detective Wink, there you are, go ahead and take a seat over there." I was in a meeting room mostly empty except for a long table where everyone sat. I was directed to sit alone on one side of the table, while Light, the Captain, and the others sat looking at me. I didn't really have much choice, so I sat down and looked out at the masks of the men and women who would be judging me.

"I trust your feeling better, Detective, because if you're not up for this now we can always reschedule," a man wearing a mask with a long, elephant-like nose and built in glasses said to me. I noticed the political sticker above his eyes.

"No, I'm feeling much better, and there are some things we need to talk about." I was trying to sound polite and on their side but it was obvious by the table what side I was on. I looked at the Captain and could see the bags under his eyes, even with the mask on his face; he must have been up all night.

"We'll get to all that, Detective, but first I think introductions are in order." The man with the nose shuffled some papers and made a tiny mark on one of them before continuing.

"I am your Chief of Police, but don't feel bad for not knowing that—I know you've been out of the loop for some time. To my right is District Attorney Elisa and Senator Darwin, and of course you already know Detective Light and your Captain." I looked at Elisa and mused over her gold and red mask that swept up like a burning fire, which matched her black suit with red undertones. Her mask showed that she had lots of money and even a little bit of power. The senator wore a mask that looked like a primitive man, more like an ape than a man in certain light.

"Pleased to meet all of you, even under these circumstances," I managed to say, not really sure if I was in trouble, or if they just wanted answers from me. I wanted to ask if I needed a lawyer present or not but I guessed the DA was as good as it got.

"Alright, there are a few things I would like to talk about this morning, but first I would like to hear about what happened to you last night." "While I listened to the Chief's question, I couldn't help but wonder what Detective Light was doing in the room. I knew he was my partner but it just wasn't standard protocol for a partner to be involved like this.

"It was an interesting night. Where would you like me to start sir?" The pressure was getting to me and I wasn't handling it well, as I could tell by the angry sound the Captain made.

"Why don't you start with why you didn't check in with your partner or any of your fellow police officers that were involved in last night's sting?"

"I was instructed to check in with my partner, but no one else. The Captain wanted us to stay low key to avoid notice by the local partiers. I tried checking in with my partner but wasn't able to and I didn't want to wait so long that I missed my chance to catch the killer."

"I've been made aware that you were contacted by Detective Light and that you were the one who wasn't answering the phone," the Chief continued. The part of me that had decided to like Detective Light now hated him again; I wanted to call him Judas right then and there.

"I can't be certain of when anyone made the phone calls. All I know is that we had trouble getting into contact with one another and I acted."

The Chief noted a few things down on his paper and in unison everyone did the same, even Light.

"Ok so you entered the party and being the only police officer there, you weren't able to stop the two murders that happened at the masquerade."

"Wait a minute, there was a second murder?"

"Yes, I guess you weren't aware. Why don't you tell me about the murder you do know about."

"I don't know anything about a second murder but I witnessed the murder that happened in front of the center stage."

The Chief lost interest in his little notes and gave me his absolute full attention. "Tell me about the killer—what did you witness?" The Chief spoke carefully, in a way that revealed nothing.

"His height was average and every inch of his body was covered in black from the plain black boots to the black gloves. The only thing special about the killer is the mask he wears, which can only be described as the face of a demon."

"You mean to tell me the killer walks around with a demon mask on and no one notices?"

"Look I know it sounds crazy but I'm telling you what I saw. There is no mistaking the fact that it resembles a demon."

"Alright, Detective, why don't you continue on with last night's account after you saw the killer stab the victim in the chest."

I told the entire story to the group sitting at the table from the chase to the fight in the small room and my getting trapped inside. I wasn't proud of my mistakes but I told the group everything, no matter how embarrassed I was. No one interrupted, but only jotted down their notes and listened. The truth was I really needed to tell someone what happened anyway.

"That's about it, after that I was rushed off to the ambulance and now I'm here. So could someone please tell me about this other murder?"

The Chief looked over to the DA Elisa, indicating that it was her turn to talk. "Well, Detective, honestly you were looking like suspect number one not too long ago. Being the only person at every murder and the only person to actually see the killer in action, it was starting to look more and more like you. Last night we were notified that arresting you would be the best practice if only to be safe. I'm sure you understand." I didn't understand and more than anything I wanted to defend myself but didn't interrupt her.

"To make the case against you even easier, you were the only one let into the party even though you were carrying the same fake invitation as the other officers who weren't allowed access. But then you were fortunate enough to be locked away inside of that store room." Elisa nodded over to Detective Light, who took that as his turn to speak, and he stood up, directing his voice to me.

"We believe the second murder happened after you were locked in the store room. All the other murders were perfect stab wounds to the heart that ended life almost immediately. The murder in the mirror room was sloppy, and almost appeared rushed."

I was happy to have been cleared only moments after being implicated. Now I was fully interested in the second murder. "I don't understand. How was it rushed?"

"The killer missed with the initial stab and only wounded the victim rather than dealing the killing blow that we've seen in the past. There must have been a struggle because in the end the victim was stabbed in the back, along the spinal column. This caused the victim to be paralyzed and eventually bleed to death." After everything another person died because of my actions; if I had only been smarter another life wouldn't have been lost.

"After finding the second dead body," Detective Light continued, "a thorough search of the underground was conducted and eventually, after some time, I found your pistol on the ground. That's when I started yelling and eventually found the door with the key jammed in the lock." Another mystery, if the killer didn't want me found why leave bread crumbs in the form of my pistol on the ground.

"The murderer could have killed me at anytime: instead of cutting my hand, he could have stabbed me in the back, and my gun was on the ground, so he could have just shot me." I felt like this was something the group of important people at the table needed to know.

"What makes you so sure the killer is a he?" Elisa asked from behind her notebook.

I thought about this for a moment before answering. "When the killer kicked me to the ground there was some real force behind it. I can't say for certain, but it's either a man or a very powerful woman." Elisa seemed content with this answer but I wasn't sure what she writing down in her little notebook.

"Anyway, Wink, you were in pretty bad shape when I found you. Whether he meant to or not, the killer cut a pretty good vein, which is why you were so out of it. The medical team said you lost a lot of blood and the oxygen in that room was bringing you down even more than you know. The killer was closer to getting to you then you might think—maybe he just wanted it to be slow and painful to send a message or something."

Even though I didn't really agree with Light, what he said made some sense. I mean if you were the killer wouldn't you want the cops to know you were untouchable?

"I guess we have enough information about what happened last night. I think it's time we move on and talk about some other matters of importance," the Chief said, making it clear there were other things on the agenda today.

"After some debate we've decided these murders are becoming a real problem and it's time to bring you and your partner in on whom the victims are."

Finally, I breathed a sigh of relief; I was so tired of the guessing game; I wanted real facts to go on.

"All of the victims involved in the masquerade murders are officials on the masq policy election board. This means these are the very people who will decide in a couple of weeks, whether or not the masq policy is going to stay in effect long term."

Immediately my mind went to suspects and the people I would be questioning first things in the morning.

"Everyone already knows the officials are leaning towards extending the masq policy, so it stands to reason that someone is trying to stop that from happening." No one was writing anymore; it seemed my time was over, now it was time for the real work to begin.

"Detective Wink, if I were to keep you on the case as the lead detective, tell me what steps you would take to find the killer before the next party."

"I would look into the unmask group, the one they call Face. I think there's a good chance that one of them has gone rogue and is finding other methods beyond just protesting in the old fashioned way." It all made sense and I marveled at how much easier it was to get those all important leads now that I had the information about the victims.

"Perfect, that's what I like to hear. That means you and Light are still leading up this case but now you're under my radar and my jurisdiction. You have one week before the festival masquerade party so that means you have one week before the killer strikes again."

"Why don't we just tell Funny Bunny to shut down the parties so that these murders come to a stop?" Light asked. From the Chief's body language, I was glad I hadn't been the one to ask the question.

"Honestly, Detective, if these murders have a political agenda, then the killer is just going to find another time and place to kill the voting members of the masq policy. Why would we take away the only knowledge we have, and that's when and where he will strike next?" I couldn't have said it any better myself, and oh how I wished to see the look on that puppy's face, when the Chief kicked him down.

"Alright, gentlemen, that's all for today. I suggest everyone get some sleep before the next work day. Thank you for your time." The Chief gathered up his papers and with a few nods and handshakes he and the other two big wigs were out of the office. I was more than relieved, until the Captain, who hadn't said anything during the meeting, finally spoke.

"I am far too tired to even begin with you Wink, so I'm just going to let you know, if you can't find the killer in a week we're going to be having a long conversation." He slammed a hand down loudly on the desk and then rushed out of the room like an angry bull.

"Looks like we got our lead, Wink. Better get some sleep; we have a lot of work ahead of us tomorrow." I wasn't even thinking about how much I hated Detective Light and how I would resent working this case with him. My mind was in other places, for example the unmask group and how difficult it was going to be tracking down one rogue killer.

"Actually I think we're going to have one hell of a busy week."

Thirteen

All the stress, frustration, and regret from the day before melted away. Today I had a lead; today I had purpose and that purpose was to get my killer. To find whoever was behind this mystery, I would have to start from the bottom and work my way up. If Face was really a part of this, I would need to start talking to people who were connected, and soon. Unfortunately there was one more thing I had to do before I could even get started on actual ground work. A good background of research was vital to any case and this one was no different. If I wanted to find the right people, I would have to start by gathering some information.

To start my dig I went to the biggest social networking site on the internet, aptly named Maskbook and started looking around for anyone who supported the group known as Face. For the first few hours of this all I could find were stupid kids complaining, acting like they knew something. It was we support Face this and masks are for conformists that, a never ending complaint line. Just when I was starting to think about working this from another angle, I found something interesting.

Anyone who is serious and ready to do something about the masq policies, write to my link here. I can give you all the local listings for what you can do to help our cause. It wasn't much and I normally wouldn't have taken much interest, but it was the nature of the profile that kept me involved. The profile picture was of a face—but not a real face, only a mask of a real face. It was creepy enough to make a statement and it meant this guy was brave enough for everyone to give him a second glance. Beyond that there were only fake identifiers, bogus addresses and phone numbers, nothing personal about this guy. I only had the name on his profile TrueFace80k. To get to the actual link I had to leave Maskbook. This was another good sign that meant this TrueFace80k didn't want just anyone contacting him. After clicking the link the net brought me to an all-black web page, with a spot to type in the center. In bold gray lettering the website demanded I answer a question before I would be granted access to the site.

What do we hide beneath a mask? I barley even read this question before I instinctively answered, typing in the word face. I realized how foolish this was when I saw an error message pop up in red letters, stating that I now only had two of my three attempts remaining. Face would have been too obvious but it was too late to question what I had done. Getting access to this site was my one and only concern for that day, so I started taking notes. I wrote out the question and began brainstorming possible answers. I figured I would jot down everything I could think of and then I would narrow the list down to the final two. Words began pouring out of me like a wildfire and after a short rush of nonstop writing, I had something close to twenty words. I started feeling a little overwhelmed, considering I didn't even know if the site called for a single word or an entire sentence. I thought about calling for a tech guy, but I wanted to believe I could handle cracking the code on my own. I read the question out loud, this time trying to find some kind of hidden meaning.

"What do we hide beneath a mask?" I thought for another moment and then made my selection, this time with more thought behind my answer. I typed the word personality and pressed the enter key, only partially confident that it would work. The already too familiar red error message dropped into view and let me know I had one attempt remaining. I wanted to keep thinking of an appropriate response but instead quickly typed the word emotion into the box and hit enter. The red error message came right back, this time stating that I was all out of attempts and that my IP address was locked out of the system. I knew a thing or two about computers but I wasn't all that sure about passwords and how this worked. Still I could always just contact the tech department if I really couldn't get in on my own. I decided I would try again when I got home, since the police station IP was locked but not my personal computer.

"Any luck getting any leads?" Detective Light asked in his cheery voice, only making my day worse since so far I hadn't come up with anything.

"Not yet, but I did have a question. If I were to ask you what we hide beneath these masks, what kind of an answer would you give me?"

The blue mask on my partners face was my window into his soul, only this particular window was closed. "I would say we hide all that we are." A dull silence caught in the air, as if there was some kind of significance to those words, perhaps beyond that of a simple question.

"Anyway if you get onto anything let me know, I'm itching to get out there and track down our killer." Light walked away and once more left me feeling suspicious and confused. Throughout the rest of my work day I made a list of possible answers to the question and continued to ask everyone what they thought. Most of the answers I got were the same as the ones I had already tried but a few of them had potential. I narrowed the list down to my three possible answers, trying to stick to what was simple because that just seemed right to me.

I left the station then, eager to test my new ideas on my own computer. "Alright True Face let's try this one more time." It didn't take long to retrace the website and return to the screen that had blocked my passage into the next stage of my investigation. I typed the first suggestion I had, the one at the top of my list: identity. I pushed enter and received the red lettered sentence that I was really beginning to hate. Only two of three attempts remaining and two more sentences scribbled on my little list. As if out of nowhere it became clear to me then and I simply decided I wouldn't need the list I had spent all day making.

"We hide everything beneath a mask," I said while typing the word everything. Only a second later I was inside the website. This time I wasn't even thinking about the website or the case or even the murders. All I could see was my daughter and the masks of the evil men who had taken her from me. My definition for the question became clear to me and in a way I understood the people of Face a little bit better. Beneath a mask we not only hide the good but we hide the evil and by doing this we protect them.

The site opened like a pair of automatic double doors at the grocery store. Only at fist glace it looked like nothing more than angry kid's rants and raves. This was followed by yet another child complaining about the same thing. Upon further inspection I could see a series of links to all sorts of well-connected Face members. It was hard to tell how long it would take to sift through the countless links and pages but it had to be done and soon. At the top I spotted a page that opened on a series of MaskBook accounts and noted one in particular. The account had a small picture next to the name and I could just make out a face of true beauty. There wasn't anything so remarkable about the face, except that it was the woman's actual face. It brought me back in time.

*****

The horse pulled on the carriage, flexing its muscles with each rhythmic step. It wasn't a chore to the horse, but instead was its purpose. The white carriage rocked as it carried us over the cold stone on our journey through a sea of lights. It was Christmas time and we were on our way to see all of the year's Christmas lights. I shuffled in my seat to get a better view of my amazing wife. The red leather-like cushion, that reminded me of a Buick's vintage interior, squeaked when I moved and added something awkward to the moment. I looked at Danielle and saw that behind her was a sea of color—the Christmas lights were particularly bright this year. The light gave off a glamorous glow that surrounded her and left that smiling image of her face forever trapped in my memory.

*****

The picture of the girl looked very similar: you could tell it was truly her face but the lights that surrounded her fogged it enough to make it hard to see, but at the same time surrounded the woman in a glow that made her look beautiful. The name next to her picture was only one word and it fit the girl in the photo better than I could have described her myself; her name was Angel.

I searched the site for some time and everything returned to this mysterious woman. The more I looked, the more certain I was that she was well connected with Face. Of course this was assuming that the website was the real deal and not some high school kid's afterschool project. I had to get a better handle on how I could get involved with the group, so I started to build a plan.

"You want to do what?" I was back at work the next morning and was busy pitching my plan to Detective Light. As expected, he wasn't on board with the idea. I had spent the night trying to come up with something that would work in our time frame; it all came back to one idea.

"I don't think I feel comfortable doing that, I mean it's a little too much don't you think?"

I started shaking my head in response even before Light could finish trying to get me to see his point. "Look, we don't have the kind of time we need to walk around questioning people. It could take a very long time to build a case against Face. If it was going to be easy the local cops would have done it already." Light was my partner now and I had to get him on board if the plan was going to work, though that didn't mean I'd let him stop me from going through with it. Still I knew how much easier it would be if he was on board, as it would save me from having to sneak around.

"It just reminds me too much of all those cops trying to pull undercover drug stings, only to end up doing tons of the drugs themselves and never really getting out." Light was referring to my idea, to pose as two new members of Face.

"How about this, if you really have a problem let me do the dirty work. All you have to do is watch my back; I will be the one to take off my mask, not you." I could see the idea weighing heavily in his eyes; he had to know it was the right answer.

"Come on, it's the only way were going to make this work." I didn't have much faith in my partner but I reminded myself that he had saved my life; that should be enough to give him the benefit of the doubt.

"Alright fine, let's do it your way." I had the impulse to do a little half jump and yell out a yes in excitement but decided against it. I wasn't a teenager anymore, after all.

"Tell me what you have in mind, Wink. How do you plan on joining up with the group?" I reached into my desk and pulled out the folder I had been working on, the one containing information on the website.

"Right here is a list of important people I want you to go over so that you can get familiar with the players. Pay close attention to the woman called Angel. I have a pretty good feeling she has a large part to play with Face." I opened the folder so that Light could see the pages as I flipped through them. I stopped on the last page and started explaining the steps we were to take in my plan.

"This is a list of possible meeting areas; this one in particular caught my interest because it's a convention room near the courthouse. I made a call and found out that a support group meets there called 'Dealing with the Mask Transition.' It would be the perfect place for supporters of Face to pick up new members."

"Alright, this is actually sounding pretty damn good." I heard a touch of surprise in Lights voice, mixed with something I wanted to think was jealousy.

"So I figure I go in there and start sending out signals. I can make sure the people there know that I am fully against the masq policy, and with some luck Face will come to us. All I want you to do is listen in on a wire that I will be wearing." Light was still listening as he went through my lists of people I thought were potentially part of Face.

I had spent most of the night looking through the website, reading comments, looking at photos, and jumping from one link after another. I could have kept on going but after collecting about eight names that I considered to be part of Face, I thought I could call it a night. The one thing I noted was that all of these names were somehow connected to the woman named Angel.

"This woman seems to come up a lot in your reports. Why is it that you think she is so involved?" Detective Light was flipping back and forth through the pages but kept on coming back to the large picture I printed out of Angel's face.

"She came up on every page that looked suspicious and is at the top of every one of these guys' lists. Besides, just one look at her and I know something is up—no one is brave enough to post their face like that, no one but a member of Face.

"Ok, so when do you plan on running this by the Captain?" I was hoping that Light wasn't going to bring that up; it was just one of those things better left unsaid. On my own I never would have bothered the Captain with this kind of thing, but of course that was all a long time ago.

"Honestly, I was just thinking I would wait and tell the Captain after I had the information we need." I let the statement hang in the air and wondered how Light would respond. I kept thinking about how difficult it was to read him, as he truly was a mystery. Just then I heard footsteps behind me, and the look in Light's eyes was fearful.

"Wink, would you mind stepping into my office for a moment?" The voice of the Captain sounded off from somewhere behind me. I nodded but felt a ping of panic; it reminded me of school and getting caught by a teacher while you were in the middle of doing something bad. Light had been trying to warn me that the Captain was behind me; he just didn't come out and say it. Now he couldn't even look at me, and was instead looking off in the distance like he could no longer associate with a trouble maker.

"On my way Captain" I muttered under my breath, even though the Captain was already waiting for me in his office. I couldn't be certain as to how much the Captain had heard, so my plan was to play this like a criminal and not say anything to incriminate myself. I turned from my partner, who was still staring off at something he pretended was important, and I headed for the office.

"Alright, Wink, it's about time we get this over with." Standing at the back of the room a man had his back to me; all I could tell was that he was staring out the window. I didn't know what was going on, so I only nodded to the Captain and sat down in the chair facing his desk.

"Good to see you again, Detective Wink. Tell me, how is your case going?" The man at the window turned and I saw the half man, half monkey mask of Senator Darwin. He hadn't said a lot at the previous meeting so now I didn't know how to gauge my response to him.

"We've compiled a lot of information and I think we're going to have something concrete soon."

The Captain sighed a little from behind his mask before stepping aside so that the Senator could get closer to me.

"That's good to hear. I hope I am posted on the activity of your case as you get closer to nabbing that killer." The man seemed formal, with a large portion of pride that only came from the assumption that he was better educated than most. Again I only nodded, not wanting to let out any extra information, information that could get me into trouble.

"I'm guessing you're wondering why I have called you in here, so I will just cut right to it. I don't want to waste your or your Captain's valuable time; I know what it means to break away from important work for even a minute." With this the Senator reached into his suitcase and pulled out a folder with a set of instructions and a place for me to sign.

"I need you to look over this document and sign it so that we have it for our records. I take personal care when it comes to this matter and like to make sure the police department doesn't shy away from any mandatory laws. No matter how small or silly they may seem."

I looked at the form and saw right away what I was signing. I almost let out a laugh at how terrible the timing was for this.

"Here you are, Wink. Now you need to have this on your mask immediately. The day after your waiting month is over, the department and you will be hit with a barrage of fines," The Senator explained as the Captain passed a large sticker stuck between two sheets of thin transparent plastic towards me. I looked at the NY police department logo and the item that identified me as a cop and cringed.

The Senator spoke again, possibly noticing the irritation in my body language and wanting to make sure I understood the agreement. "You need to have this sticker on your mask at all times, whether you're on duty or not and you won't run into any problems."

I hated the slimy bastard and the masq policies all over again but I really didn't have a choice. Or maybe I did. I had so many questions about how dangerous it was to identify ourselves with the stickers, but asking would only lead to the same result. For whatever reason people were committed to the masq policy, and anything I said would only cause problems.

"Ok, I'm going to put this thing on first thing when I get home today. I still have a little time before the month comes up and I want to make sure the thing is on my mask right," I said in a rush while signing the form and handing it off to the Senator. I stood up from my chair, making cheerful nods at the Captain and Senator as I made a slow movement towards the door.

"Wait a moment, Wink. I want you to take this seriously and put that sticker on. It is a requirement of the department." The Captain could tell I was up to no good and from the sound of it he wanted the Senator to know he was on top of things.

"Oh I know, Captain, don't worry. The next time you see me I will have the sticker on my mask." With that the Senator and the Captain thanked me and I was clear to escape the office where I had to lie and lie some more. I walked out and found Light eagerly waiting for me to come out and tell him how much trouble I had gotten into.

"So what was that all about? Did the Captain go for the undercover idea?" I had a moment of doubt about my plan and questioned the choice I had made to bring Light in on it. Unfortunately he already knew what I was up to, which meant I had to take him even deeper into my plan that would either solve this case or get me fired.

"Look, Light, my plan is going to work. I can almost guarantee it's the only way to go if we're going to get to the bottom of this. I need you to make a choice either to help me do something that isn't exactly legal with the police department's new masq policy, or to get out now while you still can." I expected a long silence or a conversation weighing the pros and cons of the situation, but I was wrong.

Detective Light answered me as soon as the words came out of my mouth: no doubt, only determination. "Finding the killer is far more important than following some rules. I've thought about this enough already, I'm on your side one hundred percent." I will admit I was a little shocked by this answer, but now looking back it does make sense that Light would follow me on my mission.

"So what's the plan, Detective Wink?" I stuffed the sticker with the department logo into my desk drawer, making sure that no one, including Light was watching.

"I think we need to get to that meeting, but first we need to stock up on some supplies. The more recorded information we can collect, the better this is going to look when the Captain gets involved." Light was nodding while I searched around for all of my papers and notes; I wanted to be ready for my performance. I knew there was a lot of preparation that needed to be done fast if we were going to make this work.

"Come on. The sooner we get this stuff checked out the sooner we can start setting up," I said to Light before I started my power walk to the elevator. Light followed me out of the building, matching my pace. I didn't even think twice about the New York City police department badge that sat buried in my desk drawer.

Fourteen

It didn't take long to check out the materials we needed; with such a low crime rate, it was easy to get a hold of all of it. Only we didn't have the time to get the full work up for a sting, which included a van with video and sound surveillance. Instead we got a high quality listening device that I could wire underneath my clothes.

The meeting started just before seven and we didn't get out of the office until after five thirty. In a normal city this might have been fine, but in New York this was barely enough time. I had to attach the wire while Light drove, and spent the rest of my time sound-checking the equipment. I lined the wire underneath my clothes, taping a small section so that it would stay in place and go unnoticed. There of course were other, easier ways to record conversations, but this method gave the highest quality recordings.

We pulled into the parking lot and didn't waste any time starting the next round of sound checks, so that Light could listen in to everything that was going on. It took a couple of minutes to get things set right and after that I actually had a couple of minutes to kill before the meeting. This should have been spent casing the place and preparing, but instead it was wasted on talking to my partner.

"So what makes you think Face is really going to expose itself at this thing?"

I wanted to explain myself but I really couldn't, it didn't make the best sense for a rebellion to meet in such a public way. All I could say to defend this whole quest of mine was that I had a gut feeling and more than that I had to find a lead and fast.

"Look, this is the only option we have to solve this thing within the time limit. How about we stop asking what if questions and just act on the hunch as if it were actual facts? It's all we've got." Light didn't pursue the matter further and I was glad because I had to get in there before it started. I wanted to get a handle on the people I would be baiting.

"Alright, if for some reason something goes wrong I have my phone on vibrate. Other than that make sure you listen close for something that might help me get in with the right group." I didn't wait to see how Light felt about the onslaught of orders coming from his partner, partially because I was in a hurry, but mostly because I didn't care.

I made my way to the double doors and entered the building without looking back. The farther I got from the car the better I felt about my mission. There was a long hallway with dull brown carpets and a ceiling that used to be white but now looked dirty and smoky. Despite the atmosphere, I felt refreshed, like that first jump into a swimming pool on a hot summer day. This was the kind of thing I loved, the kind of thing that helped me to forget my past and only enjoy the moment. A lame sign made out of a white piece of construction paper read, Dealing with the Mask Transition, conference room at 7.00. I didn't know where the conference room was but I figured I would find it somewhere along the way, so I headed down the ugly hall. I passed by several empty rooms, their lights off. Whatever purposes this building served during business hours seemed to be already done and over with. The hallway broke off into two directions and I wasn't sure which way to go, until I saw people walking around at the end of the hall. I headed in their direction and ended up right where I wanted to be, at the conference room.

"Go ahead and take your seats around the circle. We still have a few more minutes before we can get started," a woman in the back of the room said, in a voice that sounded better suited to addressing a group of toddlers. A circle of chairs was set in the center of the room and already over half of them were filled up with mask-wearing people. A table of refreshments sat in the back of the room: stale cookies and what looked like cheap punch. No one was interested in the refreshments; instead people were taking their seats and eagerly awaiting the speaker. I started my search of the room, scanning every person from head to toe, looking for some kind of signal that they were involved with Face. Once more the mask policy prevented me from being able to identify anything more than a series of my masks.

"There may be a few stragglers but let's go ahead and get started. We have a few things I want to go over tonight that I think are a very important process in this adjustment. But first I would like to go around the room and meet up with the couple of new masks that I see out here tonight." The woman wore a mask that warmed the heart a little bit. It was difficult to describe but it reminded me of a fifties wife, only more plain. She had a poof of curled hair with a big clip and her dress was covered with flowers and blue stripes. Her mask was painted with makeup that highlighted rose-colored cheeks and red lipstick, and even matching eyeliner gleaming around the eyes of the mask.

"You can go ahead and start—we just want to know your name and a little bit about yourself, maybe why you're here or what's difficult about the masq policies." Her voice was grating, but I now heard a soothing undertone that made it seem more like a caring mother than it did earlier. The guy she was speaking to stood up and took off his cowboy hat and held it tight at waist level while he spoke to the group.

"Hi everyone, I guess you can call me Rooster—that's the name I've been using lately and all. I um came here today because I keep having nightmares about all these masks." Rooster shifted uncomfortably and couldn't speak; he swallowed hard and continued awkwardly with his introduction. I watched his mouth move from beneath his bandit like mask, which really was only a cloth bandana tied around his head, probably not enough of a mask to be legal.

"You see I have this dairy farm upstate and I have to hire a lot of extra hands every now and again, to help me get things done on time and all. I guess I'm just having issues trying to work with these men, when I look out and see a sea of masks all over my field. Every time I look out there my first instinct is to grab my shotgun. It just isn't right what's going on nowadays." Rooster sat down while putting on his cowboy hat in one fluid motion, and I could see real terror in his eyes as if he was back at the farm staring out at those masks.

"A lot of you know similar pain in dealing with the mask policies. I want you to know, Rooster, you're not alone in this fight and were all going to help you through this," The mother of this group spoke but I was only faintly listening as I eliminated Rooster from my list of Face members. I had one job to do here that required me to analyze and eliminate anyone I thought could be involved and I meant to do it right. I was busy looking over the crowd when I became aware that everyone was staring at me in a strange way.

"Sir, it's your turn to introduce yourself. You don't have to of course but trust me, it really helps if you just get past being shy and join the group." I didn't realize it was my turn to speak and suddenly I did feel embarrassed. I snapped to attention after my brief moment of panic and the flash of memories long forgotten.

"I'm d- Wink." I stumbled on my words and almost announced myself to the crowd as Detective Wink, which would have blown the case right then and there.

"I just go by Wink now and my reason for being here is simply because I'm having trouble adjusting to the way things are and I hate wearing this stupid mask." I heard a sound in the back as I went to sit down; it was a rush of air that made psshhhtt sound. Someone in the crowd was blowing off my statement as complete crap and they were right to do so. Maybe at a different time I would have let it go but I was desperate to find the answers surrounding the masquerade murders. I looked at the woman who made the sound; she was across from me and wore a raggedy army jacket with a series of mismatched patches. Her mask was entirely covered by a large peace sign; the eyes were built into the left and right gaps and the mouth in the bottom gap. She was an obvious candidate for Face and already I had lost her by not telling the truth to the group. I had to impress her and there was only one way to do that.

"You know what, that isn't the truth and it isn't even what I meant to say," I burst out to the crowd as I stood back up and readied myself for something extremely painful.

"The truth is, the truth is, I was at home when a couple of masked men knocked on my door. I wasn't ready for them, I messed up bad." I felt the words come out in broken chunks, my voice cracked, and I felt tears sting my eye. I had come to terms with a lot of things but never had I said any of this out loud to anyone. I gripped the laminated C and let it give me strength to continue on with my speech.

"I opened the door, my daughter should have been in bed but she heard the door and came down the stairs to see who it was. I didn't have a chance there was a gun in my face and all it took was that one bullet to graze my eye and continue on to kill my daughter. I would give anything to go back and put my face just a little bit closer to that gun. The bullet should have killed me and only me." Silence hung in the air like a rain cloud; no one could save me from where I was. No one dared say anything good or bad to bring me out of that moment. I felt more emotion than words can describe; I had to save myself or rather Cali had to save me.

"This is something of hers I carry with me, this letter C that she made at school." I held out the laminated C to the crowd like some kind of badge, a badge that meant more than my real one.

"Every time I look at a mask I see the monster who put a bullet in my eye and into my innocent daughter. I will do whatever I have to do to end the masq policy somehow. Adjusting to this thing is a joke, the only answer is to rise up and force the world to reveal its face." I sat down full of real emotion; in that moment I meant every word, and I knew the right people had heard me.

The meeting continued with a few more introductions but I was so red in the face and hot with emotion I couldn't seem to calm down enough to listen. I had said so much more than I had intended. Before the meeting I hadn't really thought about how I would get the attention of Face, I just knew I could. After the introductions the mother of this little meeting got up and started spewing crap about the bunch of steps that were necessary to follow in order to accept this whole thing. Before I knew it the lady was telling us that prayer would help us and that looking to a higher power could get us through these trying times.

"Now, let's hear from a few of our long time members and see what they have been doing to make it through the day to day adjustments of the mask policy."

I was glad to see the girl in the peace sign mask stand up in response to this. "I just want to say that it isn't easy getting through the day to day of dealing with this mask crap, but just take comfort in knowing that better days are coming."

The meeting mother didn't seem to like this and quickly interjected before the girl could on. "Emmeline, remember what we talked about before: there is no reason to believe the masq policy is going to end any time soon, so please do not give false hope to these good people." Emmeline turned to look at the meeting mother and I saw her short blonde hair that just went passed her ears, and I wondered what her face looked like underneath her mask.

"There is no reason not to hope, everyone," Emmeline said and the meeting mother put up her hand like one more word would send her to time out.

"This class is about coping with the masq policy and learning to accept the changes. If you are not here for that then you're not ready to face the truth." The meeting mother had obviously had enough of these outbursts and wasn't going to allow it to continue.

"Ask yourselves what people hide beneath their mask," Emmeline said and turned to walk away from the room. When she did several others jumped up to join her. I counted six out of the room who were ready and willing to follow her out of the meeting. I knew they were members of Face even before she made that last comment and now I had all I needed to join them.

I was the last one out of the room and felt awkward following a group that I wasn't really a part of. Still I knew this was my chance to make my mark with Face and it would be the only opportunity I would ever get. Not a word was exchanged between them on the journey out of the building and into the parking lot. Once we got outside two of the men in the back turned on me and made sure to get close enough to seem very aggressive.

"Who are you man? I don't think we know you," asked a tall man with long hair and a mask that reminded me of a pirate with a mustache and beads dangling from its goatee. The other had dreadlocks and a mask that was more like a biker helmet that covered the whole face and only showed a hint of the person behind a visor.

"Look, I'm just interested in some of the things Emmeline said in there. I just want to talk and see if maybe I can be of use to your cause."

The man with the motorcycle helmet joined in then and I became aware of his muscles and the absolute pride in his movements. "And what is it you think our cause is?" he asked. I didn't know how to answer: if I said they were part of Face they could assume I knew too much, and if I said I didn't know they may think I knew too little. This was a strange predicament, one that would decide the fate of this case, which was enough to keep me from answering right away.

It was Emmeline who spoke then, saving me from having to answer. "I heard your story in there; I know that you meant every word of it. Still you have to understand why we need to be careful. I need you to come out and say what it is you're looking for." Things got a lot more comfortable with Emmeline asking the questions rather than the two brutes who were still in my face. I had to speak. It was now or never.

"I don't know if you guys are members of Face, but even if you're not I have a feeling you might have some ideas on what I can do to end this mask policy. I just want nothing more than to stop this. I don't care who is opposed, I'm with them. I just need to join the right cause and I need to do it now."

"Fair enough, that's all I needed to hear. Come with us. We can't exactly talk here but if you really do want to get involved with Face now is your chance." With that Emmeline walked away and the two brutes backed off in silence, while I followed. A black van came into sight; it was the typical vehicle you would picture for a group of radicals attempting to stick it to the man. Emmeline pulled open the large sliding door and the van opened up revealing a couple of benches on the side and a large open area in the center. Either they had stripped the van, or this was a work vehicle with added seats.

"Not too bad, Emmeline, not too bad," I said, following the girl into the back of the van along with the other members. The guy with the motorcycle mask jumped into the driver seat and he didn't waste any time firing up the vehicle and bolting out of there like we were already on a mission.

"How do I know you are who you say you are?" Emmeline asked once the van turned the corner and headed onto the main street. I thought I'd already proven myself to the team but apparently I needed to do more.

"I know what you said in there was real, but that doesn't just give you an all access pass to people who have every reason to remain anonymous."

I didn't have any way to prove that I was sincere, especially considering I really wasn't. "Look, I can't prove anything to you by speaking. Anyone can lie, but I'm not going to do that. Instead I'm just going to tell you that I am serious about this and I'll do whatever it is you need me to so that you can trust me." Bold words from a detective, however it was necessary to get the group—mainly Emmeline—to believe me. She smiled from below that peace sign mask and it wasn't comforting, but instead looked full of mischief and disobedience.

"Let's just go ahead and see how serious you are about bringing down the masq policy. There's an easy test that I like to do." For a second I was worried but then I saw I had no reason to be, only another reason to be grateful for taking on this mission. Emmeline reached up and lifted the peace mask from her face, slowly and carefully as if she were revealing more than just a face. She lowered the mask and I looked at pale skin with small freckles dotting the area between her nose and cheeks. She had high cheek bones that became more pronounced when she smiled, and a bubble nose that was small and extremely feminine. Her lips came alive while surrounded by her cheeks and chin in ways that I had never seen before. Emmeline couldn't have been older than twenty, but she had small age lines on her face that were clearly beyond her years. The simple sight of a face told a story, one that I hadn't read in a long time. It was beautiful.

"That's all I really needed to see, Mr. Wink." I didn't know what she meant at first, I was so distracted by what I was looking at I didn't see anything else. But I had small tears brimmed in the bottom layer of my eye. They weren't much but Emmeline apparently noticed. I felt like the day ended in the blink of an eye, when she put her mask back on it was night once more.

"For now we have to be careful and keep our masks on most of the time. All it takes is one person to reveal information to the cops and everything we're working for falls apart. I'm telling you this so you don't walk around with your mask off and end up getting arrested." I finally felt like I was recovering from the sight of her perfect face when the van pulled into a warehouse complex.

"Where are we going?" I had been blinded by the moment for so long I hadn't thought to take a second to ask some important questions. A couple other people in the van started talking to one another, which I took as a good sign like I was truly accepted now. The two talking were women, neither of them all that interesting to me; they were the grunts and I was after the big fish.

"To our home base, of course. If you're going to get involved you need to know our protocol and how to contact us." We reached the end of a warehouse district and pulled up to a large building that reminded me of a steel mill, or a production plant. The van pulled around to the back and parked next to a large eighteen wheeler truck that had its back open inside the building, for loading something. I just didn't know what. The van opened up and Emmeline waited with me for everyone else to exit the van and head inside the building.

"Now what you're about to see is to remain between us and other members of Face. I have worked way too hard giving our kind of people a safe haven for some random guy to ruin it." I absently felt for the wire beneath my clothing and when I touched it I felt a ping of guilt so great I wanted to come clean with Emmeline right then and there. Just the thought of Light leading a sea of officers into the heart of the resistance sent pure anger running through my veins.

"Are you sure you're ok with this, because you suddenly don't look so good," Emmeline said with a touch of curiosity and a pound of mockery. I shook the feeling off, vowing to myself to stop Light from ever disturbing this place.

"Yeah, I'm ready. I just started feeling a little overwhelmed for a minute. I'm not used to this kind of stress in my life these days." Emmeline blew out some air just like she did in the meeting earlier, like she knew I was full of pure bullshit. She hopped out of the van and signaled for me to follow; I did as I was told.

Emmeline walked past the semi until she reached an all white plain door. She grabbed the silver handle and walked inside holding the door open so I could follow. I took my first steps into the biggest criminal organization in the area, and it was all I could do to keep from smiling.

 People were running all over the place lifting boxes, driving forklifts, talking into radios—all jobs that looked normal for a factory like this. People were actually working, going back and forth with the real determination of any real factory worker.

"I don't understand. I thought this was the headquarters for Face?" Emmeline was standing by, waiting for me to catch up after I took in the sights of the place. As she continued walking, she ducked under a certain spot where a series of pallets were resting on a metal beam. Emmeline was moving though this place as if it was her actual home, and maybe it was.

"This is the headquarters for Face, but it's also Packered Distribution. We specialize in taking large orders and shipping them out in much smaller quantities. You would be surprised by how many people pay money just to have us separate and bring to them what they could have bought themselves." Emmeline had some kind of pride in this warehouse; I could tell by the way she looked around it—for her this place meant something.

"Here, follow me this way." Emmeline was excited as she moved beyond the workers; she was young and vibrant and something about her gave me hope for the future. We came to a break room where I thought we would stop, but instead she kept on moving. A back storeroom came into view, a large space full of pallets and boxes but no people. It was quiet and even a little cold. A set of stairs were tucked in the back corner and Emmeline didn't waste any time running down them.

"Okay, just down here and then you're right in the heart of Face." At the bottom of the steps I opened up a door that led into a room beyond my wildest dreams. On the walls were cork boards with locations and plans all laid out in the proper police fashion. People were flipping through papers—some of them looked like typical hippies while others were in business suits and looked like lawyers. All of this was interesting but none of it mattered to me, not at first anyway, because I was far too busy looking at all the faces in the room. That's right: no one inside of this place was wearing a mask, no one.

Fifteen

"Pretty crazy isn't it?" Emmeline said from behind me and when I turned, once again I could see that perfect little face of hers. She even bit her lip in a sort of, I know you're looking at me, type of performance, and she was right.

"I can't even handle what I'm looking at. It seems so wrong that I feel the way I do." So many faces filled the room but instead of feeling joy I felt conflicted and had this strange sense of longing to be one of them, to be fighting against the man and not for him.

"Here, have a seat. We can just take this one step at a time. First, let me explain how this place works." Emmeline pointed me toward a chair and I fell into it as if it were a bed that I had been waiting all day to collapse into. She placed the chair expertly so that I was only facing her and not all the mask-less commotion going on behind me.

"Upstairs is a real business—I wasn't joking about that— but down here we're in the business of unmasking America. We do have the radical protesters here that work in ways that may not seem important, but they are. The protesters rally the people and put the media's attention on us and our cause." Instantly I thought of the people running around town without their masks on that I had seen on TV just the other day. Curiously I remembered the green jacket and the patches that Emmeline wore.

"On the other side of things we have people who file appeals, write up letters to important officials, and look for loopholes in the system that we can use to our benefit." All of this was far more intriguing than I ever thought it would be. I had pictured nothing more than a group of kids in some basement planning free the animal type missions. Still, as impressive as this all was, I found myself thinking only of Emmeline and how she fit into it all.

"So where does that put you in all of this?" I asked.

Emmeline smiled and blushed a little at the same time. I knew then that hiding her face was a true crime. "I guess I'm sort of a boss, or, I may not be the boss, but I'm definitely the number two in charge around here." She was so young, and so petite, it was almost comical seeing this tiny, beautiful woman boast about being at the top of the movement's leadership ladder.

"I'm just going to take a guess: does that mean this Angel woman I keep hearing about is the person in charge of Face?"

Emmeline changed her expression immediately, to a jealous, "here we go again" type of look.

"Angel is the boss of this place, but she doesn't really show herself and never goes out on any missions like the rest of us do. In fact, I don't even think she should be the boss. Alright that's not really true but she's my big sister so I guess I'm allowed to talk a little crap." I suddenly realized who I had been talking to the entire time.

"You're Angel's sister? Does that mean you could arrange a little meeting for me?" The look on her face came right back, and it was sour as a face could look. I was striking a very sensitive subject.

"Sorry, I can't really do that. I mean you haven't even been on a mission with us or anything and I'm not even supposed to bring you down here until then." I didn't know if Emmeline was serious or was just trying to find an excuse, so I let it go for the moment.

"So why did you, bring me down here so fast I mean?"

Emmeline blushed a little bit and I took it in, enjoying how much of her emotions came out on her face. "Because I desperately need another body who hasn't already been arrested. A lot of my guys have a rap sheet and they can't get into trouble again. There is something I have planned for tomorrow morning and I wanted to give you the crash course before you helped out with something so serious." Once more I touched the wire and wondered if Detective Light would approve of me doing something illegal for information.

"I'm ready for anything you can throw my way, the sooner we get to this the better." I was eager to get on with this; I didn't have the time for a long investigation. Emmeline nodded and then stood up, holding up her finger to indicate she'd be back in a moment, before she walked across the room and started going through papers. I watched the other members moving around the room and couldn't believe how much there was to see in every person's face. All the crinkles of age and the lines of wisdom looked natural and amazing. The flaws of every man and woman could be seen and each and every one of them seemed important. Even the facial hair on a man's face defined him, set him apart from the others with different styles and distinguishing features. I stared in wonder while Emmeline found what she was looking for pretty fast and came right back to me.

"Take a look at this." She handed a couple of pages over to me that contained a few black and white pictures and a few lines of information. I knew what I was looking at but I didn't really understand what I was supposed to be seeing in the pages.

"I don't really know what this means."

Emmeline shook her head like I was just some simpleton, but being more playful than rude. "Don't you see, there's a televised event about the masq policies and an update on what to expect in the coming years when the masq policy is extended. It's the perfect time to break in there and give the people a chance to see some faces." I looked back down, not to look at the papers but to decide if this was really something I wanted to get involved in.

"The Mayor, the Chief of Police, the District Attorney—just about every important official is going to be there. It's the perfect chance to stick it to the man." Emmeline laughed and I started laughing with her, only because I was thinking about the room full of important people that I was just with the other day. How hilarious would it be for the lead detective to show his face on TV to the world with all of his superiors present?

"I guess I see your point. When does this thing start?" After the laughter I got back to the questions and Emmeline did the same, cutting away from the fun and focusing on reality.

"According to those papers it goes live at nine in the morning, which means we need to be ready way before that. So if you are interested we plan on meeting at the news station about seven." I didn't even give it any thought. I was excited to do something with Emmeline, and more than that I was still trying to solve this case.

"I'll be there; it's about time I did something with all this energy that I feel towards the cause." The response I got from Emmeline was that of pure pleasure that I was willing to go with her after only just joining up with Face.

I wanted to stay there all night with Emmeline, but things don't always go the way we want them to. For starters I knew Light was listening on the other end and to make things worse there was a lot going on at the factory. I hoped there would be time later to be around her but reality had a way of bringing such fantasies to an end.

"Okay, so how do I get back to my car?" I asked this sometime later after we had gone over the plan and I knew what was to be expected of me the next morning. The operation didn't frighten me one bit; the only thing I was afraid of was dealing with Light after this.

"Oh, I'll take you back to your car, sorry to keep you here all night. I guess it is starting to get late. We better end this if we're going to pull this off in the morning." I was shocked that I was the one who'd ended the conversation. I followed Emmeline out of the factory, but we didn't go to the van. Instead we went to a brand new green Prius and she jumped into the driver's seat.

"It figures you would have this car. Isn't it a little out of your price range though? I mean, being a rebel against society can't be all that profitable."

Emmeline put the car into gear as I spoke, but she didn't answer right away, she only started to drive. This was the first time I had seen her be serious all night, or maybe she just seemed serious with her mask back on.

"Why didn't you take off your mask while you were at the factory?" Emmeline suddenly asked me and I really didn't know how to answer.

"Come to think of it, I didn't even notice. I guess I was so busy looking at all the faces that I forgot about my own." I laughed a little bit at how strange it was for me to forget such a thing, and how weird I must have looked in there, the only one wearing a mask.

"The reason I have this car is because I own that factory. Well, my sister and I own the warehouse. My father is no longer with us and he left his business to Angel and I. It's part of the reason we keep it running, and also part of the reason Angel is so busy."

Just when I thought I knew Emmeline, she revealed a secret that surprised me. The respect I had for Emmeline went up tenfold in that moment. Here was a rich girl, not some poor hippie but a rich girl fighting for a cause she believed in. "I'm sorry about your father," I said in a low soothing way and Emmeline smiled but it was a hurt smile, a wounded smile.

"My dad was a great man, but the masq policy was hard for him and with my mother already gone there really wasn't many options left for us. It's a terrible feeling when you're alone. I can't imagine what I would do without me sister, she's the only real family I have left." Emmeline focused on the road and I could see a shimmer of tears in her eyes reflecting off other car headlights. I wanted to say something to soothe her but I already used the sentence I could think of saying and repeating that again just seemed pathetic. However, Emmeline broke the silence for me.

"I guess now we're even: we both know about the saddest moments in each other's life." If we hadn't pulled into the parking lot where I left Light, I would have told her the truth right then and there. I was feeling a lot of guilt for involving this girl with me and my case; I knew only bad things would come of it.

"Thanks for everything, Emmeline. I will see you in the morning for operation Face Flash."

Emmeline laughed a little bit at my made up name for the mission while she parked the car by the doors where I first followed her to the van. "I like that—Face Flash. The name works. I guess this is goodbye for now then."

I looked at Emmeline and her peace sign mask and wondered if she was hoping for something romantic from me. I would have killed to be with her but I already felt bad enough as it was, I didn't need to make matters worse by getting involved like that.

"Goodnight, Emmeline," I said and with a single touch on her leg I stepped out of the car and tried not to look back as I walked to where Light was waiting. I couldn't stop myself, though, from shooting one last glance at her, and she smiled right back at me.

"You took long enough, didn't you? Do you know how long I've been sitting here listening to you flirt with that criminal?"

I sat down in the car and didn't even have a moment to speak before Light was bombarding me with his anger that had built up in the past hours. "I have to get in good with them; if you can't handle the time then I will find someone else to listen in. Anyone can do it, except maybe you, it would seem."

Detective Light peeled out of the parking lot, obviously too angry to talk, so instead he only drove me straight to my car. I enjoyed the silence while we traveled back to the police station; it gave me time to reflect on all that happened, and mostly to think about Emmeline.

"You need to think about how far you're willing to go just to obtain some information. Maybe if this was a real case that the Captain and others had signed off on. Then you could do something illegal, but the way we are doing this, I don't think it's such a good idea." Light pulled me up to my car after giving me his two cents and I made a decision right then and there.

"I'm not really going to go with Face and get involved with some criminal action; I'm just going to make something up as to why I couldn't show up. Come on, Light, I just want information and if a couple of white lies get me there then so be it."

Light let out a sigh of relief before holding out his hand for my wire that I had been wearing all night. "That's good to hear. Now hand me that wire so I can take this stuff home and finish my notes for the department."

This was the part of the plan I was regretting; I couldn't let Light bring down Face. It just wasn't right.

"I was thinking we wouldn't bring down Face after all this. I mean, we're here to solve a murder and that's all; we don't want to do anything more than that. I'm not going to run off busting them, but just in case we can't solve this thing I want something to show for our efforts. Bringing down the majority of Face would be a massive achievement, one that would offset our failures on this case." There was no reason to argue with Light right now. I would save that for another time; I knew there would be one. I handed over the wires and he put them with the rest of the stuff he had been working on.

"Alright, I will see you back at the station in the morning," I said before stepping out of the car before giving my partner any more time to speak. I didn't want him to ask any more questions.

"See you in the morning, Detective Wink," I heard before I shut the door and went straight to my vehicle, wondering if he was watching me the whole time. The sooner I got away the better I felt. I had every intention of joining up with Face in the morning and I didn't want Light to know that.

I spent the rest of the night in a very good mood, thinking only about seeing Emmeline again. For the few hours I slept, I was out like a baby. Thinking about her was like being back in high school and being on a date for the first time. Even though it was all just an impossible dream, at the time it felt real, and like everything could work out in the end.

*****

I was early to the meeting spot; with so much pent up energy, I just couldn't wait to do this. I finally had a place to put all of my hatred for the masq policy. The familiar van pulled up right on schedule and Emmeline jumped out and moved into a hug before I was ready.

"You actually came; I was worried you wouldn't show up."

I looked down and saw her batting those deep blue eyes; I hadn't noticed how great they were before. Today she was wearing all black, from black pants to black boots and even a tight black shirt. In fact, they were all wearing black and I suddenly felt very out of place in my gray hooded sweater and jeans. Emmeline turned and grabbed something out of the van, all the while still keeping one hand on my side in a small awkward hug.

"Here, put these on. You don't want to go in wearing anything that people can identify later." Now I would fit in with an all black outfit topped off with a peace sign mask that was also all black. I jumped in the van and changed as quickly as possible, not wanting to keep my team waiting. It was a good thing that I hadn't worn the wire because the driver of the van watched me the whole time and would have caught me right then and there. After getting dressed I stepped out and saw the members of Face already in a huddle, with a space left for me next to Emmeline.

"What do they hide beneath a mask?" Emmeline said to the group after I joined and put an arm around her back, completing the circle. In unison we spoke like football players psyching one another up with a chant. Even I knew the answer and I said it along with everyone else, as if this was all meant to be.

"Everything!" I yelled with the group and our hands went down and the team burst into action. I went with Emmeline and a couple of other guys to the back of the news station while the rest of the team headed to the front of the doors, a difficult spot to enter. Our path was much easier as we simply entered by a dumpster to a service door and were inside. Immediately I could hear words echoing inside the main chamber of this place, and I wondered if things had started early. We came to a corner facing the main entrance to the press conference and saw two security guards holding a post at the doors.

"Come on, we need to find the doors to the back of the stage area," Emmeline whispered and turned back around so that we could find another way. We were darting down a hallway when I saw two police officers coming toward us. Emmeline pushed through a side door and we ended up inside a kitchen, staying just out of sight of the officers.

I felt pure adrenaline rush through my veins while we moved from hallway to hallway until we saw the wide double doors that obviously led up to the back of the stage. We were still early, but now that I was close enough to listen to the voice I had heard earlier I realized it was just a mike check. One guard was posted at this door for the moment but I knew it wouldn't be long before a lot more officers arrived. Emmeline looked at one of her people and the girl nodded—she already knew that she had a job to do. The girl pulled off her black peace mask revealing a smaller back up mask that barely covered the center of her face. She pulled off the black shirt and pants and stood up in just her underwear.

"Thank you for your sacrifice. I will not leave you in there for long," Emmeline whispered and the girl nodded as she headed down toward the guard. The security guard saw her but didn't act, instead only looking her up and down not sure what she was going to do. She pulled the mask off of her face and stuck her tongue out in a comical display that sent the guard chasing after her. The girl was fast and she didn't let running around without a lot of clothes on trouble her one bit.

"This is our chance—come on," Emmeline whispered and we all made our move on the door, entering quickly and quietly into the staging area. Behind the doors there were stairs at the top of which was all the equipment necessary to light the stage and power the mikes. Emmeline found a spot at the back for all of us to hide and wait for the signal, when we would move and make our mark. For now it was only time to wait in the silence, with only one another's breathing to comfort us as the minutes passed.

One after another people showed up and took their seats for the conference; every few minutes I could hear people walking back and forth to get to their seats on the stage. That meant the people closest to me were bosses and superiors at the police station. If I were to get caught right here in this moment I didn't

know how I would explain the situation. That made this simple—
we just couldn't get caught. It took awhile for things to get
underway but once they did we didn't waste any time springing
into action. Emmeline had an ear piece firmly placed with a
connection to the other members of Face and she waited for their
go ahead. I waited listening to the muffled voices beginning the
speech for the live TV audience.

"Alright, I have the signal. Get ready everyone—you know
what to do."

My heart started beating faster than I ever remembered it
beating, and for a second I wondered just what the hell I was
doing. Just then the lights to the building went out, followed by a
rush scared sounding noises from the crowd, as we began to move.
Emmeline had night vision goggles on and she led the way. All we
had to do was stay close and follow. We reached our position and
then spread out creating a full line across the front of the stage so
the crowd and cameras could see us.

"People of America, do not forget the sight of a face,
because if you do all will be lost," Emmeline spoke to the crowd
and cameras, her voice signaling the lights to be turned back on.
There we all stood in front of everyone, our faces exposed, my face
exposed. I gripped the peace mask in my hand, wanting so badly to
put it back on. The masked faces of the crowd only looked up at us
in awe, just as I did the night before when I first saw Emmeline's
face.

"We hide everything beneath a mask. Don't be slaves to the
government: make a stand, unmask here and now." Her confidence
amazed me. This young girl was speaking out to the world, and in
our current situation she was naked, her face exposed, yet still she
was defiant.

"Over there, get them." I heard officers pointing as they ran up the stage only moments away from arresting all of us. With a flash the lights to the building went out once more and this time we started our run for the exit, Emmeline leading the way. I had my mask back on and was running with all my might, and I figured the other members of Face were all doing the same. Emmeline kicked the doors open and we smashed our way through the two security guards who were waiting on the other side.

"Come on, it's this way! Hurry, we have to hurry." Emmeline urged us on but not all of us were as fast as she was, and I started to fall to the back. I was supposed to be in shape but most of these kids were in their twenties; I just didn't have the energy they did. We pushed open the doors and were flooded with light, the sun already high in the sky and promising we would escape.

"Get on the ground right now!" Police officers had formed a perimeter and weren't about to let us get away easily. Emmeline had already a set path for us to follow and there weren't enough police to catch us all. Still I felt panic; our path led right through the center of the police, so they were definitely going to catch a couple of us. One guy got tackled, another girl got grabbed, but Emmeline was in the front and dashed passed them before they could get her. I was in the back and they had plenty of time to prepare for me.

"On the ground now, do not make me use force." The officer talking to me didn't get the chance. I put my knee into his groin area and hard. He collapsed and I felt terrible, but I had to escape. I couldn't imagine what would happen if I actually got caught. A couple others got away and we cut across two parking lots before we came to the van. Everyone jumped inside and the driver took off. Immediately everyone started changing their clothes.

"We made it; I didn't think we were going to for a second there." Emmeline was laughing hard and naturally the rest of us did the same. We all felt amazing as we threw down the black clothes and masks we wore and put our regular stuff back on. I was panting from running and laughing and from trying to talk. Everyone was in the midst of changing their clothes and I shot a glance at Emmeline who had her back to everyone so no one saw her chest. Still I saw her from the back and when she turned she noticed I had been staring, I had to quickly save the situation by talking to the group.

"I think I might have kneed a cop in the crotch. I don't know what the hell I was thinking." I didn't know why this was so funny but everyone laughed as though I'd made a hilarious joke.

"I didn't bring my car; do you want to take me back to the warehouse in yours?" Emmeline asked me once we reached my jeep that was parked closer to the police station than it should have been.

"Yeah, that would be great," I said happily. Already today had been better than I could have hoped, and to top things off I was going to get more private time with Emmeline. We got out of the van and went straight to my jeep, not wanting to be out in the open if we could avoid it. I started driving but didn't know all that well how to get to the warehouse, so Emmeline had to give me directions. After we were on our way I started to have questions and thought Emmeline wouldn't mind answering me.

"So what's going to happen to the people who got caught?"

Emmeline immediately got serious. "I won't leave them in there for long. I have certain people I use just to bail out and pay off the fines of Face members. Of course those who got caught won't be usable for some time, since repeat offenders get harsher punishments, which leads to deals being made and all of us getting caught."

She was smart, I had to say that much. There was a good reason why Face hadn't been brought down yet: it was Emmeline.

"So what's on the agenda for the rest of the day?" I wasn't really serious but I did want to stay with her if I could, even if that meant I didn't show up for work today. For some reason I didn't really care anymore. I was getting caught up in the moment. Once Emmeline answered me, though, she reminded me why I had starting this little endeavor with Face in the first place.

"Well I was thinking if you still wanted to, you could get your chance to talk with my sister." Angel, the one person who would know everything about Face and their involvement with the masquerade murders—she was the whole reason I was here.

"Do you think she would talk to me?"

Emmeline smiled again with that jealous look. It made me sad, but I really did need to speak with Angel.

"Yeah, she would be happy to talk with anyone willing to stand up on camera and announce that they are a member of Face." I got my meeting with Angel and in record time, but I did think Emmeline was wrong. There was no way Angel was going to be happy with the questions I was going to ask. I could only hope Emmeline wouldn't pay for falling victim to my lies.

"Talking with Angel would be great, thanks Emmeline. I appreciate everything you're doing for me." I hated what was about to happen, and I could only hope at the end of all of this I wouldn't lose Emmeline forever.

Sixteen

Angel was already waiting for me in a different part of the warehouse, a part I hadn't seen yet. At the other end from where I was standing the previous night was an office where Angel apparently spent most of her time. According to Emmeline, her sister was not only the head of Face but was also the head of a major distribution corporation and that kept her busy most of the time.

"So after you have your talk with Angel, we should go out and get a cup of coffee or something." Emmeline was asking me on a date of sorts and right before I was about to interrogate Angel and possibly ruin any confidence Angel had in her sister. My heart sank at the thought and for a long time I couldn't decide what to do. It occurred to me that I could just quit being a detective and just let things happen the way they would without me. It most certainly would be a better life, especially if it meant I got to spend my time with Emmeline.

"Yeah, if you still want to, I would absolutely love that."

Emmeline smiled and I continued to think things over in my head; I really didn't know what to do. Running around with kids and pulling elaborate pranks on the world was fun, but the idea of catching my murderer was even better. I always loved bringing down a killer and so far I'd had nothing but bad luck. Here and now I had a chance at some real information. There was more to this life than having a little fun, and besides I was too old for the young and rebellious Emmeline.

"Alright, I'll be out here. Oh, and my sister can be a little mean, so just don't take it personally," Emmeline squinted up her nose in distaste for her sister and I almost laughed out loud at how ridiculous it looked. I was standing there in the warehouse basement with my mask on and decided there was something I wanted to do before I went inside. I pulled the mask from my face and exposed my old age, my flaws, and even my missing eye for her to see.

"Emmeline, thank you for everything, I can't remember the last time I had this much fun."

She smiled widely and pressed her lips to my cheek, just a little peck but it was enough to make me regret what I was about to do even more. In some way I knew things would never be the same between us so I just wanted to feel something with her, if only for a moment.

Finally, I walked away from her and went over to the office door at the back of the room. It was plain wood with nothing more than a small window with the blinds drawn closed. I knocked three times in the rhythmic way as Emmeline had instructed and I heard the expected answer.

"Enter," a strong female voice said, and I did, taking care to open the door carefully and shut it in just the same manner. I had my mask off; I didn't want to be disrespectful to a leader who felt pride in showing her face.

"Emmeline tells me you have something you want to talk to me about, so what is it?" The woman at the other end of the desk had long blonde hair and a face that looked like a model's. She didn't wear a mask but instead had thick lines of silver makeup that shined like glitter next to both of her eyes. She wore a tight fitting suit jacket and skirt, and I could tell this woman was more business than pleasure, at least at this point in her life.

"I was just hoping to ask you a few questions about something in particular, if you have the time that is. I can always come back later." Angel stood up from her desk and placed a folder in a stand at the top of a file cabinet, revealing to me how tall she was. Even though she was wearing silver heels that matched her makeup, it was clear she didn't need them. She sat back down and let out an awful, annoyed sigh that made me want to leave rather than ask her anything.

"No, I don't think I want to keep a Detective down here in my warehouse. It's bad for my business if you know what I mean."

I had walked into a trap; the leader of Face already knew exactly who I was. In fact I was starting to wonder if everyone already knew who I was from the start. Was Emmeline only toying with me? Was she just trying to see how far she could go by playing with my emotions?

"So if you already know who I am, why agree to see me?"

Angel shook her head as if she had all the answers and I was only wasting her time with each passing moment. "Don't worry, I didn't know the entire time, or trust me you never would have made it this far. But now I have information against you. There is no way your department would sanction you showing your face on camera, not to mention assaulting an officer. I also know you have a thing for my sister. You wouldn't want her finding out the truth, now would you?" She had me by the balls and there wasn't much I could do without risking myself and ruining everything I had with Emmeline.

"Okay, fine, you have me there, but what I want to ask you is serious and it is worth whatever punishment I have to face with the department."

Angel nodded and seemed a little surprised that all of her threats didn't scare me; at least that's how I acted.

"Fine, go right ahead, ask and you shall receive whatever you want to know. Careful, though, Detective—you may not like what you hear. Trust me I am not one to lie, no matter who I'm talking to."

Experience told me she meant every word of that, which meant it was now or never to get the answers that I came for. "Alright, look, there have been a series of murders that have taken place at these mansion parties and I have it on good authority that Face is involved somehow."

Angel remained still and emotionless, looking at me like she was staring into my soul. "I am aware of these murders you're speaking of and for you to even think for one second that Face would be involved in such things is just ridiculous. You have spent time with the primary members of our organization and during that time have you seen anything close to murder plots. Take a good look around: we're an activist group doing our part to restore society. We would never stoop so low as to kill anyone."

I felt as small as a person could. While I may have been wrong to think Face was involved, she hadn't really answered my question. I wanted more. "Listen, I know the group I've been with wouldn't kill anybody but I'm not talking about one of your close members or even your sister. I want to know about any Face members who seem violent, maybe ones who thought a more active force would solve the problem faster." I wasn't about to lose my nerve to this business woman. I had authority and she had a lot more to lose then I did, whether she knew it or not.

"Actually there has been one new member to Face that has shown violent tendencies and is a liar of epic proportions."

I knew where this was going and I didn't like it.

Angel continued, "You are the only person I have ever had serving me who has assaulted an officer, and you are the only one who has consistently lied to my sister and the rest of Face."

I was tired of having the blame shifted on me just because it was convenient for everyone and I wasn't about to take it anymore. "You listen to me: all I have to do is make one call and this place will be shut down forever and then your daddy is going to turn over in his grave because you fucked up. Trust me, devil, you have a lot more to lose then I do." The tables turned and I took over the conversation, making it very clear that I thought she was the opposite of an angel.

"If that's how you want to play it, very well Detective. I will tell you everything I know." I could tell she was full of anger but she was a business woman and would remain calm and collected when necessary.

"Good. Let's start with anyone who might be a possible suspect." I took out my notepad and pen and prepared to write down names and numbers. Time was of the essence if my answers were even going to matter.

"Let me be as clear as I can to you, Detective Wink. I don't want you to take offense because I really do not want police shutting down my factory. I personally know every person who has been here and is still here working with Face and none of them would be responsible for murder."

I didn't want to believe it, no matter how sincerely she said it, and I just couldn't walk away now. If I'd ruined things with Emmeline—the best thing to happen in my life in a long time—I had to come away with some answers.

"That's impossible. How do you know for a fact that no one has had a change of heart and decided to start killing to get the point across?" I was angry at her, but mostly I was angry at myself for wasting everyone's time and destroying everything with Emmeline. Getting answers wasn't even the point anymore. Now it was all about proving that I hadn't been wrong.

"If you haven't noticed, the kinds of people who work with Face aren't the murdering types. They're here to make the world a better place, not to kill people."

I knew she was right but it wasn't something I could face. Now of course I wish I would have just listened to Angel.

"Look if you really don't believe I can let you ask the very person involved with each and every member of Face and she will set you straight."

She was talking about Emmeline. Unfortunately, my pride wouldn't let me just face the facts and walk away; I had to hear it from Emmeline herself. "Just bring her in here. I am only here for answers and that's exactly what I'm going to get." As the words left my mouth I regretted every one of them, but it was too late to change what I had done. I'd ruined everything. Angel picked up her phone and sent off a text message before I could get the courage to squash my pride and stop this from happening.

"What did you need?" Emmeline said from the doorway. Her voice was small and weak, like a mouse's in a room with lions. I put a hand on my face from the sheer embarrassment of the moment that was about to get even uglier, thanks to me.

"Your buddy here has some questions for you. It seems he isn't satisfied with my assurances, so he wants to hear from you."

Emmeline had seemed powerful, confident, and strong, but now looked worried, confused, and sad.

"Look, this isn't easy for me but I have to ask." I was trying to find the right words to make this more soothing for Emmeline, the person I had been lying to this whole time.

"Quit trying to sugar coat the whole thing and just ask the question," Angel said, making damn sure that I wouldn't be able to save the situation. She wanted me to suffer for threatening her.

"Fine, here it is. Emmeline I'm a detective and I need to solve some serious murders that may be connected to certain members of Face." The words stung my lips like poison. It had been a long time since I hated myself the way I did in that moment; the look on Emmeline's face broke my heart.

"So everything has been a lie? You set me up from the beginning. You even made up that stuff about a daughter and that she was murdered, and I can't even believe I trusted you." Emmeline was lost for a long moment in the lies I'd told.

I tried explaining, to make her see that it wasn't as bad as it looked, but it was all in vain. "Emmeline, it wasn't like that and not everything was a lie. I just needed information and this was the best way to get it. You have to know everything else was the truth.

I was with you at the press conference you know and I meant the things I said." I wanted Emmeline to know the truth but she wasn't going to have it, at least not in this scene, not at this moment.

"No, don't worry about explaining yourself, Detective; I'm sure you have plenty of immunity to do whatever you want, as long as you get the information. You want the truth, that's fine, I can give you whatever answers you want, but that's all you're going to get." This wasn't a movie and it didn't end with the guy getting the girl. This was real life and that meant I wouldn't get a second chance.

"As far as your stupid murders go, let me explain something to you, since you didn't get it while you were out with us. Face isn't here to kill people. I am not here to kill people, and I can personally guarantee to you that not one of our people has killed someone for our cause." Emmeline had taken all that sadness from the betrayal and turned it into pure anger.

"If you don't have any more questions could you kindly get the fuck out of our warehouse, Detective?" Out of everything she said, the word detective stung the most, sounding the way she said it like a joke, like I was nothing but a joke to her.

"Emmeline I promise I won't bring the police here, you guys should be fine." I was trying to explain to Emmeline that I was just doing my job but Angel cut in before I could really get to what I wanted to say.

"Detective, you have the information you came for. Now get out of here before this becomes a legal issue for the both of us." We knew things about one another and this was the last stop before things became a whole lot worse. I had to get out now while I could.

"Goodbye, Emmeline," I said but she didn't even look at me, but instead stared at the wall like it was far more interesting than I was. I waited another second for her to say something but when she didn't, I took the hint and walked away.

*****

Later that night I slept alone in my apartment. I didn't even bother going into work the next day. I didn't have any intention of letting Light know why I wasn't there so I turned my phone off. All I wanted to do was escape the world with sleep and with dreams. There were so many things wrong in my life and getting a taste of something amazing only brought me back to earth in the worst way. I didn't care about the police department anymore that was for sure. I was finished trying to be something I wasn't. Those were my thoughts as I spent the evening sleeping, with my phone off and my mind in another place.

I awoke the next day in the middle of the afternoon. I had slept something close to seventeen hours and I was ready to get back to some more. Except I was woken up by someone banging angrily on my door. For some time I lay there, knowing there was a good chance it was someone I didn't want to see, so there was no reason to answer. But then a thought crossed my mind that maybe Emmeline had a change of heart and tracked me down here and that everything was going to be just fine. I knew it was a long shot but just the thought of things being that easy was enough to get me out of bed.

"Hang on, just a second I'm coming," I said, though not really loud enough for anyone to hear. I was still mostly dressed and I grabbed my mask on my way to the door. I pulled open the door already half expecting to see Emmeline and that peace sign mask waiting for me on the other side.

"What the hell were you thinking?" Detective Light yelled at me, showing yet another side of him I hadn't really seen yet. He stepped inside and shut the door behind him. I didn't move an inch so he was right in my face when he started speaking again.

"Showing your face on national TV and with the mayor and the chief and god knows who else all standing around and watching. You have made me responsible for you by involving me with your undercover mission and then you pull a stunt that could land you in prison?"

I never thought of myself as an overly aggressive person, but I really almost hit Light right then and there.

"To make matters even worse you don't even show up for work twice in a row and you leave your partner hanging to answer all the questions? People have seen your real face and it isn't going to take long for the Captain to figure out that we were both involved in this." Light the angry dog was pushing me too far.

"Listen up, Light, I don't need you telling me how to act. I did what I had to for information and I got exactly what I was looking for. So why don't you just back up before I get really pissed off." Light did change his tone then, not because of the threat, but because he thought I knew something important about the case.

"What did you find out? Do you know who might be involved in the masquerade murders?"

I really wished I knew the answers then, not for the sake of the case but just to have something to rub Light's nose in.

"I can tell you for a fact that Face has no involvement with the murders," I said plainly, letting Light take in my attitude. I wanted him to know that I really didn't care.

"Well isn't that just convenient for you and that precious little Emmeline. I wouldn't believe a word of anything you found out. It's pretty obvious how lost in the moment you were with that little hippie bitch."

Veins were standing out in my neck and only sheer restraint was keeping me from tearing that two-faced fuck's head off. "Watch it, Light. You're a little young to be barking off like you know anything about what I'm doing. I've been putting criminals away for a long time I don't need you in my house telling me what I do wrong." Even I was shocked at how calmly I was handling this situation, though some part of me did know Light had a point.

"I guess you're right. I mean it really isn't all that bad." Light dropped the macho man thing and starting acting a little bit more normal, a little too normal and a little too fast. "We can always just give up Face. Then the bosses can't be too mad at us for not finding anything out involving the murders."

Something kicked in then and restraint was impossible. I ran at Light and smashed him hard against the wall of the apartment, shaking the wall and knocking a couple of pictures to the floor.

"That's exactly what we're not going to do. If you even try to bring them down I will personally make sure you pay for each and every one of them." I looked Light deep in the eyes and made sure he knew I meant every word of it; I could tell he believed me. I held him there for another moment before releasing him and taking three steps back, waiting for him to talk.

"Well, I guess there isn't anything else to say other than I'll see you in the Captain's office in a couple of days." With that Light turned around and headed out of the apartment, and a second later the door slammed hard enough to knock the last picture off the wall.

No matter what I said or did when Light came over that day I knew that he was right. How could I explain what I was doing to the Captain, or make the mayor see that I was in the right by breaking the law right in front of him? I had a lot of questions, but the one that stuck with me was, how did Light know it was me? How was it that he knew the sight of my face? Was it the missing eye? Had it been so easy to see in the video? Of course I wasn't watching it when it happened and I had yet to actually see what I did on camera. I had a lot of questions but they faded away with time just like everything else did. Time has a funny way of stealing our true emotions.

Truthfully the hunt for Face had been a complete waste of time. I believed that they were not involved in the murders and that meant I was no closer to solving the case. There wasn't much time left to find the answers I was looking for, and that meant I was going to be back in the office as a failure. The Captain and all the other bigwigs of the police department would not be happy with another let down, and I had no idea how they were going to act this time.

I would have gone back to bed and just let the world do its thing; I would have enjoyed my rest and forgot the pain but something got me back on my feet. The festival masquerade was coming soon and that meant more than just fun and games; it meant it was time for another murder.

Seventeen

Luck was finally on my side because the Captain never talked to me about my face showing up on TV. In fact, he never mentioned anything I had done over those past couple of days. I even had the government sticker on my mask, so there was no reason to get into any trouble. Things actually went pretty smoothly the next couple of days at work following my two day hiatus.

Light and I avoided each other like the plague, communicating only through glares of hate and disgust. This was another reason to feel lucky, and now that luck was running in my direction, I was ready for yet another masquerade. In fact, everyone was getting ready for the masquerade—the entire department was going to be involved this time. Even the mayor was having some involvement, doing his part to make sure everyone had access to the party. This meant issuing everyone temporary masks without the government stickers. By the look of things the festival was going to have more police at one time than the entire city of New York. I just wished I would be the one to get my hands on the wicked killer and not some random police officer who happened to be in the right place at the right time.

During the last couple of days at the police department I wrote a very long and carefully worded report that went to the Captain and then on up the chain of command. This report detailed my findings in the Face organization and the conclusion that they were not involved. I had to leave a few things out here and change some details there, but all in all I think I made the right decision. At least my way we weren't going to get called in to discuss things, which would have given Light a chance to expose me right in front of our superiors. The Captain received the report and even though he wasn't happy, he accepted what I had found as at least a means of eliminating some possible suspects. The other higher ups didn't even care anymore, since all their attention was on the coming masquerade party.

I can't be sure what Light was up to on those days but I can say he was busy. Most of the time he wasn't even at the office but was out doing some kind of leg work instead. When he was at his desk the guy was a man possessed and spent all of his time working on some large report. I could only assume he had his own letter to write for the Captain but with the time he was taking on it I wasn't worried, yet.

I drove by the warehouse a couple of times and thought about trying to talk to Emmeline but it just seemed too difficult and I knew it wouldn't amount to anything. She had been a distraction from my life, but already she was fading away piece by piece.

All my time and energy, along with that of the rest of the department went into preparations for the festival masquerade party. Only when the day finally came we discovered that none of us were really ready for what was about to happen.

******

I walked into the familiar scene of the masquerade party, with my pistol tucked into my holster and my backup knife sheathed where it belonged at the bottom of my pant leg. Tonight the mansion was filled with festive decorations, similar to something you would see at a cheesy Hawaiian hotel party. Security didn't hassle me on the way in; in fact no one seemed to have a hard time getting into the festival. People were moving freely around, which struck me as very strange.

"Greetings, party goers and welcome to the festival. Try to enjoy the party but remember to be safe and stay in groups whenever possible." Funny Bunny spoke to the crowd with a little less pizzazz then I had grown used to. Even Rosie seemed like dead weight at his side. His voice lacked emotion and there wasn't a lot of spectacle to go with his display. The only thing I could think was he was tired after all the police and murder investigations.

"The party is going on all night so just stay right where you are; you never know what surprise may be coming your way." Funny Bunny ended with a bow and both Rosie and he retreated back up the stairs and disappeared out of sight. It was the first time that Rosie hadn't bothered to come say anything to me and I wondered why. I still had the same mask on, so she would have recognized me, and I wasn't even wearing the police sticker.

"Don't get any ideas. If you see Wicked let me know—there is no reason for you to take him down by yourself," Light said from behind me and I turned to see his blue mask, only now missing the government sticker that had gone so well with it. He spoke in a tone that suggested I couldn't handle things and that I needed him for this.

"Get out of my mask Light; I don't have anything to say to you." I didn't give my partner a chance to say anything, but walked right past him and on to the next section of the party. I looked around and noted that the Captain was present as well as several other officers I recognized by their masks. I started to count the masks I knew and found the number to be startling. Over half of the party goers here had to be police; it was the only explanation for why things were so dead around here.

I started to feel frantic. Where were the drug salesmen shouting out for buyers, where were the drugged out lawyers, where was Chops and his attitude? This just wasn't adding up. Funny Bunny would never throw a dull party and based on what I knew he would never sell himself short. There was only one real solution, which I didn't have time to explain to Light or anyone else.

I bolted from the dull party and ran outside, continuing to run until I reached the parking lot—not the one for people like me, but the one for the rich. I saw exactly what I'd hoped to: a long black limo pulled to the side of the curb. A security guard was talking to a man I couldn't see who was sitting in the car with his window rolled down. Seconds later the guard nodded and the man rolled up his window, while the limo started to pull away.

The question was obvious: why would this particular rich guy decide suddenly not to attend Funny Bunny's party? The answer was simple. This party was nothing more than a fake, a ruse set to trick the police into thinking they were monitoring the real thing. Funny Bunny wasn't about to let the police ruin his string of parties, no matter the cost; the real party was somewhere else.

The limo finished turning around and began its decent out of the parking lot and on towards the main stretch of road. This would be my only opportunity to find out where the real party was, but to follow the limo I would once more have to go out on my own. I didn't stop and think about what to do; I was already running to my car as fast as I could go.

Even I was shocked at how fast I was in the car with the engine running, but the limo was already on the main road and was disappearing fast. I had to catch up if I was going to see where it was going and that meant peeling out and speeding after the thing. I touched the phone in my pocket as I turned the corner and raced after the escaping limo. There wasn't time just yet—I had to at least catch up and then I could call the Captain and let him know.

I hit the gas hard and caught up to the limo just as it turned onto the freeway leading away from town. It looked like the car was heading for the water and I didn't waste any time falling in line right behind it. I had to fight my way past a couple of cars, but after a few moments I felt pretty confident that I was close enough. I fumbled with the phone in my pocket and finally got it out.

The limo was picking up speed and I had to do the same. We were already well over the speed limit and I wondered if the car knew it was being followed. I glanced down and looked for the Captain's number, keeping an eye on the road at the same time. I briefly thought about calling Light when I passed his number in my contacts but decided against it, knowing there was no fixing the damage between us. I finally came to the Captain's number and went to press the dial button, but I didn't get the chance.

I felt my whole body rock forward and the phone slipped from my hands and fell to the floor, somewhere near the pedals. I looked back in my rear view mirror and saw a large black truck with a giant silver grill on the front directly behind me. The windows were tinted and I couldn't see who was driving the beast of a truck but I knew they were after me. Still the situation didn't quite register until I watched the truck ram me a second time.

The limo quickly changed lanes and then immediately exited onto a different freeway, all in an attempt to lose me. I floored the jeep both to get away from the truck and to keep up with the limo. The truck was on my ass and wasn't letting up; for every mile that I increased my speed the truck seemed to double that. The truck slammed into the back of my jeep again but this time I almost lost control and drove into the opposite lane.

I reached down to find the phone while keeping my foot all the way down on the pedal, a dangerous move but I had to get in touch with someone before this got worse. I thought at least for the moment I would be able to keep my distance from the truck while I felt for the phone. A slam came from the side and this time I went up against the guard rail, hearing the scrape of metal on metal before I even knew I was pinned on the rail. An all black car was now at my side with similar tinted windows and it too was slamming into me from the side. I flipped the wheel hard back into my lane and forced the car back onto its own side of the road, starting to feel a little outnumbered.

I gave up on the phone, deciding it was too risky to try for it again while there were two cars trying to run me off the road. I silently pleaded with passersby, looking for someone to call the police or to help me in some way. No one seemed to even notice what was happening to me. We were going fast and I wondered how much more I could take before a driving mistake would cost me everything.

The limo suddenly exited the freeway and I barely had the time to dart off the road and follow. The black car didn't even have a chance to exit, but the truck didn't have a problem and was on my ass once more in a matter of seconds. The limo was heading down a beach access road that wound down and shared a lane with oncoming traffic. This was the last place I wanted to be for a vehicle showdown and I started to feel for my gun instead of the phone. I caught up to the limo and the truck caught up to me; if they'd been communicating properly they could have smashed me right then and there.

A side road appeared almost out of nowhere and the limo turned into it. Not wanting to lose the car, I did the same and it almost cost me my life. The jeep lifted off the ground on one side and the whole car almost flipped right over. With two wheels in the air I kept on the limo and with a little luck landed safely back on all four tires and continued my pursuit. The truck slowed down a bit for the turn and this gave me precious breathing room to gain some ground on the limo.

The road was getting worse as dirt and gravel began flying up into the air and I could barely see with all the limo was kicking up in its wake. I could only imagine how badly the truck would be dealing with the combination of the limo's dust and my debris. I looked back and saw the truck was losing ground which worried me because I knew it was best suited for the road conditions.

The limo kept on moving and now I could see trees and water around us and I wondered where the hell we'd ended up, since during the commotion I'd lost sight of where we were going. The limo blew through an intersection and I followed, except I wasn't lucky enough to make it through. An exact clone of the truck behind me had been waiting for me and it smashed into the side of my car with expert timing.

My whole body shook and my head bounced off the driver side window, the car spun around and I was facing the west side of the road, whereas the limo had been heading north. The passenger window shattered, the windshield took a nasty crack, and the entire passenger door was bent inward. My poor jeep took a beating and I felt the repercussions of that very beating as I wished to God I had gotten a phone call off.

My head was spinning and it took a few long moments for me to get a grip on what had just happened. The reality of it all didn't sink in until I saw the second truck pull up next to the one that had hit me, both in excellent condition. Their grills were designed to withstand this kind of punishment, which meant these trucks were made for this sort of thing.

Once I got the stars out of my eye I went to start my car back up—it had died in the midst of the accident and I really needed to get moving. Both trucks moved forward and started pushing me from behind, each truck taking a section at the back of my car. They weren't moving fast but we were going down a hill and every second were gaining speed. This was either some kind of scare tactic or they really had a specific reason to push me in that direction. I slammed on the brakes and started to skid until the trucks revved up their engines and I went back into a full push.

Turning away from the trucks, I looked out at what was ahead and saw a downward hill that ended with water surrounded by trees. Nearby I saw a large residence and, closer than that, at the bottom of the hill, a farm house or a large storage shed of some kind. I assumed they meant to push me into the water and I wasn't about to let that happen. I reached down and pulled the pistol out of its holster. It came out smooth and I lined up the shot.

It doesn't happen often that a police officer gets to use his weapon; most of the time it's just there as back up and more importantly it's there to discourage criminals. I hadn't shot to kill in a long time but this time I wasn't here to play games. I wanted to live to fight another day. I opened fire twice into the driver's windshield of the truck on the left side and then a second later did the same to the vehicle on the right. Bullet holes broke into the glass and the loud popping sound was followed by the sound of glass cracking. Only I didn't hear any cries of pain or anguish and the trucks didn't slow down.

I was out of options and out of time, so I did the only thing I could think of. I opened my car door and dropped out at the first sign of clear grass and a place I could land without breaking something. I rolled on the ground like a rag doll and my limbs felt just like that by the time I stopped, feeling as though I'd broken every bone in my body.

Only seconds after my roll I heard a sickening crunch, followed by more breaking glass and then the revving of engines. My car had veered off the path toward the water and smashed into a tree, and now the powerful trucks were trying to fix that. The side of the headlight smashed off and the jeep came free of the tree as the trucks continued to push. The jeep lifted up on one side and this time it didn't return to the normal position, instead ending up on its side before beginning to roll fast towards the water.

I realized the trucks were backing up and I knew it was time to stop gawking at my vehicle and find somewhere I could hide. I went to move but was interrupted by the jeep once more as it crashed into a series of tree branches and ended up back on all four wheels. I reached for my phone and remembered it was in the car, having flown from my grasp earlier in the chase. I realized then that I had missed my opportunity to hide. I was as good as dead and I knew it. Except one of the trucks stopped moving then, and the driver of the other truck stepped out of the vehicle.

He was muscular, and wore all black starting with an all black mask that even had a black mesh shield over the eyes; nothing could be seen of the man. On the passenger side of both vehicles more men stepped out; with their all black clothing on it was difficult to distinguish between them. I counted three in all and assumed there was another one, probably dead from my gunshots. The men took one look around and then turned in unison to stare right at me.

"You need to come with us right now!" One of the men yelled in my direction, I knew this meant they wanted to kill me quietly and probably somewhere far from here. I did what any smart person should do when approached by this situation, I ran. I had one place in mind: the giant barn I'd seen, and which I assumed stored equipment of some kind. Gunshots followed my dash but luckily the men had a much slower reaction than I had expected. Maybe they thought I had given up, or maybe they just weren't ready. Either way you look at it I was extremely lucky to make it into the tool shed without a bullet wound.

I ran at the door full bore, not bothering to try the handle. The door caved in and I fell to the floor, hoping to avoid the barrage of bullets; so far I had counted five shots. I hit the floor hard and thankfully, the door slammed and latched back into a closed position behind me. I crawled across the floor and then stood up and ran into the darkness of the tool shed. I walked past tractors and lawnmowers and other tools I couldn't identify in the dark. I even thought I saw a pair of four wheelers. Who ever owned this place was probably extremely rich and kept the barn just to store some of his expensive toys.

The door burst open and I could see the rush of bright light coming from somewhere behind me as the three men entered the storage room. It was three against one and on top of that I realized they would be better hidden in the dark than I would be. But I had time on my side: they needed to find and kill me fast, before anyone discovered what they were doing. I knew just biding my time would be the best option, so I found the perfect place to hide:

the back of a boat in the far corner of the building that was covered with a tightly fit tarp that I managed to slip under.

I heard the men whispering, clearly trying to sneak up on my in the dark. I didn't move I didn't even make a slight sound; I only stayed where I was and listened. One of the men came close to me and started looking under and over a stack of large boxes until he eventually reached the boat. He stood up on the front end of the boat and lifted the tarp, looking inside and waiting for a long moment, like he was waiting for his eyes to adjust. If he could have seen clearly he would have spotted the back end of my body crouched in the center of the boat. Instead he saw nothing but darkness and ended up continuing his search elsewhere. The three men were growing antsy and their frustration grew until they were sick of lurking around in the dark.

"Enough of this shit—you can't stay hidden forever. We're going to find you and when we do we're only going to make you pay for every minute you made us waste." Bold threats, but I knew that there was no way I could safely give myself up to these men. The speaker had pure confidence in his voice and he reminded me of every typical hired mercenary I had ever seen in the movies. I would not show myself; I would wait for as long as I needed to. My survival, I knew, depended on it.

"Fine, Detective—stay hidden, but remember, every second you waste here with us is another second you're putting someone's life on the line." The thug wasn't just some hired gun. He actually knew about the masquerade murders. This time the threat worked; I couldn't hide while another murder was committed, one that I could actually stop this time.

"That's right, Detective, I know everything that you want to know, so come on out and we can have a chat. Hell, I'll even let you interrogate me if that's what gets you going." Sarcasm and laughs from the group of mercenaries sent to stop me from breaking this case wide open. I decided then that there was no point to hiding because I had nothing to lose; it was the thugs who should have been scared. Earlier I didn't want to kill anyone, but now I needed answers and I already knew which one had them, which meant I only needed one alive.

I rolled out of the boat and used my upper body strength to ease myself to the floor, taking my time and making sure I didn't make a sound. I pulled my knife out of ankle holster and gripped it in a backwards fashion, perfect for throat cutting. Together I wielded knife and gun as if they were one—they had to be for my plan to work.

"Enough of this shit. Let's just burn the place down or something," one of the other thugs said nice and loud, revealing his position for me and my blade. I crept along until my eye focused in and I saw him. It was like I was becoming someone else, someone other than a detective. It was as if I were channeling the killer, like I needed him to complete my bloody mission.

"Come on, you chicken shit, show yourself," the lead thug said as he started firing random shots into the barn, away from his comrades. This was my perfect cover and I didn't waste any of it. I climbed up a nearby stack of crates and then jumped on top of the thug using my weight as an anchor. He was big and tough but, surprised, he fell to the floor and I buried the knife all the way to the hilt in the side of his neck. He coughed a little and spit out a little pool of blood from between his teeth, but no one heard him over the gun shots.

"I'm done with this. Come on guys, we're going to have to torch this place after all." I had a clear view of the speaker from across the room and knew the perfect way to wound him. I cocked back and threw the knife with everything I had; it flew in between boxes and tools and smashed into the thugs shoulder. He cried out and hit the floor in obvious pain, squeezing off an accidental round that bounced on the ceiling.

"Boss, where are you?" the other thug cried out, looking for his wounded commander, not realizing he was the only remaining mercenary who could stop me. I quickly slammed the butt of my gun against a metal pipe creating a sound that had to be investigated. The thug started coming my way just as I had expected and I readied a headshot that would end his cruel life in an instant.

"I'm over here, you idiots. Get your asses down here and help me get this thing out of my fucking arm," the lead thug groaned with the injury but didn't seem as bad off as I had originally hoped. To make matters worse, the other thug headed in the other direction, ruining my clean shot at him. I would need to get a shot off before they had a chance to regroup and use the time against me. I went back to my familiar boat and did my best to speedily climb to the top, no longer bothering to be silent.

"Why am I surrounded by complete amateurs? Fine, I will just handle this myself." The lead mercenary tore the knife from his shoulder and every rip and drip of blood could be heard in the building. I reached the boat and saw the spotlight attached to the top of the center bar, and for a second pictured this as a fishing boat out on a lake in the middle of the night. I flipped the switch and the light came on revealing both of the remaining thugs.

"Shoot him!" the leader cried and the thug responded by launching a series of gunshots in my direction. The light, though, had blinded him and not one bullet came close to hitting me. I took my time, aiming a clean shot and letting out a nice calming breath just at the right time. The bullet did what I knew it would: a clean headshot that killed the man instantly, putting a solid hole in his mask. I felt a level of pride in killing the two men, imagining for a moment that those men were the ones who had killed my daughter. I knew they deserved to die.

"Die, you son of a bitch!" The wounded thug now had his arm back; the knife lay bloody on the floor beside him. This mercenary was smart and didn't bother trying to hit me with a random shot while he was blinded by the spotlight. Instead he did something I didn't expect, before I could even register what had happened. He shot out the light and instantly exposed me while at the same time hiding himself. Now he fired and this time the bullets were close, too close. I fell off the top of the boat and felt hard concrete catch me.

I didn't pass out, but I did lose a couple of moments in the blurriness and confusion of the moment. I could hear the thug and knew he was close and more then that I knew some time had passed since I had fallen. I forced my body into a standing position and I wiped the blood from my eyes.

"Should have known better then to challenge me, Detective. Should have known you were already dead when we ran you off the road." The thug was just mumbling, using his own words as motivation. He was still bleeding after all. I had taken a good spill but I was getting my senses back and that meant I could still get this guy in a position to give me some answers. I heard footsteps so close they made me shiver; I reached for my pistol and discovered that it was gone. I had dropped it when I fell.

"I can't tell you how much cash I'm going to make when I bring your badge in to collect, and now I don't even have to split it with those other fools." I knew he was only a grunt and I would have to keep him alive to get enough information to bring down the real master minds. Even if I didn't plan on actually killing him, I would still need my gun to be in charge. I couldn't beat this guy without a weapon. I started scanning the area but it was so damn dark there was no way I would find it. I moved away from the footsteps and my head swayed with the confusion, I felt dizzy vomit warm up my belly.

"I know you're there, Detective," the man said, sounding more like a demon than human. In my present state I almost could have believed that was the truth. I thought about finding a weapon like a shovel or a wrench but against an experienced gun it wasn't likely to work. He was right behind me so I turned a corner just missing the bullet that was meant for my back.

"Just keep running and the next one is going to hit you in the dick." I tripped and landed on something warm and squishy and realized it was the guy I had knifed earlier. There was no time to get up. I could only turn just in time to see the gun rise up and become level with my head. I had no more time to think and only a split second to react.

Time froze and there in the darkness, somewhere in a storage shed, a gun went off and a bullet tore into an exposed chest.

Eighteen

I actually thought I was dead. I could feel the intense pain in my chest and the drowning feeling spread into my lungs, then on down to my stomach. I felt sickness and weakness that soon became my whole world. Only, it was the thug who had fallen over on his back with a bullet wound in his chest. The pain I felt was first from thinking I had been shot, and second from the realization that I had just killed the only information source I had.

The gun in my hand was unfamiliar but it had saved my life. I had landed on it when I tripped, and lifting it in that final moment had been relatively easy. I knew I had to kill or be killed, but the fact that I had just shot my own case down made me wonder if it had been worth it. Only then did I feel remorse for the people I had killed, and the mistakes I had made. I rushed over to the lead thug and discovered nothing more than a dead body. I had shot him directly in the heart, which was either good or bad luck, depending on how you looked at it. There wasn't anything else I could do for these men so I rushed outside and left the corpses to rot in the storage shed.

I opened the door and was greeted by more darkness. The moon hung in the sky emitting a white purple glow that shed some light on the world I lived in. I reached the destruction of the vehicles and without thought I approached the left truck and looked inside the driver's door. Another dead body sat in the seat with twin bullet holes in his chest; he had died whereas the other driver had known what was coming and got out of the way. I took a guess and figured it was the lead thug who had been driving the other truck. He had seemed smart enough to avoid an attack like that. I checked the guy for a phone but found nothing, so I ran to the chaotic remains of my jeep and searched for my phone and again found nothing. I realized then that even if I had found the phone it would have been destroyed along with everything else.

I knew then that I had only two options in front of me. I could run to the nearest house and use their phone to call the police to the storage house. That would mean a crime scene and a very long time that I would have to spend here explaining what happened. Or I could take one of the trucks and head in the direction the limo had gone in the hopes that I was close to the masquerade and still had time to stop another murder from happening. Without a gun, a phone or even a clue, I jumped into the truck and found the keys waiting in the ignition. The truck fired up with a roar and I let the power of the vehicle flow into me as I peeled out on the gravel.

I was on my way up the road and already forgetting what happened in that shed, at least for now. The truth was I had a lot more on my mind than that place. All I could think about was the murder, hoping there was still time to stop it. I hit the road hard and turned the corner even faster, heading in the same direction as the limo had gone earlier.

Only a minute or two passed by when I came to a hill that overlooked the water and a number of giant houses built along the shore. The gravel turned into smooth paved roads and the truck felt even more powerful in my hands. I sped down the hill in a rush hoping for a sign to lead me in the right direction. At the bottom of the hill I came to a stop sign and another choice: which direction to a take. Every second counted I couldn't choose wrong. Looking down the streets, I noticed a massive increase in the amount of cars parked on the right side of the road—it was as good a guess as any.

"Whoa, I am so freaking wasted!" someone yelled just a short distance up the road. I knew I was right where I needed to be. Up ahead I saw smoke drifting in the air behind an incredibly large house, and the amount of cars there gave it away immediately. There was no way to get close and there wasn't even any real parking nearby. I pulled the truck over as far as I could and then I ditched it there, knowing more important things were waiting for me on the inside.

There weren't a lot of people on the streets but there were enough to know something big was going on. I knew these were only the people who had hit the party too hard and too early. I walked past them trying not to draw attention but moving fast enough that I probably looked questionable. I had been in such a rush I forgot all about the injury to my head, now I remembered but only because each hurried step made my head throb with pain. I heard the familiar chants getting louder and I knew I was home, a strange way to feel but it was the truth. I could smell the smoke of a bon fire, and the flames and the food reminded me of old times and high school parties by the river.

"Dude, you missed it, Funny Bunny man, he is so awesome he was just like, I mean you know, like he was all about it," a drunken man started saying to me as soon as I reached the driveway. He didn't make much sense and I didn't really care. I pushed on, moving around the house and toward the backyard where the commotion was coming from. I didn't bother with the inside since it looked like this time the main attractions of the party were outside.

I looked out over a sandy landscape, a grassy backyard, and a sea of people in the water and everywhere else I could see. A giant bonfire was the center of the commotion, with an even bigger fire pit was built around it, making it the biggest and safest bon fire I had ever seen. Torches lit the way and every path was flooded with people in skimpy clothes and bikinis, even though it was too cold for that sort of thing, although that was nothing compared to the naked bodies skinny dipping in water so cold it could kill them.

"Rosie," I said when I spotted the women with the rabbit mask, though she was far away and would not hear me calling her name. She wore a summer dress with black and white polka dots and you could see her matching swimsuits straps poking out the top of the tiny dress. Funny Bunny and Rosie sat on a makeshift throne as if they were the island gods of this place. Even though I was still taking in the sights of the masquerade I heard hushed and worried voices speaking.

"Hey man are you alright, can you hear me?" As I drew closer to the bon fire I could see a crowd gathering around something, or someone. I spotted several Tiki masks, creepy African masks, and even one that reminded me of a Kokopelli figure. I was trying to listen in on the crowd that was gathering but as I moved closer the sounds were drowned out by rock music. It was coming from inside the island bar, which looked just like the one from the first masquerade, where I took that drink to clear my head. I recognized the song and knew I was listening to Ronnie James Dio and his classic hit Holy Diver. The music was drifting by me just as I was walking by the bar to get to the crowd of people.

"Holy Diver, you're the star of the masquerade, no need to look so afraid," Dio sang as I walked by and the line struck me as almost too fitting for the moment. I finally got beyond the bar and arrived at the back of the crowd that was now almost twenty people strong.

"He probably just drank too much; quit making such a big deal about it." I slipped in around a couple people and got a straight view of a man face down on the sand. I was a step above and couldn't get to the guy as more and more people took an interest and the crowd grew.

"Just flip him over and make sure he's okay. What the hell is wrong with you people?" a newcomer to the situation said before she stepped out and crouched near the guy. She had a painted mask that had hieroglyphics on it but it didn't take away from her serious demeanor. She pushed and the guy flipped over onto his back revealing a gaping wound and a pool of blood soaked into the sand.

Screams and panic followed, and everyone started to run as if the killer were chasing each and every one of them down on a personal vendetta. At first I tried to approach the dead man but there was far too much commotion to even get close. My spirit was officially broken. Failure was the only word that continued to pound through my aching temple along with the sounds of screams.

*****

I sat on the sidelines of the party as the police arrived, who got there sooner than expected because someone had already called in a noise complaint. When more calls started coming in about murders and killers the rest of the police force made it here within ten minutes. I saw the Captain and made sure to duck down somewhere hidden, keeping out of sight of anyone who might have recognized me.

I just couldn't handle the embarrassment anymore; I was starting to think pretending that I never made it down here was going to be the better decision. I honestly hadn't seen anything—I had been too late and facing the questioning just didn't seem worth it. I really didn't want to run into Detective Light and since I hadn't seen him yet, I took my chance to get out of there. I found a random mask on the ground in the shape of a Tiki man; I figured there were lots of them floating around so I used it as a cover. I put the Tiki mask on and walked out of the party with the rest of the crowd.

"You are under arrest for impeding a criminal investigation." The Captain and some other officers were reading Funny Bunny his rights, who was being arrested for tricking them into attending the wrong party. It wouldn't stick and wouldn't affect a rich man but they wanted to send a message to Funny Bunny for screwing the department over like that. I didn't stick around to hear the rest; I just wanted to get out of there as fast as I possibly could.

I thanked God despite my frustration that the black truck was where I left it, since I needed something to drive back to the barn. Plus having the vehicle back where it belonged at the crime scene would only make explaining things a lot easier. A few cars were honking, the drivers getting angry with the truck for blocking part of the road and slowing down traffic. I heard some obscenities while I hopped in but I ignored them, feeling numb to the world. Truthfully I hadn't felt so low since the day my daughter died.

I drove back down the hill in a daze, but still managed to park the truck so that it was pressed up against my jeep just as it had been before. I stepped out and sat there on the ground, my back pressed against the truck's tire staring up at the stars. I watched the world from a different point of view and saw that nothing mattered. I had given up. I lifted my body enough to look in the side mirror of the truck and at the mask missing an eye. I couldn't even remember putting my real mask back on, but there was the bloody tear, haunting me.

"So you returned to the scene of the crime. I would have thought a detective would know better than that." A door shut and Detective Light stood in the doorway of the large shed. I had to peer out to see him and just missed whatever he was holding as he tucked it away. I had come back only to run directly into the last person I wanted to see. I at least hoped that he had just arrived.

"Good to see you, Wink. You would not believe the night I've had." He sounded enthusiastic when he spoke but I couldn't tell if it was sarcasm or truth. I decided I better stand up for this conversation.

"Whoa, why don't you just stay right where you're at, Wink?" Light said when he saw me get up. I even saw his hand reach back and graze the handle of his gun; he seemed jumpy and afraid of what I might do.

"Relax, Light, I didn't do anything crazy. I was forced to defend myself and that's all." Without being sure what was going on in his head I just wanted to make it clear that I wasn't in the wrong, no matter what it looked like to my partner.

"I get it, Wink, I really do, but I think it might be best for us to head down to the station so we can explain all of this to a few people. I already called this in so the regular cops can collect any information they might need from the scene, you know the drill." Was Light asking me to go with him to the station or was he telling me—I wasn't really sure.

"Actually, I don't think I'm ready to go back to the station just yet. I think I'll just sit here for awhile if it's all the same to you." Detective Light looked at me as if he was trying to see beyond my face, like he was peering into my soul.

"Detective Wink, I do not think it is a good idea to stay here. I will ask you one last time to come with me back to the station."

"Light, I'm not going anywhere so just back off man." I thought I was being clear with my partner but he didn't budge, and instead only stood there for a long moment preparing for what was coming next.

"Detective Wink, you are under arrest. You have the right to remain silent. Anything you say can and will be used against you in a court of law. You have the right to an attorney. If you cannot afford an attorney, one will be appointed for you. You have the right to remain faceless under the masq policy guidelines." Detective Light pulled his gun out of its holster but he didn't lift it. He stood still, breathing deeply for a moment before he spoke again.

"Do you understand your rights?" I didn't know how to respond to any of this. Everything was happening so fast and now I was under arrest by my own partner.

"Yeah, I get my rights but why don't you tell me what I am under arrest for?" Aggression was the only thing I could feel and right now I wanted to take every ounce of it out on Light. He didn't back down and up to now I never would have guessed Light would have the guts to arrest me.

"Detective Wink, I am placing you under arrest for suspicion of murder. I didn't want to do this here but you leave me no choice—you have to return to the station with me." I took a step around the truck so that Light and I were only a stone's throw away from one another.

"Light, I already told you these men attacked me. I had to defend myself. I didn't want to kill anybody but I did what I had to." I was trying to persuade him to believe me but really I just wanted to get close enough to arrest him before he could arrest me.

"Despite how this scene looks, I mean a knife to the side of a man's throat, your gun on the floor of a warehouse containing two gunshot victims, that isn't what I'm talking about. You Detective Wink have had opportunity, motive, and the means to commit every murder at each masquerade." Already I was beyond anger at the man for pointing unnecessary blame at me, but to point the finger on something I had worked day in and out to stop was simply incomprehensible.

"How dare you even try to throw that shit on me? I could say the very same thing about you. Every single murder you have had some part to play in. How do I know you didn't just join the department to set me up? In the end it's going to be my word against yours and I am the senior officer so who do you think they're going to believe?" Light didn't seem impressed but I meant every word of it and I was going to tell the Captain the same thing when we got to the station.

"You still don't get it, do you Detective? How are you supposed to solve cases when you can't even see what's right in front of you. I mean, I am good but come on, even I know that I slipped up a couple of times. How did you miss all the hints?" I felt like Light was mocking me about something but I still didn't understand what he was getting at.

"Here let me drop you a hint that you just can't miss: Good luck, Detective Wink." Light said this in an ominous tone that sounded familiar but I couldn't remember something so small with everything going on. He shook his head and laughed for a moment before he started walking away from me and towards his car.

"Hang on, we might as well make this as dramatic as possible for fun, since you seem to be confused and all." Light opened the trunk to his expensive car, which he had expertly tucked in the corner, where I just missed it when I pulled up. He ducked his head down and I saw the back of his mask come off and an entirely different one come on. He turned and looked at me in this creepy three faced mask that looked familiar but took me a moment to place.

"Man you really are fucked up in the head if it's that hard to remember a cab driver from just the other day," Light mocked and finally I did recall the driver who already knew my name, but this didn't really answer any of my questions.

"Think about it, Wink. Why would I be watching every move you make if I were a rookie detective just made your new partner?"

I knew then what was happening but didn't see the point in answering Light.

"Here let me reintroduce myself, I am Detective Light of internal affairs. Pleased to meet you." Everything I had done wrong since returning to the department was becoming real for me; I could almost see my mistakes as if they were a movie.

"Wink, did you really think you were just going to come back to work without having someone assigned to watch you? You were shot in the face and your daughter was murdered by masked men, so aggression towards the policy was expected from the start. And since your record already stated your disregard for rules and procedures in the past, we could only expect the worst."

I wouldn't let the rat drag me through the mud. I wasn't a criminal or a killer, I was doing what I was supposed to do and I refused to think my mistakes would cost me everything. "I had to do things back then that were questionable because the crime wave was out of control. We all had to do something or nothing good ever would have happened. And I don't care who you are, there isn't any evidence to arrest me, so you can just go fuck yourself." If I had my gun I probably would have tried to arrest Light but from where I was standing he held the cards.

"That's fine with me, Wink. If you want to fight your murder charge rather than admitting it, that's your right. By the time the banquet party happens you will be in a cell and then we really will know for sure if you are the killer. It's simple really: with you behind bars no more masquerade murders will happen and I will show everyone that I was right about you." Light was right, another murder was going to happen and if I was locked up I would never have the chance I needed to solve the case.

"Sorry, Light, but I don't give a shit. You can't arrest me for a murder just because I was doing my job by being there and you can take that back to your bosses." I started walking away. I didn't have a car but I figured I would walk until I made it to a phone and from there I didn't really know.

"Wait, Detective, I'm not finished with you. In fact I have a lot more to say." I tried to keep walking; I didn't care what he had to say, until I heard the click of his pistol as he loaded a bullet into the chamber.

"What are you going to do, shoot me?" I turned to face the man who had been my enemy all along and I looked right down the barrel at all three of his faces.

"Wink, you are under arrest. I have plenty to hold you on until the murder charges come through, which is only a matter of time."

I bounced back into the conversation without even missing a beat. "What could you possibly arrest me for, huh?" Light or three faces or whoever the hell he was now reminded me of all those times I had wondered about him, and now I knew. My instincts were spot on with him; I cursed myself for ever trusting him.

"You supplied a suspect with drugs, you broke into a criminal witness's house without a warrant, and you began an undercover operation with a domestic terrorist group without authorization. Hell you even buried the information and made sure none of your criminal buddies got caught for what you discovered. Oh and I can't forget to mention your faceless stunt in front of all of our superiors." Light was laughing at how foolish I had been during our time together and he was right—I would be locked up for sure.

"Don't worry; if you're not the murderer then I'm guessing you won't be behind bars for too many years. The only thing you're going to have to accept is that after I arrest you I'm going to arrest every member of Face, including your best friend Emmeline."

I had been confused about what I should do going back and forth in my mind until Light said this. "Fine, you win Mr. Internal

Affairs. You have done your homework and have me right where you want me. But if you want me to come peacefully then I want a promise that Emmeline and the others are left out of this." I waited eagerly for a response but Light wasn't in a hurry; he wanted to absorb every second of this.

"Fine, we have a deal," he answered finally. "Now put your handcuffs on and toss me the keys." I knew Light would never follow through on our deal but I put the handcuffs on anyway. I tossed the keys over but they went a little too far and he dropped them onto the ground. As soon as he bent over to pick them up I was out of there, running faster than I ever had ever before.

"Get back here, you criminal! You're only proving that you're guilty!" Light was yelling which meant he didn't know where I'd run off to, which was a good sign. I slipped around the house and started making my way along the trees and other shrouded areas.

"All units: our suspect is on foot proceeding down the west shoreline. Move in to apprehend." I heard Light speak into the radio and immediately the sky was filled with blues and reds and my ears were drowned out by sirens. Light already had a team of officers waiting to take me in as soon as he had the cuffs on my hands and the keys in his. I ducked down and quickly pulled the spare key out of my pocket and removed the handcuffs; I couldn't let them slow me down.

"You're a fugitive now Wink, do you hear me? A fugitive!" Light was yelling somewhere back there but I was already gone, using every ounce of knowledge and timing to escape. Again Light was right: in the eyes of the department I would be a fleeing criminal and that meant my life was already over. Still there were just a few more things I would have to do before I could let them arrest me, and the first step involved Emmeline.

Nineteen

I can't say getting away from a police trap was easy, but I knew a thing or two about how things worked and that helped me make it out. Getting away didn't really involve being the fastest person or the quietest. It was more about finding a good place to hide where you would never be found. Or at least a place where you could hide long enough for the police to move on, but not long enough for them to get the k-9 unit to sniff you out. I did just that after creating some distance between me and them, finding a spot in an overgrown gathering of plants. It may not sound like the most elaborate plan but it worked well enough for my escape.

After getting by the cops I had to take a very long walk out of the boonies and back to civilization. I could have gone the way of the festival masquerade but I assumed lots of police would be going back and forth all night and I didn't want to press my luck. I marched back, taking my time and staying close to the tree line where I wouldn't be seen. It took me well into the morning to find a gas station which of course did not have a pay phone. I had a feeling that I wasn't ever going to find one so I ultimately decided just to ask the guy at the desk to use his phone. It wasn't the smartest move considering cops were already looking for me but I couldn't just stay out in the open and on foot.

I picked up the old white phone that looked like it hadn't been used a whole lot, since people used cell phones and the gas station business didn't receive a lot of calls. I turned my back to keep the guy at the counter, who was wearing, fittingly, some kind of gas mask, from overhearing my conversation. I called the only person I could trust, the only person I kept close outside of work. The phone rang and my stomach cringed along with it.

"Hello." At the sound of her voice, which sounded as if she had been deep asleep, I just about hung the phone up. Instead I paused and waited for a moment, which only caused her to become even more irritated.

"Hello?" She was my only option, and I had no choice but to man up; if I could kill four dangerous attackers I surely could ask my ex wife for help.

"Viola, its Wink, sorry to call you so late but I need a favor and you're the only person I could think to get a hold of." I heard her clear her throat and wipe the sleep from her eyes and when she came back it was as if she had been wide awake all along.

"I guess I'm really not getting any sleep tonight. What's going on, Wink? Why do I have detectives calling my phone looking for you?" Questions that I wanted to answer but couldn't in my current location. It just wasn't smart.

"I'll explain everything, but I really need you to come pick me up first, and maybe bring a car that I can barrow for a little bit, if that isn't too much to ask." I recoiled to protect myself from the approaching blow like it was an approaching fist.

"Yeah that's fine, where are you at?" I wanted to ask how she had a vehicle just readily available for me but thought better of it. I gave her the address of the gas station and to my surprise she knew right where it was, even though I didn't even know where I was.

"Alright, just stay there Wink. I'll be there in a couple of minutes." It was a kindness that could have saved a relationship, or maybe it was something else, I wasn't sure.

"Thanks, Viola, I really appreciate this." With that I hung up the phone and she did the same. I slid the phone back to the man and he only glared at me like he knew something that I didn't. Everyone was an enemy from my current position, so much so that I thought everyone was glaring at me, even through their masks. Still eyes are the window into the soul and the people around me seemed to have the worst intentions. I didn't want to stay in the public view, so I thought waiting outside was a better idea.

Sitting out there in the back of a gas station I really let my mind wander, and it did, right into paranoia valley. If Detective Light had been watching me the entire time, it made me wonder who else had been watching me. Why was I chosen for the original masquerade party if the department was so certain that I was unstable? Who else knew about Light and more importantly, who had been working with him to bring me down? I did recall the Captain and Light having private conversations that I wondered about then, and now I really wondered what went on. I guess I had my answer as to why no one would work with the kid: he was internal affairs and most of the department probably knew.

I questioned many things out there, sitting on the side of the curb, watching the approaching cars, waiting to get somewhere safe. The murderer came to mind as he always did; even in my situation I still felt determined to find the killer. I knew

I wasn't the murderer, even with the black outs and the knife that I carried that could have matched the kill weapon. I knew the killer had a motive and it came from a hatred of the masq policies. However I still didn't have anything solid, in fact I didn't really have anything.

A large group of cars drove by in the darkness. I could see headlight after headlight and I envisioned a sea of cop cars surrounding the building and trapping me here. The cars passed and I wondered if maybe Danielle had sold me out. What if she had called Light right after speaking to me? I was really losing my nerve and trusting an ex wife just didn't seem all that safe from where I was sitting. I was getting ready to take off; I figured taking my chances alone would be better than getting arrested thanks to a betrayal. Just then a dark blue town car pulled up and the window rolled down, revealing Danielle, just as she promised. I let out a sigh of relief and a little bit of confused laughter before running to the car.

"Thank you so much for coming. You didn't have to stick your neck out for me and I just want you to know that I really appreciate it," I said to her from the side of the window while I hoped she would step out and let me have the car.

"Get in," she said and I did, noticing how serious her tone was. It reminded me a little bit of those nights when she'd be pissed that I got home late, or not at all. Right when my body hit the seat and the door shut the car sped off and hit the road, heading for the city.

"I'm going to let you borrow the car but I want to get somewhere I can get a cab first if you don't mind." She sounded so serious, like she already knew my situation though I hadn't explained anything to her yet. I looked her over and saw a regular pair of jeans and a t-shirt, even her mask was plain but I could see a lot of makeup around her eyes.

"Well, are you going to tell me what's going on or not?" I felt like a kid in trouble whose mom had already talked with the principal.

"Yeah, I just don't know how much I should tell you. I don't want you getting too involved and end up in trouble yourself." That was part of it, but mostly I just didn't know where to start or what to say on the subject.

"I already am involved if I'm letting you use my car, and besides a Detective Light already said it was serious enough that I could be in danger." I hated Light more than ever learning that he had been calling people and making sure they knew I was a monster.

"That son of a bitch, you can't listen to that shit! It's nothing but a...I don't know what it is but I'm basically taking the fall for something I didn't do." It sounded silly to say I was involved in a set up but that's really how I felt.

"I obviously didn't believe it or I wouldn't have agreed to help you, so just spit it out already and tell me what is happening." Danielle sounded sincere and I knew if I ended up arrested I would regret not telling her the truth while we were alone in the car together.

"I am wanted as a murderer. Detective Light is an internal affairs investigator and he thinks I am responsible for a series of masquerade murders." The car shifted a little bit and I assumed it was from the shock at such a crazy thought.

"You, the murderer? You Detective Wink, the murderer? That's what they really think?" Danielle started to chuckle and then she laughed long and hard. I was confused and didn't really know what to say. She pulled over near a busy street where she could easily get a cab and then wiped the tears of laughter from her eyes.

"I'm sorry, I just can't believe they would actually think you were a murderer. After a lifetime of catching those kinds of people, that's how they repay you?" I didn't really find it all that funny but I could see the irony.

"So what are you going to do, prove your innocence somehow?" Danielle asked from the driver's seat and I realized I didn't really know how to do that.

"Eventually, yes, but there is something else I have to do first." In that moment thinking about Emmeline felt wrong, like I was cheating on Danielle or something. Somehow she picked up on the vibe though, because she didn't dig any deeper.

"Well, all I can say is good luck and I hope this turns out ok. If you need me for anything else you know that I'm here for you."

Friends were hard to find, but I guessed the loss of my love wasn't so bad considering she was my only real friend. "Thanks Viola, you've helped me more then you know. I'll give you a call when this all blows over, and don't worry, I'll take good care of your car." I was grateful to her but I was aware of the clock too; I had to hurry if I was going to save Emmeline and the rest of Face. Danielle stepped out of the car and I did the same. We didn't say anything else to one another but as I crossed the car to get to the driver's door we came face to face and hugged one final time. I pulled her close as the cars rolled by and in that moment I didn't care about my problems. I only wished for a life that wasn't mine anymore.

I didn't bother driving to my apartment; I already knew it was crawling with police, or at least Light waiting outside. Since I no longer had my phone and wasn't driving my jeep, in the modern world I was a ghost. I had a list of things to do but the one at the top was getting to the warehouse and to Emmeline before it was too late. Detective Light wasn't playing around; he was out for blood and the moment he realized he wasn't going to find me, he would hunt down Face. I didn't let my mind wander about what was to come or what was already lost. I had a mission and I wouldn't fail.

In the borrowed car I made it to the warehouse easily. To my surprise the police hadn't made it to the hideout yet. At least, I didn't see any police lights, and a raid of that size would have definitely given off a sign. I pulled the car up next to the others, cars I knew belonged to members of Face. I locked the car and stepped out into the early morning air; it was still dark but soon the sun would make morning clear. Nervousness took over the moment I approached the entrance to the warehouse, a feeling I hadn't prepared for. Grabbing the cold steel handle took everything I had, and I froze before pulling it open.

"What do you think you're doing back here?" An angry voice spoke from behind me and I quickly turned to see a mask like a motorcycle helmet and a baseball bat. It was one of the men who had been with us during that first meeting and later on at the mission.

"Look, I need to talk to Emmeline. Something terrible is about to happen." The black visor shielded the man from view so I couldn't tell what he was thinking. I took a step towards him to try and plead my case but he only lifted his baseball bat menacingly in my direction.

"Listen, I am a police officer. Do you really want to be responsible for bashing a cop or do you want to help Face because that's the only reason I am here."

The motorcycle man seemed to be thinking for a long moment before he lowered the bat down to his side. "I'll let you in but Emmeline is going to be pissed, so if she tells me you have to leave then that's what you're going to do."

I didn't know if this guy believed that I would actually listen to him once inside, but it didn't really matter either way. "Fair enough, but time is really important here so can we get moving?"

With an annoyed sigh he unlocked the warehouse door and led me inside. He took me all the way to the back room where I had been before, only this time people weren't working or running around busily. Instead the room was all silent and empty except for one man reading a newspaper and sipping a cup of coffee. He looked up and the sight of his face seemed wrong somehow, and I realized how unprepared I was to see an actual face.

"What's this?" the man asked, throwing his paper aside and standing up, looking shocked. The motorcycle man set his bat down and waved a hand for the man not to worry so much and then walked away down to a part of the building I hadn't yet seen. This left me alone with the man and his confused look; I wanted to explain the situation delicately.

"I'm a friend of Emmeline's. I just have some information for her." The man had thick gray eyebrows and he looked too old and tired to be involved in this kind of rebellion. Nonetheless he seemed to believe me because he sat right down and went back to his paper as if nothing had happened. I didn't take long after that for Emmeline to come running up the hall confused, obviously just coming out of a deep sleep. I saw her with no makeup on, her hair a mess, baggy pajamas, and sleep still in her eyes and still she looked beautiful.

"What the hell are you doing back here?" She spat at me in a wicked tone that was not her own, and even though I knew she had the right, I couldn't even believe that she was so angry.

"Emmeline, you know I wouldn't be back here unless it was for something important, so please just listen to me."

Her look of annoyance on her face didn't change. "Well, what have you got to say, Detective?"

I never thought the title of detective could be so horrible to hear, but it really was. "This isn't going to be easy to say but I'm pretty sure there isn't a lot of time left before you're going to have every cop in the city kicking in your door."

Her eyes went from tired and annoyed to big and worried. "What are you talking about? I thought you said we were going to be fine? You promised me that you weren't going to turn us in." A tiny line of tears lined her eyes.

"It's more complicated than that. I will explain everything to you soon but first we need to get out of here."

Emmeline took a second to process the information and then transformed from a hurt girl to a powerful rebel. "Start waking people up right now. I'm going to get my sister—she'll know what to do," Emmeline ordered motorcycle man and the old man, and then all three ran off. I waited, thinking it was going to take a few minutes but instead Angel came around the corner already dressed up in a white business shirt and skirt. She had an all white mask on that was streaked with silver and had a pair of wings drawn onto its sides.

"How long do we have, Detective Wink?" She didn't sound angry or lost. Angel had been ready for this from day one and she was happy to have some kind of advance warning.

"I can't be certain, but if I were to wager a guess a warrant has already been issued and the cops will be here within the hour."

Angel nodded and then waved for me to follow her as she walked down the hall to her back office. The door closed behind us and Emmeline was already inside waiting for us. She had on her army jacket and peace sign mask, and was too busy throwing papers into a shredder to notice Angel and me.

"Wink, I just wanted to thank you for coming back and letting us know what was about to happen. I was angry with you before but now I can see what your priorities really are." Angel was saying things I never would have expected but it was Emmeline who was listening with obvious confusion. She looked up to her sister, which was good for me since it meant Emmeline could be thinking about giving me a second chance. At least, from the way she was looking at Angel and I, I hoped she was.

"Now, we have a way out of this warehouse so I am not really worried about the police catching us, but if we can get some of our vehicles and incriminating evidence out of here things will be even better. Wink, please help Emmeline with the rest of this room. I'm going to rally my troops and get as many of them out of here as possible." Angel left us in the room and I just stood there awkwardly watching Emmeline stack papers for the shredder. This was the chance I had been waiting for to make this right with her, to make things right with someone I cared about.

"Emmeline I never meant for any of this to happen. You weren't ever meant to get hurt in all of this. I just wanted to stop a killer, no matter what the cost."

She didn't respond right away, but I could tell she knew I was sincere. Finally, after a few moments, she spoke. "You said before that you wanted to explain everything to me—here's your chance. I want to know about these murders and why you're here." I sat down beside her and started moving papers from her pile into the shredder, and at the same time I told her a simplified version of my story. The shredders whine made it difficult but I spoke over the sound as loud as I had to, feeling that Emmeline had to know and understand my story.

******

"Please tell me you're close. The cops are here, and right on schedule." Angel was standing in the doorway and Emmeline and I were working our way through more plans and evidence than I thought possible. I had told her the bulk of the story and she seemed to understand a lot better the events that had led me here. I didn't have time to tell her about Calliope, but then she already knew most of that and it was too sad to tell over again.

"We're close, we just need a little more time," Emmeline pleaded with her sister but Angel only shook her head and beckoned for us to get up.

"Stop where you're at. You need to get out of here. Wink, I had your car pulled around to the other side of the building—get to it and get Emmeline out of here."

"What about you? The cops are going to arrest you for sure," I said, moving my mind beyond the logistics of our escape. Emmeline jumped up and seconded my comment; she didn't want to leave her sister behind any more than I did.

"Someone needs to be here and who better than the CEO, just spending the night working late?" I couldn't argue with that and luckily neither could Emmeline, who hugged her sister instead of talking.

"You don't have a lot of time. I would get out of here while you still can."

Emmeline nodded and pulled my arm until we were outside of Angel's office and running. The members of Face who were caught would only end up in jail for maybe a year; I however was facing much more time. I ran like a convict escaping a maximum security prison all the way down the hall and out a back entrance that opened onto a service tunnel. We passed a sign that said Maintenance Service Entrance and Emmeline turned onto a large opening in practiced fashion.

"Come on, we're almost there," Emmeline said, nearly out of breath. I was too winded to even respond. I was so damned tired from the day's activities I just wanted to pass out somewhere and not wake up for a week. The tunnel sloped and came out on a work garage that housed several transport vehicles and forklifts. To the back my car sat untouched and ready for our escape.

"I just feel so bad leaving my sister to deal with all of this," Emmeline said but I didn't really think we had any more time to waste discussing what had already been decided.

"She's going to be just fine. Chances are, there's nothing even left for her to get in trouble for. It's not illegal to work late." They weren't the most comforting words but they were enough to get Emmeline in the car and give us a chance to get away safely. A ramp led us out of the garage and into an open field of dirt just outside of the warehouse limits. In the dark early morning sky I could see police lights flashing all over the area surrounding the warehouse from front to back.

"Holy shit, your partner isn't playing around trying to capture you, is he?" Emmeline knew that Light was after me but neither of us really understood the extent of his search until that moment. I saw a flashing light somewhere in the distance and recognized an approaching police helicopter.

"We have to move right now. Do you have somewhere we can go?"

Emmeline nodded and I sped off in the opposite direction of the police force and the approaching helicopter. I left the lights off hoping that the chopper wasn't already looking in our direction. Maybe it was luck or just good timing but no cops followed us and we made it to the road, leaving the warehouse behind. Still, I could picture Light questioning Angel and the thought sent shivers through my spine—the man was a monster, one who could trick just about anyone.

"So what are we going to do now?" Emmeline asked after we had been driving for a short while and were getting closer to her house. I didn't know if this was a shot at letting me know I could stay with her but I heard the word we in there somewhere.

"Well if it's okay with you I'd like to lay low for a week while I wait for the grand banquet. It's my last chance at clearing my name and catching the killer once and for all."

Emmeline pointed at the next turn and we came to a large house sitting on its own large piece of land. It was secluded and perfect for hiding out for awhile; it was far from town and far from police. The house even looked a little romantic in the sunlight that was now pouring out over the land, promising better things were to come.

"I think it's more than okay with me. I would love to have you stay with me for awhile," Emmeline said in a voice that didn't sound familiar to me: it was slight and feminine, different but still amazing in its own way.

"Thank you, Emmeline. You don't know how much this means to me."

"Yeah, I do—it means you have somewhere to stay that doesn't have bars for a door." Emmeline jumped out of the car and ran to her family home, throwing her mask and jacket off as she did, letting the sun bounce off her hair and light up her face. I watched her run in the sun and the yellow field that surrounded her and for the first time in years I felt like I was home.

Twenty

Sleep was an amazing thing but it was even better with someone I really cared about sleeping right beside me. The night had been one nightmare after another and the giant bed in the back bedroom of Emmeline's house was a relief. The moment my head touched the pillow I passed out; over-exhaustion had taken its toll. I slept deeply and comfortably with no memories, no dreams, just perfect uninterrupted sleep. To make things even better I awoke to find Emmeline in the bed with me sleeping just as perfectly.

"Emmeline, are you awake?" I asked even though I knew she was asleep. I didn't want to wake her but the room was dark and I wanted to know how long I had been there. I rubbed the sleep from my eye and tried to focus in on the room I barely remembered in my confused exhausted state. It was like the part of my memories where I walked from the car inside of the house and into the bedroom was missing.

"Yeah, I'm awake. You've been sleeping for at least twelve hours. I thought I would join you a few hours ago. I hope that's okay."

I wanted to yell out that it was more than okay but I didn't want her to get the wrong idea. "Yeah, it's okay, but if you need me to go I can sleep on the couch, or if I have to leave your house that's okay too. I don't want you to feel responsible for me." I looked for my mask while I spoke but I didn't see it anywhere. It was strange how accustomed I had grown to it. There really was some kind of craving to hide my face. It was almost addicting.

"I already told you that you can stay here for the week while you wait for the next masquerade thing to happen, the grand banquet I think is what you called it." Emmeline was more than accommodating and I wondered how I got so lucky to find a friend like this. I sat up and leaned on my arm and felt pain shoot down my head and flow all over my sore body, the effects of the previous night catching up to me.

"Urgh," I muttered and fell back onto my side. It was a pretty pathetic attempt at getting out of bed. I was starting to feel a lot older than even my years and wondered what I was doing in bed with a young healthy woman.

"Take it easy, you went through a lot yesterday. Just calm down—it's not like you can go anywhere, since you have to lay low, remember?"

I let out a breath of relief, having forgotten that I had a week to rest and stay out of trouble. That meant I needed to calm down and forget about the people out there trying to kill and arrest me. If anyone was going to get me out of the dark funk I had been in, it would be Emmeline.

"Alright, so what do you want to do today?" I said in a new cheery tone, one that threw Emmeline off. I wondered if she had ever heard me be happy before this moment.

"Don't worry, I'm sure I'll think of something."

I was really starting to like the sound of the upcoming week with Emmeline.

*****

I got up from bed and went straight to the shower, which could only be described as simply wonderful. The warm water surrounded everything and washed the pain and agony of the previous day away and with it all the bad memories of my past. While it wasn't able to fix all of my problems, it was the closest I was ever going to get. I left the shower and dressed in some basic jeans and t-shirt that I assumed were Emmeline's father's. I wasn't even finished getting dressed when I was rushed by the smell of eggs and bacon spreading through the house.

"How do you like your eggs?" Emmeline yelled from down the stairs and I came around just in time to see her standing there holding a spatula. She wore a yellow summer dress that had pink and brown flowers on it and showed off her legs and bare feet. I froze there and couldn't even answer, her presence was so overwhelming: her bright smile, high puffy cheeks, lips with a light shade of pink, a small button like nose, and big eyes that look up at me confused but happy.

"Alright, I guess it's up to me to decide what you're going to eat." She mocked me and walked away laughing, knowing full well that I had been frozen by her looks. I walked into the kitchen and sat down taking time to look at the white walls and red floral patterns that felt warm and homey.

"Those clothes look good on you; it's nice seeing them worn again."

I knew they were her father's but I didn't ask. I thought it might be too soon or maybe I just couldn't handle the thought of Emmeline being sad.

"Thank you for everything. I mean, you don't have to go to so much trouble just to make me feel comfortable." I wasn't used to someone taking care of me; I was starting to feel a little awkward, like I was doing something wrong just sitting there.

"It's no problem. The way I see it I owe you pretty big for saving us from the cops, you didn't have to stick your neck out like that."

I didn't tell her that I didn't have much of choice, seeing as I was already screwed.

"Did you hear anything from your sister yet?" I asked instead, not wanting to focus too much on the things I did for them or the things she was doing for me.

"Not personally no, but one of our people dropped by and said that she didn't get arrested and on top of that everyone from Face was able to get away. Apparently she is being watched so she thought it would be best if there was some distance between us for now."

I thought of Angel back there fighting off the cops with threats of law suits and laughed a little bit at the thought of the sisters. They were a tough couple of girls and messing with them really was a bad idea.

"Here's your breakfast, Detective," Emmeline said and placed a plate of delicious scrambled eggs, bacon, and toast in front of me and then did the same for herself. We sat together and talked about things far from the masq policies and the bad things we were going through. I didn't even correct her on the fact that I was no longer a detective.

*****

Emmeline and I spent the evening outside by a small duck pond hidden at the back of the house. I had slept most of the day away and by the time we were finished with breakfast we were just in time to watch the sun go down. A picnic table was placed outside beside the pond and we just sat on top of it together under a blanket. The sky went from orange to a deep red and then into a swirling purple. I put my arm around her as the sky became dark and tiny dots of starlight speckled the atmosphere. I pulled her close and felt warmth spread across both of our bodies. I didn't move any further that night but just stayed close by her side and talked about different times in our lives, happy times.

Later on that night we were back inside and ended up sitting on the floor across a coffee table playing board games. To make things interesting Emmeline had dug out some beers from the fridge. They were girly drinks but anything sounded good to me. We played Clue first but realized the game couldn't really be played with only two players so quickly threw it aside. Next we tried our hand at Monopoly but we were both already buzzing pretty good and couldn't take the game very seriously either. Finally we decided just to play with a deck of cards, which was only second to our talking. While I don't remember everything we said while I was there, we spent a lot of time talking while we were together at that house.

"So do you share this house with your sister or is it all yours?" I asked after a large gulp of the cherry flavored drink I was holding.

"My father left it to the both of us, but Angel's never here. She lives at the factory—it has everything she needs. Dad put a small apartment in the back when he had nowhere else to go and it works perfectly for her." Emmeline looked down at her drink and I could see the sadness in her eyes; I had struck an unhappy nerve even if I hadn't meant to.

"I'm sorry, I wasn't trying to bring up bad thoughts. I was just curious about this house." I tried to reset the tone in the room which only moments ago had been filled with laughter and card games. Emmeline smiled and looked at me from across the table, not seeming all that upset about things after all.

"Actually, I really don't mind. You can ask me anything. I recognize you're just trying to get to know me better." She smirked and for once I was able to just enjoy the moment. We did just that, and before the sun had even come up there were beer bottles everywhere. I didn't know how many we drank, all I remember was Emmeline suddenly lying on her side on the couch and passing out. I got up and put a blanket over her while the world turned and I almost fell down.

"Emmeline, are you okay? Do you want me to get you some water or something?" I asked her in a confused slur of my own words and I still wonder if she had even heard me right.

"I'm really happy you're here, Wink," she said and fell asleep in the second. I looked at her for a short time and realized I was just as happy. I could have crashed out on the bed upstairs but I wanted to be close to Emmeline. The floor beneath her worked just fine.

*****

The next day the sun was shining bright, the birds were chirping somewhere in the distance, everything was warm and beautiful, except for my hangover. The shower was a very useful tool when you woke up feeling like shit, and I definitely felt like shit. That was the price to pay when you spent the day drinking, though. I took a long and wonderful shower that washed away the grime of yesterday and began another day alone in the house with Emmeline. I found my old clothes that had now been washed and put those on, not knowing where to look for more of her father's clothes. After the morning rituals I went to check on Emmeline who was still sleeping on the couch.

"How are you feeling today?" she asked from in-between half closed eyes and with a smile that showed how happy she was to see me this morning.

I looked at her and my hangover went away just thanks to the happiness I saw in her face. "I feel pretty amazing and you look just as amazing."

She pulled the blanket over her face and rolled over just enough for the blanket to lift up and give me a shot of her panties. "It's too early for me to look like anything but a zombie." She couldn't have been more wrong.

"You look beautiful, no matter what time it is." I knew I was falling in love and I knew Emmeline felt the same way; I wasn't sure how I knew, but it was just something I could tell by looking into her eyes.

Emmeline had to leave for a short time and get some basic items that we would need for the next couple of days and sadly I couldn't go. I watched her get ready while we talked about various things, enjoying the morning until Emmeline put her mask on and I remembered what kind of a world we lived in.

"Don't worry, no one is going to follow me. It's not really that big of a deal."

I wasn't all that afraid of Light following Emmeline back to the house. It was a more a fear of breaking apart our little romance, tucked away in this house. It was difficult to explain but I felt like her leaving would force me back into the real world and I really wasn't ready for that.

"Just be careful and if you see a really nice blue beamer behind you, watch where you go because it will be following you."

Emmeline left me alone and I recalled what it was like to really be in love again, when you start analyzing everything and worrying about the smallest things.

I had to pass the time and even though it was against my morals I found my way into the study that I figured belonged to Emmeline's father. It was sealed off but I opened it anyway and discovered a good sized library and a nice oak desk. I sat in the leather chair and opened the top desk drawer revealing a black snubnose Smith and Wesson 38 special. I didn't take the gun out but I looked it over and, noticing the box of shells right beside it, wondered if I would need to use this gun. The next drawer was a large one containing folders and a stack of papers pertaining to the warehouse. A small drawer at the top center had a collection of pencils and pens and a small leather book. I picked up the book with some kind of dread because I knew exactly what I was holding. I flipped through the diary to the last page and read.

Take good care of my business, girls. There are a lot of good people counting on you to keep things together without me. I just can't stay in a country that wears a horrible mask. I know you won't understand but it's just for the best that I don't have contact with anyone from America. Some day things will be better there again and I will return to you but for now you two will have to do your best without me. Just remember we hide everything beneath a mask. Don't trust anyone until you see their face.

I shut the book and put it right back where I found it, trying not to lose my temper at the coward for leaving his daughters to fight his battles while he hid in another country. I tried to tell myself that I couldn't have a real opinion just from reading one short passage. Still it did answer the big question as to why Angel and Emmeline had been working so hard to bring down the mask; they wanted their father to come home. I felt a moment's regret that Emmeline had led me to believe her father was dead, but I guess that was easier than the truth.

Emmeline made it back to the house just fine and I didn't mention what I had seen in the study. I only hoped she would reveal to me her past when she felt comfortable. We spent the day playing house as if we were a real married couple and this was the house we would live in until we grew old. I knew it wasn't possible but right then and there it didn't really matter, all that mattered was us and the time we had together.

"I don't think you should involve yourself so much with the case. It seems like you're better off just getting away from all of that chaos. After everything you did to solve the murders and all that you've been through, your partner just turns on you. It's terrible." Emmeline and I were sitting at the table enjoying the dinner we had prepared together, a colorful collection of steak, mash potatoes, and broccoli. We set the table up nice and were pretending we were out on a real date at a real restaurant.

"I don't think we really should talk about my problems anymore. I'm sorry. I just want to know more about why you have this house and why you and your sister run Face." Emmeline was trying to slowly turn me from going to the final masquerade but I wouldn't have it, and now I just wanted to avoid the question.

"I'm not finished trying to get you to stay here with me and forget the case, but for now I'll drop it if that's what you really want." Emmeline was wearing a lacy see-through black shirt and if you looked you could see her teal undershirt that matched her earrings and belt. This was the most dressed up I had seen her and it was as impressive as the rebel I had grown to care so much about.

"That's exactly what I want," I added after swallowing a full bite of steak and taking a drink of the wine we had set out on the table. I'd never really understood drinking wine with dinner, since I thought it tasted terrible and kind of ruined the meal. But it was supposed to be the romantic thing, so I tried to enjoy it for Emmeline's sake.

"If you really want to know why Angel and I started Face then you would have to know my father and you can't really do that because he isn't here. It's hard to explain but my dad didn't deal with the whole mask thing very well. In fact, it made him pretty crazy. At first he tried wearing the mask but he was constantly scared, like there were issues none of us could understand. He would try and run things at the warehouse but instead he would hide in his office and avoid everyone. Eventually he could only hide in his study and flat out refused to wear a mask of any kind, or look at anyone with a mask on." Emmeline paused for a moment not wanting to explain this to me. It was obvious she didn't like being vulnerable and this made her just that.

"He just had to leave is all. It doesn't sound like he is the best dad, leaving us like that, but if you could have seen the way he was, well you would know it was the best thing for him." Emmeline hadn't been eating while she spoke, but now she took a few big gulps of her wine like she was trying to swallow the way she was feeling.

"Truthfully I have been scared since my dad started acting so strange. It didn't get better when he left and even running with

Face didn't make things improve. The first time I didn't feel scared anymore since the country put a mask on was when I met you. When you spoke of your daughter and the things you went through I knew you were speaking from the heart. You were saying the things that I wanted to say—you weren't exposing your fears but were standing out against them."

I stood up and went to Emmeline and she leaped from her chair into my arms and we started kissing each other, alternating taking the lead.

"You don't have to be scared anymore. You don't ever have to be scared," I whispered into her ear as we backed up to the couch. I took off her lacy shirt and started working on some of my own clothes at the same time. We were getting even more comfortable with each other on the couch and we both knew where this was going.

*****

The rest of my time spent at the house with Emmeline was something of a dream, but I know that my day to day life there with her isn't the important information that you need to hear. So just like all the other good things in my life, this too came to an end.

"Please, you have to just hear me out. This isn't your fight anymore. It's time to move on just stay here with me." Emmeline had shown a different side to me and beneath the powerful exterior was someone who'd been scared before, and was now afraid of losing me.

"I don't know how to explain to you why I have to do this but it's just something I have to finish. I don't know why, but I have a part to play in this."

Emmeline looked down for a long moment and then went over to a shoebox she had sitting on the counter. "I finished what I was working on for you."

Inside the box was a mask, but with a different design than I had ever seen. I pulled it out and looked it over, wondering if this thing would pass a legal inspection by an officer. The mask was split down the middle in a jagged fashion so it only covered half of the face, the half that was missing an eye. On the cheek, pressed into the mask's design was Calliope's laminated C.

"I found it when I was washing your clothes. I thought you should display her for the world to see, along with as much of your face as you can. You know, stand against your fears. I think it suits you well." I held it out to the light and felt pride in the first mask that I had ever really liked to look at.

"Thank you, Emmeline, it's perfect. And now I won't have to get caught in an instant walking in there with my old mask on." I went to put the mask on but instead Emmeline stopped me and we took the time to enjoy a long passionate kiss. I put the mask on then and looked at her with a new level of pride; somehow I felt more complete while wearing it.

"There is one more thing," I said. "I don't really have a gun and I may need one. You wouldn't happen to have one around that I could use, do you?" I had been hoping the gun in the drawer would come up at some point but it never did.

"Yeah, I have just the thing. Hang on," Emmeline said in a very sad tone that hurt my heart before she ran up the stairs. I watched her go and felt a longing to stay. I wanted badly to turn back the clock and start the week over from the beginning. A second later she returned with the snubnose 38 special in her hands, the one I had been hoping for.

"Here, it was my father's. I hope it helps."

I held the gun to get comfortable with the weight and popped it open to check to see if it was loaded. She handed me the box of bullets and I accepted them; there was no telling how many I might need.

"Emmeline, I really care about you and wish there was a way that I could repay all that you have done for me. I guess I just want to say thank you so much for everything." I wanted to have some kind of a special good bye moment, but there were no words to explain how I was feeling and there just wasn't enough time in the world.

"Stop talking like this is your final day with me or something. Just catch the killer, clear your name, and then you'll be back here with me."

I smiled and nodded but with my track record since the beginning of this case, I had a feeling it wasn't going to end well.

"Alright, let's go, they're here," Emmeline said and walked out the door. I followed only a lot more slowly than she; I wanted to get a last look around the house. Outside the van was waiting with a couple Face members who were going to help sneak me past any watching police. I couldn't afford to get caught now and if Emmeline and her people were willing to get me closer to my objective then I was going to let them. I had to leave Danielle's car behind, but I knew she would be able to get it back once this was over, however it ended.

"I hope I get to see this place again," I said to Emmeline while looking at the house one last time, taking it in with the setting sun shining on its rooftop. I experienced so much happiness in that house that I would never forget. Emmeline held my hand for a long moment before I realized that there were more important things to do than stand there reminiscing. I snapped back to reality and opened the van door and piled into the back with Emmeline right behind me. I hadn't planned on bringing her with me this far but she insisted that she at least get close enough to the party to see me off.

"Ok, we're ready. You can take us to the grand banquet," Emmeline said and the van did just that, turning away from the house that was my safety and my love for the past week. On we drove to what would be the most difficult decision of my life.

Twenty-One

The familiar scene came into view out of the van's bulky windshield: the large landscape filled with cars and people walking to the party. I wanted to get my game mask on but it was difficult leaving behind the dreamlike week I had just had. Occasionally I would look up at Emmeline and then look away as if I were a high school student too embarrassed to get caught staring. Of course I was tempted to just walk away from this whole case, to stay hidden with Emmeline forever in that other world we created. The van was being driven by the motorcycle masked man, who had become a familiar presence within the Face organization. He drove the van as close to the entrance as possible and then waited for me to get out and on with my life. I had so many things I wanted to tell Emmeline, so many emotions I felt for her, so many feelings I wanted her to be a part of. I didn't come close to what I wanted to say, though, and instead I stepped out of the van onto the street and said, "Thank you for everything, Emmeline. I'll see you again when this is all over."

She nodded, a little surprised at how quickly everything had come to end. I didn't wait long for a response; I chose to walk away before my emotions got the better of me. I walked away from her and the van and straight for the mansion's main entrance doors. The doors were shut tight and standing in front of them were four security guards dressed in tuxedoes and visor like masks that resembled giant sunglasses.

"I'm sorry, sir, but only certain special guests are allowed inside for today's grand banquet. If you will, please step down the stairs and head to the back lawn where the other guests have gathered. Thank you for your compliance." The other security were gathering together around the door and making damn sure that I didn't try anything stupid. I turned to walk away and thought how important it was that I got inside the building, so I decided to reach for my badge.

"Look, gentleman, my name is Detective Wink and I have been called here by Funny Bunny himself to make sure this masquerade goes off smoothly. I'm sure you're all familiar with the string of murders we've been having and I need to ensure that nothing of the sort happens tonight." I held the badge out for all the security to see but they didn't budge and even worse they didn't really seem all that impressed.

"With all due respect, Detective, I have been informed to be on the lookout for police officers and am to deny any and all access even if there is an emergency. Apparently Funny Bunny has been informed of some phony police officers going around and causing all kinds of problems."

I didn't move from where I was standing, finding it hard to believe that Light would go as far as telling Funny Bunny that I was no longer active with the force.

The guard continued, "Sir, as an officer I am sure you're aware that I have the right to deny you access without cause to a private residence. If you will please step back down and go around back with the other guests."

He was right, there wasn't anything I could do from right here so I did just as he asked and stepped down the stairs and out of this way. I didn't head to the back lawn however, since I already knew that what was going on back there had nothing to do with the killer. Whatever was going on tonight would happen inside with the big time guests and the grand banquet I had heard so much about. I chose to take a step back from the mansion and try to get some perspective, to see if I could find a window or some other way inside. I walked out onto the street and saw her standing there looking at the ground in an awkward nervous stance. Emmeline was having her own battle: whether or not to run after me and fix the silence that had passed between us in the van.

"Emmeline, I can't believe you're still here. It's great to see you again." I stepped up to her and as her eyes met mine the world around us melted away and for a second nothing else mattered. I kissed her with every ounce of emotion that I had and the bodies of those walking by became a solid blur.

"I just don't have a good feeling about this; I can't shake this feeling that something bad is going to happen to you." Emmeline was worried just like any new love would be about my current situation, but I wasn't going to let it stop me from what mattered.

"Then help me. I've run into some trouble getting inside and it would make things a lot easier if I had a few more bodies to keep security off of me."

Emmeline nodded with excitement for she always was ready for a chance to stick it to an authority figure. She ran off to collect her partners in Face, while I started searching the building for a way inside.

I could hear the music in the distance coming from the back lawn but it was nowhere near as loud as when I had first come here. It seemed as though there was a lot less interest in the actual party and more focus on what was to come on the inside, during the grand banquet. I couldn't tell for sure but it looked like there was an alternate door on the left side of the mansion. It was sealed off but after a jump over the fence I wouldn't have far to go to reach it.

"Alright, what do we need to do?" Emmeline asked from behind me and I turned to see Motorcycle man and another standing at the ready just waiting for Emmeline's command. It was strange but remarkable to see such a small woman capable of leading a group of soldiers into battle.

"First we need to get over this fence; I think there is another way in over there." With a simple nod the group got into position and after a quick boost I was over the fence. This was the opposite side of the mansion and there was little activity, but I could see the door up ahead. I thought about just heading for the door on my own but then I saw two more security standing by this entrance keeping a lookout just like at the main door to the mansion.

"Alright, send Emmeline over," I whispered through the gate and they did just that, lifting her up and sending her right over and into my arms. The other two worked together quite well lifting one another up and over the gate until we all stood ready to break in.

"Okay, so what's the plan?" Emmeline asked and I prepared to tell her when she should distract the guards and when the rest of us should jump those very guards, when someone else walked into view.

"Hey, what the hell are you doing back here?" It was one of the security guards from the main gate and he knew exactly who I was and what I was doing. With another guard on the scene, most likely performing a random patrol, that meant we had three men to deal with. Motorcycle man didn't waste any time and threw a right hook into the approaching guard and a brawl broke out between the two men. I watched the motorcycle helmet smash into the guard's face and wondered how the security guard was still standing, let alone fighting.

"Call for back up!" the man yelled and unfortunately the two standing at the door heard his cries and went straight for the radio to report our little attack. I couldn't let that happen so I rushed with everything I had and speared the guard holding the radio, taking him to the ground. He started struggling wildly and I could barely hold him down, and to make matters worse the other guard was grabbing my back and started pulling me off of his friend. Emmeline reacted then by jumping on to the man's back and clawing at his mask, keeping him at bay easily. Our third guy jumped into the fray and helped Emmeline restrain the man she was dealing with but I was having trouble of my own. The guy I had pinned below me was superior in strength and energy, and I was going to lose hold soon.

"Enough, I'm through playing around with you!" I yelled pulling out the 38 special and sticking it into his mask. Immediately he stopped struggling and realized it wasn't worth dying to keep us out. It wasn't the cop thing to do but I really wasn't a cop anymore and I knew that every minute I wasted out here was a minute the killer had to work out his evil plot.

"Now tell me, is that door locked over there?" I waved the gun in his face as I looked over my shoulder to see that we had a hold on all three of the guards.

"Yeah, and we're just posted out here for safety. We don't even have a key to the door, so joke's on you, dumbass." The cocky guard started laughing and I reached into his vest pocket and found a key that looked like a perfect for the side door.

"Sorry, buddy, but the joke's on you, now that you don't have any information that I need." I reared up and pistol whipped him hard on the side of the head, knocking him unconscious with one blow. I ran to the door and tried the key, my heart beating with fear that it wouldn't be the right one after all. Thankfully the key worked and the door opened.

"I can't leave the bodies here or they're going to be on me before I can get anywhere in there, but I'm worried that I don't have time to clean this up." I didn't want to ask for more than I already had but it seemed like the only solution for the situation.

"Don't worry, we can tie them up and put them somewhere safe until this is all over," Emmeline said and right away her faithful soldiers went to work dragging the guards and binding them so they wouldn't be able to escape later.

"Emmeline, thank you for this but you can't stay here—if the killer or even Light got a hold of you I don't know what I would do."

She nodded, making it clear that she understood and would listen to me, now that she had done her part to help.

"You don't need to worry. After this is all over I'll come find you," I said as I stepped into the doorway. I didn't go inside right away though, as I wanted to get one last look at the girl who meant so much to me. Emmeline took off her mask and smiled at me with tears in her eyes, and somehow we both knew this was goodbye. I had made so many mistakes since returning to work. The one thing I'd done right through all of this was finding Emmeline and I could never regret that.

It was time, though, to leave Emmeline behind and focus on what was right in front of me, inside the mansion. The hallway led around past some familiar ground and the banquet hall came into view. Unfortunately, this was probably the way the guests had entered the mansion and that meant the clock might be ticking. I didn't know how long it would be before someone missed the guards. The room had a white marble floor that shined like the sun, a long table stretched across the center of the room with a giant chandelier hanging above. The lavishly dressed guests talked and laughed while drinking champagne and every so often doing a line of cocaine. Silver and gold accessories lined the table from the silverware to the plates, everything sparkling off the diamond chandelier. This was the rich at its finest and they loved the company they were in at their amazing grand banquet. Funny Bunny sat at the head of the table and overlooked his fancy guests as they waited for what would be a massive feast.

I ducked down low not wanting to be seen just yet. I had no clue which of the guests, if any, were the wicked killer and didn't want to lose my element of surprise. I went into the first door I came to, which was a double door that opened like an old saloon door in a western movie. I was standing in a giant kitchen that looked more like a five star restaurant kitchen then that of a house or even a mansion. Everything was shiny and clean and there were all kinds of giant appliances that would never be seen in an average home. The room was massive and included a staging area full of refrigerators and cabinets, a dishwashing station, and extra storage. I had to walk a short distance to even reach the oven area where the bulk of the cooking was most likely done.

Suddenly I heard clicking heels so I dropped to the floor, keeping my head down and blocking my body from the view of anyone walking down the main stretch of kitchen. I was up against a marble island cabinet and I took a moment to notice how nice the furnishings were in here. I had a slight view and could see a beautiful woman in a tight black dress with sparkling red glitter that matched her shoes and purse.

"Hello, Cuistat, Funny Bunny wanted me to come back here to see how far along you are on the first appetizer."

I couldn't see the chef from where I was at but I could hear him remove the lid on something and instantly I could smell all kinds of delicious aromas: a collection of spices, potatoes, vegetables, and meat that I couldn't even describe. Whatever it was it smelled like perfection.

"Yes, of course, Mrs. Rosie. This is the first appetizer and it is ready to serve if you wish." The chef obviously enjoyed his position and even sounded like he was faking a French accent just to fit the part. Still I had a pretty good feeling this particular cook was as amazing as they come.

"Perfect, Cuistat, thank you so much. But first Funny Bunny has informed me that some of the guests want to meet the chef before partaking of the food. If you could, we would appreciate it greatly if you would go out and say hello to a few of our guests."

I heard the chef put the lid back on and take off his apron. "Of course, Mrs. Rosie, it would be an honor."

Rosie nodded with a big fake smile and the chef power-walked down the hallway, fortunately in the opposite direction from where I was hidden. I still didn't see the chef because I ducked down to avoid being spotted, but once he was gone I thought about speaking with Rosie about the possibility of the killer's return. Instead I poked my head back out and saw Rosie glance around quickly, like she thought she was being watched. She didn't see me and went right to her purse and pulled a large black thermos out of her bag. Rosie popped the lid off what I could see now was a giant vat of soup and proceeded to pour the contents of the thermos inside.

In that moment I tried to find an excuse for her in my mind—maybe it was a secret ingredient, maybe it was alcohol and was simply a joke—but I knew it was poison. I didn't know what to think. Did this mean Rosie was wicked or was it a coincidence? There were too many questions and not enough of the answers that I needed. I pulled the thirty eight special out of its holster and stood up quietly, gun in hand. I pointed the pistol right at Rosie as she put the lid back on the thermos and stuffed it into her bag. She put the cover back on the soup and turned to walk out of the room, but instead faced me and my gun.

"What the hell do you think you're doing, Rosie?" I didn't know eyes could become so big with shock but when she saw me a look of sheer surprise showed on her face.

"Detective, this isn't what it looks like. I can explain, just please don't do anything crazy."

I wondered how she knew it was me since I was wearing a completely different mask, but there were more pressing matters at hand. "Rosie, interlock your fingers behind your head. You are under arrest for attempted murder and the suspicion of several other pending murder cases."

I was preparing to read her her rights when she started speaking again, telling me something I couldn't ignore. "Wink, you don't know what you're doing. There is a lot more at stake right now than you know. Trust me, you don't want to arrest me right now, not when we're so close to finally changing things."

I knew that if I wanted answers about these murders, I would have to get them now, from Rosie. I was no longer an officer of the law, and if I turned her over it would be a months before I would be privy to any kind of information again. "I want an explanation. Tell me everything you know right now." If I could get answers now, I would feel a whole lot better about turning Rosie over to the authorities.

"I will tell you what you want to know, but we can't do it here. The chef is going to be back any second and if he sees what's going on here that soup may never get served." Rosie was obviously concerned that she wasn't going to get her chance to poison and murder people; I was worried what kind of a psycho I was dealing with.

"You can't honestly believe I am going to let you poison people now that I have caught you in the act. What the hell do you take me for?" For a moment I had lowered my gun but now it was back in her face.

"I won't let the chef deliver the soup yet. Just come somewhere private with me and I will explain everything, and then you can decide what to do. Hurry and put down that gun. The chef is on his way back—please just hear me out, that's all I am asking."

I could hear the swish of clothes and the approaching chef and quickly wondered what I should do. I had made so many mistakes and wondered whether this was about to be another one.

Was I destined to always fail? I lowered the gun and put it away just before the chef walked into the view of the two of us standing in the kitchen.

"Is everything okay here, Mrs. Rosie?" the chef asked, standing beside me. I didn't look away from Rosie, who would get a bullet at the first sign of betrayal.

"Of course, Cuistat, this is just one of our guest's private security guards, doing his rounds per his boss's orders."

I let out a sigh of relief that I wasn't going to have to shoot Rosie and this random chef before knowing his involvement.

"Ah, yes I see, well Funny Bunny wants me to serve the soup now. Thank you for your help, Mrs. Rosie." The chef went over to the soup, turned off the burner and made sure the lid was secure.

"If you would please wait to serve the soup, I need a moment to speak with this guard before we commence with the banquet," Rosie said while keeping an eye on me just as I had an eye on her to see how she would handle this situation.

"Of course, Mrs. Rosie, just let me know when you are ready for me to serve."

Rosie nodded and turned slowly, beckoning for me to follow her to a place a little more private. I was concerned this was only a set up, and at the same time I feared for the chef who might give his food a little taste test and end up dead for it.

Rosie led me to a large pantry that opened with a small door and went all the way back like a mini hallway filled with shelves of canned foods and various dry supplies. The room was well lit and Rosie made sure I knew there was nowhere for her to escape and no place for an ambush.

"Alright, this is your chance to explain. Let's hear it before I change my mind." I shut the pantry door behind me and redrew my pistol to make it clear that this didn't mean she was getting away with anything.

"Okay, Wink, just lower the gun. You don't need to threaten me. I'm going to explain."

I kept the gun in hand but I moved it down so that it was pointing at the floor rather than in her mask.

"The reason I'm doing this is to stop the masq policies from continuing. The only people who have been hurt are those responsible for keeping us trapped behind masks. All of those people out there are those remaining with the power to keep the masq policies in effect for years to come. They have to be stopped here and now and I will be the one to do it." I tried to understand where she was coming from but it didn't sound like a good enough reason to murder to me.

"That doesn't mean you get a free pass to kill people. If that's all you've got to say then I'm sorry but your coming with me."

Rosie let out a sigh like she was about to do something that she didn't want to do, like it was something that she was dreading having to do. "You don't realize how much crime still happens today. The masq policy changes nothing—the only difference is that people can hide their crimes more easily."

Rosie was telling the truth and I knew it; all these masquerade murders could attest to that.

"I have to show you something, something I have been wishing I could show you but just couldn't. Just try to keep an open mind, Wink, and maybe this will make you see why what I am doing is so important." Rosie reached up and slowly pulled her rabbit mask off of her face. I froze at what I saw. There were many things I was prepared for today but not this; I couldn't believe who I was looking at.

"No, I don't believe this. Danielle, how could you do this?" I just stood there staring at the face of Rosie, of Viola, of Danielle, of my ex-wife, of the mother of my daughter, and the wicked killer I had been hunting.

Twenty-Two

The last person I expected to be involved in something like this was standing right in front of me. Now things were starting to make sense: all the visits to my place weren't to check on me, they were to spy on me, to gather information. I had been betrayed by the one person in my life who I had thought was actually there for me. It seemed impossible.

"Wink, you have to understand I didn't want you to find out like this. I wanted you to know when this was all over, when you could actually thank me."

My trigger finger was itching and I couldn't believe the rage I felt toward the mother of my daughter. "Thank you? Why the hell would I thank you? For killing people, or maybe you mean for humiliating me time after time? Oh wait, I know what you mean— you want my thanks for taking the fall for this, for the department thinking that I am the killer!" I was yelling far too loud for the tiny pantry and I could tell it was making Danielle very uncomfortable.

"Calm down and listen to me before you make things worse." Danielle was calling to my reasoning, but at this point I didn't think I had any reasoning left inside of me. "You know that masked men came to our house and killed our daughter. Did you really think I would just live in a world that protected people like that? No, I vowed to do something about it and I did just that when I met a man who had real power over this whole thing."

The information was running through my mind, but not quickly enough to keep up with Danielle, at least not quickly enough to make a decision.

"Funny Bunny is on the voting council for the masq policies," she continued, "and he is the only one standing against them. Everyone else wants to keep the policy in effect. He tried to reason with them but it didn't work, it only made things worse. We had to come up with a plan if we were to stop them from voting."

"So you killed all the other members, or rather are about to kill them, judging by the poison and the room full of rich and powerful guests?"

Danielle had become a political killer for the right reasons, but now a choice had to be made.

"I'm not saying what I did was right and I plan to pay for my crimes, but only after America's unmasking; can't you at least give me that?"

I did what any officer would do in this situation: I lifted my gun and pointed it right at the woman that was once my wife. "You expect me to let you kill a room full of people just to satisfy your grieving process. I was there too, you know. I saw them kill our daughter, but I didn't snap and start plotting a mass string of murders." I had the gun trained on her but I never intended to shoot her. I only needed time to make a decision.

"Wink, those men are evil. The only reason they want the masq policy to stay in effect is because it allows them to get away with everything. Crime hasn't gone down; it's only swept under the rug, it only happens in secret now. I know firsthand because before I met Funny Bunny he was the same way—a man using the mask for his own gain." Tears were welling up in her eyes but I just couldn't bring myself to hear her words. I couldn't condone murder, could I?

"Danielle you spied on me to gain information, you used me like a fool." I had to find more reasons to fuel my anger toward her; I couldn't let her convince me to let her kill.

"I only did that for the right reason: once I had my way in I had to use it. I never meant for you to get hurt in all this. It wasn't my decision for you to be on our case; it just happened that way." She was more than sincere and she really believed this was the way to grieve for our daughter, and to change the world for her.

"I still can't let you do it. I'm sorry, Danielle, but this just isn't the way," I said though it went against everything I personally believed. I hated the masq policy and I hated that my daughter's killers live on in this world.

"Then I'm sorry too, Wink, but this has to happen." Danielle put her mask back on and once more became Rosie Rabbit, the masquerade murderer. Just then I heard a loud noise that reminded me of a metal pan hitting a hard surface. Suddenly I realized it was a pan and the hard surface was my head. I slumped to the floor landing right on top of my right hand with the barrel of the pistol pressed against my belly.

"What do you want me to do with the body, Mrs. Rosie?" I heard the familiar voice of the chef ask.

"Just lock him in here. We have to get that soup out to the guests immediately. I will deal with him later." Rosie stepped over my body and I couldn't even move to try and stop her, and the next second she was gone and I heard the pantry door lock.

My first desire was to just pass out and let the events unfold as they would without my presence, but I couldn't let that happen. The jabbing pain from the pistol that was buried into my stomach was enough to keep me awake. I used it and forced my eyes open and then began struggling to stand up. I lifted with everything I had and came to an almost standing position using the pantry shelves as a crutch. I stood up just in time to look out the small window and see the chef walking by with his arms wrapped around the vat of soup. Rosie was walking a half step behind him, making sure her poison reached her guests.

"Wait don't do this—you can't just kill people." I was speaking to people who would never hear me from where I was. I lifted my gun intending to blow the lock off and rush after the chef and knock that soup over before it was too late. Instead I felt a wash of wooziness and fell down on my knees. For a moment I thought I was going to throw up but wasn't sure if it was from the injury or what I was about to let happen.

"How am I supposed to decide? How can I make this choice?" I asked the silence if only to keep my head clear and prevent the concussion that threatened to come on. I had to think this through, even if there wasn't time; I had to think this through and come up with my own answers.

Calliope was killed by masked men and because of the masq policies crime rages on, only now hidden beneath the same mask that killed my daughter. Emmeline lost her father because he couldn't handle living in such a changed world, and without the policies she would get her dad back. On the flip side this was murder and letting one crime happen for the greater good wasn't right; there would always be a way to justify a crime no matter what the situation.

"I won't just hide and let the important decisions be made without me, no matter what the choice it will be mine and no one else's." I had been played a fool by everyone in my life, from the Captain and Light to Funny Bunny and Rosie Rabbit. I was the joke of this entire operation and now I would be the one to make the decision, just me and no one else.

I stood up fast and kicked the door in the same motion, and it split down the middle and the glass shattered to the floor. I stepped through, the 38 special still in hand and rushed for the open area where the grand banquet was being held. A serving girl ran past me in a rush and I knew what was waiting for me on the other side of the room.

"You're too late, Detective Wink. It's time you face the facts and just let this go. A better world is on the horizon. Who do you think you are to try and stop it?" Funny Bunny stood at the head of the table surrounded by death. Only a couple of guests still remained alive, choking for air.

"I'm the one who gets to make that choice, not you!" I yelled back and Rosie stepped out of nowhere and started coming too close for comfort.

"Wink, it's already over. You can go home now and just let this happen. I know Calliope would be so happy with all of us for this."

I had to shift my focus away from Funny Bunny and onto my ex-wife, who was still coming at me. "Stay back Danielle, or I will shoot you. I don't care who you are—this isn't your decision to make its mine!" Again I yelled and to my surprise Rosie stopped just as I had requested. Within a second I knew why. Funny Bunny had moved around the room and was only seconds from reaching me, holding the same wicked knife I had seen coming my way before. Instinct kicked in and I turned wide just in time to pull the trigger and shoot the knife expertly out of Funny Bunny's hand.

"I told you it's my decision, god damn it!" The knife hit the floor and Funny Bunny froze in place. He had been made and I would never let him get close enough to cut me again.

"You cut my hand once, you wicked fuck, and I am not about to let you humiliate me again. Now get in the corner over there with Rosie." I pointed and they both started to move to a spot where I could think and would be safe from any sneak attacks they could attempt. I looked at the room of dead and knew I had already let this happen, proof enough of the decision I wanted to make. The rich who had been laughing and having a good time were now face down in their soup or drowned in their own poisoned vomit.

"Listen to me, Wink," Funny Bunny said. "The dead are already gone. There is no need to worry about them anymore. If you arrest us here and now their deaths will be for nothing. At least right now I can ensure that the masq policy is over. By the end of the day tomorrow America will have a face once more." Funny Bunny was a clever speaker and it made sense now that I knew he was a politician on the voting council.

"I understand why my ex-wife cares about all this, but why do you? I can't see that a rich man with so much power would truly care about making the world a better place. What's in it for you, Funny Bunny, or whoever the hell you are?" Rosie and Funny were trapped in the corner with nowhere to go. At my command they would be arrested, which meant Funny had to convince me with words.

"I will admit I spent a fair amount of time loving the masq policy. As you probably know I started these masquerades back when I actually cared about the parties. I met Danielle when she came to protest masq policies and while all the others laughed at her attempts to sway our opinions, she made a believer out of me. I couldn't help but know more and before I knew it we were together and I truly believed in her cause."

I saw Rosie look away as if she were embarrassed to have me hear this story, which led me to believe it was true. I thought I heard something and turned to see if that chef was sneaking behind me with a frying pan but I didn't see anything.

"I tried and tried to appeal to the council but once you have everything you could ever want it's hard to choose to do something just for the greater good. It became pretty clear to me that the voting was never going to go my way, so Rosie and I came up with a plan." The room, so full of death, grew silent, and I was starting to believe in the pair of killers.

"So you unmask America and then disappear forever with all your money, and I'm left knowing that I let two murders run off and live it up in Morocco?" Again I thought I heard something but when I turned to look there was nothing there but death and regret.

"That was never the plan. We will both turn ourselves in when this is all over and done with." Funny Bunny was telling the truth. I didn't know how I knew but I just did, and Rosie would go with him at the end of their adventure.

"I have to know why you just didn't kill everyone at the grand banquet. Why all the theatrics?" I had more questions I couldn't let go unanswered; curiosity was getting the best of me.

"I wish it could have been that easy but my important guests were too busy to all attend this party, so I had to pick them off as they appeared." Funny Bunny seemed confident in his speaking and didn't shy away from sharing the details of his crime.

"What about Flex? He didn't have anything to do with this and I can only assume you're responsible for his death as well."

Funny Bunny answered quickly; he too wanted to get this over with. "Things took an unexpected turn and I had to handle things the best I could. He was an unfortunate sacrifice but he knew too much and keeping him alive would have been dangerous for our cause."

I still had questions, but I felt a presence hurrying me, like I couldn't stall any longer. It was time to make my choice.

"If I let you go, then by tomorrow America will be unmasked and right after that you plan to turn yourselves in and pay for the crimes that have already been committed?" I was summarizing our conversation but I was also looking for understanding between the two.

"Yes, that's exactly what's going to happen," they both answered in unison and I wondered why Danielle and I never found this level of understanding between us in all our years together. I was almost certain that I would pay for the choice I was about to make and that my place in the department would be gone forever, and I couldn't have been more right.

"Fine, both of you get the hell out of here, but I better not hear anything different than what we just discussed. Prison isn't going to be easy for either of you; I hope you know what you've gotten yourselves into."

With a sigh of relief the pair started straightening up for the planned escape out of the building and on to the next part of the plan.

But then Rosie stopped and yelled for me. "Wink look out!"

I dove to the ground and felt a sharp pain hit the side of my leg. I'd been knocked to the floor hard but I knew I had just dodged death.

"Bad choices Detective—that should be the name of your file, and hey maybe that's what I'll put on it when I send it away for good."

I rolled over and saw the blood on the marble floor. It wasn't a serious wound but it would be enough to slow me down. I grabbed my pistol and slid back until I was behind the cover of the giant table scattered with dead bodies.

"All this death and you just turn and let the murderers walk away. What kind of Detective are you? I mean, I knew you were messed up but Jesus man, you're a glutton for punishment." Detective Light was walking with his pistol in hand and wearing a mask that I remembered but not the one I had grown accustomed to when we were partners. It had three faces: one to the right, one to the left, and one dead center where his real face would be. I could see him in the reflection of a silver plate.

"Don't either of you think of going anywhere. A cop can shoot a serial killer on sight, so do not make a move." Light was pointing the gun at Rosie and since I'd put them in the corner they really didn't have anywhere to run.

"So what, Light, you were just going to shoot me in the back, kill all of us and expect to get a medal? Or are you really as screwed up as I always thought and just enjoying the kill?" I spoke hoping to buy myself some time to find a clean shot.

"From where I'm standing you're just as guilty as these two. Don't worry, I'll make sure everyone knows that I was right and that you are partly to blame for these murders." The three-faced mask was bulky and had to obscure his vision, but it also looked solid and may deflect a bullet.

"You're a killer just like these two, Light. What makes you think you're any better? You belong behind bars, you three-faced freak." I started sliding to a better angle, hoping I could just pop up fast enough to take him down with one clean shot to the chest.

"Do you have any idea how amazing it is to be an internal affairs agent when you don't have to show your face? I can be anyone I want to be by simply putting on a mask. There are endless faces out there and I can pretend to be any one of them. Just the thought of someone ruining that for me, well let's just say killing to keep my mask on is worth it."

I was in position and just needed a distraction; I hoped Rosie or Funny Bunny would provide the chance I needed.

"It doesn't take a psychiatrist to see that you need help. I knew there was something up with your head the moment I met you. I don't know if it's split personalities or some other kind of disorder, but you definitely need help, Light."

Light was angry and wanted me dead, and aimed his gun right where he thought I was still hiding. This was my perfect chance to pop up and take care of my partner once and for all.

"It doesn't matter if you think I'm sick, Wink, because the newspaper will clearly state that you were the crazy one, not me, and that's all that matters." Light pulled the trigger hitting the empty spot where I had been hiding earlier. I was up, gun in hand within a second. I fired but the bullet went high, a perfect head shot if there had ever been one. A black hole smoked dead center, hitting the mask Light was wearing right between the eyes. His head reared back and I prepared for the psycho to fall on the ground.

"Sorry, Light, but I've made my choice."

Light suddenly recovered and aimed his gun far faster then I was prepared for. I should have known that the mask would deflect the bullet.

Being shot is a strange thing. I remember the sound of the gun, and the flash of fire out of the barrel. What I don't remember was how I ended up on the ground with this burning sharp thing in my gut. My hand was pressing the wound but I couldn't think, all I felt was pain, like a razor blade was spinning inside of my stomach.

"You can't help him so don't even bother moving or you're going to get a bullet as well." I could hear Detective Light yelling at Rosie and I wanted to get up and help her but the pain in my stomach wouldn't let me stand. I had seen so many movies where the hero gets shot and then is right back in the fight, saving the day. I tried to be the hero but couldn't move, the cutting weight was holding me down.

"Get on your knees right now and put your hands behind your back before I shoot both of you." More mockery from the man I was meant to stop, from the evil that had been hiding right beside me. I felt a buzzing in my ears and realized something bad was about to happen, like maybe I was about to die after all. I realized I wasn't going to come back from this but I knew I had to leave this world the right way, and if that meant doing something wrong, well so be it. In a way I understood Funny Bunny and thought doing something bad for the greater good was okay after all.

"You are under arrest for mass murder. Both of you are going to get the death penalty for this," Light said.

I reached out for the nearest dead body and found exactly what I was looking for stuffed in his jacket pocket: a tube rolled up and filled with strong prescription drugs most likely morphine or dilaudid. Hell it might have even been a type of heroin. In that moment I didn't care since it was the only way for me to fix this. I swallowed the drug with everything I had left.

"What do you think, do you even deserve prison or should I just shoot both of you right here and now?"

The gunshot wound became numb and I felt better than I had in a long time. It became very easy to stand up and lift my gun. Light was stuffing his gun in Rosie's mask and making sure Funny Bunny was watching; he wanted to torture them for as long as possible. The world swayed and shook and the colors all around me became sounds. It was as if I could see clearly despite how messed up I was on the drugs.

"Stick this in your file, Detective Light of Internal Affairs." I wasn't sure if I had even spoken or if I had just thought the words but they fit the situation. I shot Light in the back twice, and his body shook like a rag doll but he didn't fall down. Instead he turned and lifted his gun in my direction. I responded by firing my last two shots, hitting him both times in the chest, both killing blows that would have knocked any man senseless. Except Light did not fall, but only rocked back and forth from the force of the shots and then continued to lift his gun. I dropped to the floor as a series of bullets started ringing out in the banquet hall.

My head was spinning as shards of broken wood were breaking out of the oak table, and dishes were shattering all around, but Light didn't slow down his assault. I didn't know if I was being shot or not; the ground was the sky and the sky was the chair. I suddenly had a vinegar taste in my mouth and then began vomiting. I rolled to a different spot as soon as I thought the hailstorm of gunshots was over but then they started right back up again.

I realized then that Light must have reloaded, and as the thought occurred to me, I decided to do the same, opening the chamber on my thirty eight special and letting the spent shells hit the floor. I felt very tired as I pulled the box of shells out and I accidently dumped them out on the marble floor. In a confused state I grabbed a handful and started stuffing them into the six open chambers.

"You're dead, Wink, you hear me? You're dead!" Light yelled but the sound was far away, as though he were yelling from a distant island rather than the marble room we were in. I locked my gun into place, keeping my head low so that the bullets wouldn't take me out of the game forever. I was covered in the remnants of nice things: the fine dishes, flowers, oak table, and the silk table cloth all were just dust scattered on my clothes. I didn't know if Light was finished shooting or not but I didn't care. I was through playing his games and I wanted nothing more than to end this. I stood up, gun in hand and felt this sudden ping of pain hit my side just below my ribs, and I wondered absently if I had just been shot.

In rapid succession I fired the 38 special and hit the mask six times tink, tink, tink, tink, tink, tink the bullets bounced off the mask and only dark holes remained. All three faces had taken bullets, two bullets each to be exact and for a moment all went quiet. Light dropped his gun to the floor and it smacked the marble with a loud thumping sound. Light dropped to one knee and the weight of the three faced mask hunched him over. A rush of blood leaked out of the holes and onto the white marble. In the next second he fell onto the blood stained marble and his mask made an awful banging sound when it hit the ground.

"Get the hell out of here while you still can, and you better follow through on your promise," I managed to say to Funny Bunny and Rosie Rabbit who were sitting in the corner trying to avoid the chaos happening in the banquet room. Danielle looked like she was going to say something but Funny Bunny grabbed her by the arm and they raced out of there like they were on a mission. And I knew they were.

"Sorry, Light, but you just didn't have what it takes to bring me down," I mocked while climbing on top of my fallen enemy. I ripped open his fine tailored suit and revealed a bullet proof vest that had twin slugs pressed against him.

"Son of a bitch," I cursed and almost collapsed onto his dead body when I felt something inside of his right pants pocket. I reached in and pulled out a tape recorder, one with an internal memory and a plug to fit into a computer. I looked at it for a long time and ultimately decided there was still something I had to do before I could allow myself to die.

I forced myself up and when I did I caught site of blood that was running down my pant leg from the latest wound I had received. I didn't know how much time I had left before I would bleed out so I hurried as best as I could.

Before leaving the banquet room I looked back at the dead bodies and silently hoped that it was all worth it. I hoped that Danielle would follow through, and I hoped that people like Detective Light wouldn't be allowed to hide behind a mask anymore.

Epilogue

I had many hopes for the future when I left the banquet room, but one that I didn't mention was living long enough to tell my story. I can't really explain what happened when I left but somehow I managed to bandage my wounds. It wasn't a great job but it was enough to keep me alive and that's all that really matters.

I awoke on a balcony at the top of Funny Bunny's mansion overlooking the grassy patch of land where I had once watched the man perform a speech. I had passed out there and let the drug run its course out of my system, somehow surviving the night. I held on long enough to tell my story so that not only would the world know how America managed to unmask itself, but for personal reasons as well. I take comfort in knowing that whoever finds this will know what Rosie and Funny did and will know that they have to pay for their crimes, even if it was for the greater good.

Anyway, that's my story the best that I can tell it, starting with the call I received that set this whole case in motion. I have to assume the council knew it had a traitor. I was a tool meant to be used by the department to catch Funny Bunny, but I had failed time and time again. Of course my failure was a result of my own ex-wife using me for information and arranging to have me drugged to slow my investigation. I still have some questions that I now know will never be answered, but I think I've figured most everything out.

Unfortunately I do not have the time to think through the events of the masquerades and decipher each and every event but whoever is listening to this recorder may have the time to do so.

It wasn't an easy thing to do with my wounds but I removed my mask so that I could watch the sun rise on a world with a face.

I guess at the end of all this I can only think of Emmeline and how she will be now that she can finally take off her mask and stop fighting. Her father will come home and she will be able to move on with her life, which is all I really want for her. I wish we had more time together. I really don't want to die but there isn't much I can do about that anymore. If you're listening to this, Emmeline, I hope you move on and have a wonderful life. The time I spent in that house with you meant the world to me.

That's it for my goodbyes. My final words are, don't bring back the masq policy just because it was ended through crime. By now you all know that hiding the evil of the world isn't going to change things; you have to deal with the problem for real and not just hide it. The road ahead won't be an easy one but people will always find a way.

Calliope here I come. Don't worry, you don't have to be alone anymore.

*****

"Emmeline is that you?"

"Of course, who do you think fixed your bandages?"

"I thought I was dead for sure."

"There's no reason to be so dramatic. You're going to be just fine. Now come on we have to get out of here before anyone else shows up. Turn that recorder off, if you want someone to find it then leave it where it is."

"I guess I really am going to see it."

"See what."

"The world unmasked—the world with a face."

END.